D0424353

DATE DUE

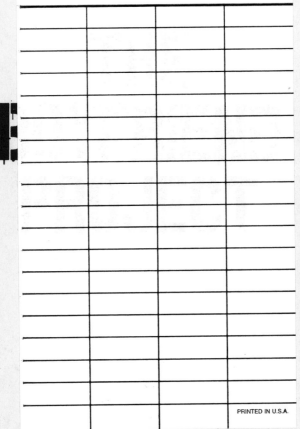

PRINTED IN U.S.A.

Books by Rachel Hawthorne

Caribbean Cruising

Island Girls (and Boys)

Love on the Lifts

Thrill Ride

The Boyfriend League

Snowed In

Labor of Love

Suite Dreams

Trouble from the Start

The Boyfriend Project

One Perfect Summer

The Dark Guardian series

Moonlight

Full Moon

Dark of the Moon

Shadow of the Moon

THE BOYFRIEND PROJECT

Rachel Hawthorne

HARPER TEEN
An Imprint of HarperCollinsPublishers

HarperTeen is an imprint of HarperCollins Publishers.

The Boyfriend Project

Copyright © 2015 by Jan Nowasky

Library of Congress Control Number: 2014955505
ISBN 978-0-06-233073-4

Typography by Jenna Stempel
15 16 17 18 19   CG/RRDH   10 9 8 7 6 5 4 3 2 1

❖

First Edition

For every girl who has known the scary, confusing, wonderful,
thrilling adventure of falling in love . . .
And for every girl who hasn't yet, but one day will . . .

Chapter 1

KENDALL

I loved Jeremy Swanson.

I loved his long, slow kisses, his dimpled smile. I loved the way one of his hands always came to rest on the small of my back when we walked.

"I love you, Kendall," he whispered breathlessly as he trailed his mouth along my neck before returning it to my lips for another searing kiss.

I loved that most of all. That he loved me, quirks included.

We were doing our contortionist impression, as we struggled to find a comfortable position in the cramped backseat of his car that was quickly turning into a sauna. Because of all the mosquitoes, we had the windows rolled up. Because of the price of gas, the car wasn't running, the air conditioner wasn't blowing.

But neither of us cared about the discomforts. We were together. That was all that mattered.

Jeremy shifted, lost his precarious perch on the edge of the seat and, with a yelp, tumbled the few inches to the floor.

I laughed, held up a hand. "Sorry."

"No, I'm sorry," he said, moaning as he shoved himself into a sitting position. "I don't know why my parents had to get me such a small car for a graduation present."

"Probably because they knew this is what you'd be doing with it."

He grinned. The shadows stopped me from seeing the little dimple that I knew had formed in his left cheek. "Probably. Dad worries that I'll do something stupid before I even get to college."

"Like fall in love," I teased.

He leaned forward and gave me a quick kiss. "That's the smartest thing I've done so far."

He tried to get up but he was wedged between the front seat and the back. "This is ridiculous. I'm glad you love me. These moves wouldn't impress a date."

I placed my hand against his cheek, leaned in, and let my mouth play over his. "Your moves impress me."

They always had. We'd been together for nearly four months, longer if I counted the friendship phase that had begun at the start of our senior year just after his family moved to town. Over spring break when my best friend, Avery Watkins, hadn't been able to go to a movie with us, Jeremy had kissed me for the first time. It had been a sweet kiss, a tentative brushing of his lips over mine as though he were afraid I'd take offense and slap him or something. I hadn't taken offense. Instead I'd moved in to welcome his advance. He'd taken the kiss deeper and I'd fallen hard.

Now, without breaking off the kiss, he tried to smoothly get back onto the seat. He grunted, shifted, pulled away, and sighed. "I'm stuck."

Ruffling my fingers through his short, blond hair, I laughed again. "And I intend to take advantage of that."

I kissed him again. He cupped my face, his thumb stroking the underside of my chin where the skin was soft and sensitive. Shivers went through me. He skipped his tongue over my lips before slipping it inside to dance with mine. He always took his time. He always went slow.

Sometimes slower than I wanted.

I tugged his shirt out of his jeans, glided my hand beneath the soft material, and skimmed my palm up his back. He groaned low, began pushing himself up—

"Oh, God! Oh, God! My back's cramping." His hand flew to his side, his head reared back.

"Okay, hold on." I opened the door and clambered out of the car, trying to give him more room to maneuver. I pulled on his legs. He really was wedged in there. We'd already moved the seats up as far as they would go. "Here, take my hand."

Finally he was able to shift slightly so he could crawl backward out of the car. Arching with his hands pressed to his spine, he paced back and forth several times. With a look of contrition, he finally straightened and laughed with an exaggerated roll of his eyes. "That car has got to go."

Although it was relatively new, it was the unsexiest thing I'd ever seen and looked like something my grandmother would drive to church. Walking over to him, I flattened my palms against his chest. "Maybe you could trade it in for a motorcycle."

"Where would we make out?"

Good question. I'd have to talk to Avery about that. She pretty much became a motorcycle expert when she started dating Fletcher Thomas.

I heard the beep of an incoming text on my phone. I opened the front door, reached in, and grabbed my phone from where it rested on the console. Speak of the devil.

Avery:

Going to B.S. Meet us?

I almost said no but I was tired of the cramped backseat. I looked over my shoulder. "Want to meet Avery and Fletcher at the Burger Shack?"

"Guess I kinda ruined the mood with my old guy,

4

back-out-of-whack impersonation."

"It's more the heat." I slapped at a mosquito. "The bugs. And I'm a little hungry."

"Okay, let's go." He slammed the back door while I slid into the passenger seat. Then he closed my door before jogging around and slipping behind the wheel.

He started off, slow and careful, backing away from the lake until we reached the road. I didn't look to see what other cars were out there. This area was pretty much make-out central, but couples deserved their privacy.

"You know," he began, "you don't have to say Avery *and Fletcher*. If it's Avery, I assume it's Fletcher, too, now."

Avery and Fletcher had started dating seriously just a few weeks ago. "I'm so glad she got a boyfriend," I said. "I think she was starting to get a little uncomfortable hanging around with us all the time." She'd been my best friend forever and Jeremy had always been good about inviting her to go places with us. I loved how considerate he was, but I had to admit it was nice that Jeremy and I had more time alone now.

"The right boyfriend." Jeremy cast a quick glance my way. "You didn't just want a boyfriend, did you? You wanted the right one."

"Totally." Reaching across the console, I touched his arm. "And you're the right one for me. That's what I wanted for Avery. Just didn't expect the right one to be him."

Fletcher had a bad-boy reputation, had needed to take a summer class to graduate from high school. Avery was all smarts, ranked third in our class, and nearly always followed the rules. The ones she broke were harmless.

"I like him," Jeremy said.

"He's a lot different than I thought." I knew Fletcher as a tough guy who often came to school looking like he'd been in a brawl. After getting to know him, though, I realized how sweet he could be—at least where Avery was concerned. The guy would do anything for her.

Jeremy pulled into the B.S. parking lot, came around, and opened the car door for me. It had taken me a while to get used to him doing that. I'd never had anyone open the door for me, but his dad had taught him to be courteous. It was a little old-fashioned, but I liked it. When we got to the front door of the restaurant, he held it open while I walked through.

Avery wasn't here yet, so we settled in a booth near the back by the window so we had a view of the parking lot. We'd barely sat down, when I saw a motorcycle with two people on it roar into the lot. My heart skipped a beat at the recklessness. Jeremy would never take a risk like that. He was sure and steady—just like me. But I couldn't help thinking about the thrill of the ride, noticing how brightly Avery was smiling as she got off the bike. Joy and happiness radiated off her.

"Is that why you suggested I trade in my car for a motorcycle?" Jeremy asked.

I'd been so absorbed watching them that I jerked with a little guilt at Jeremy's question. "It just looks like it would be fun, doesn't it?"

"A car is more practical. What do they do if they have to haul a bunch of stuff?"

Turning slightly, I looked at Jeremy with his conservative haircut. I put my hand over his, and he immediately turned his palm up and threaded our fingers together. I didn't know why our mode of transportation was suddenly nagging at me. "But it would be exciting."

"As long as you don't smile while you're whipping along and get bugs between your teeth."

"I've never seen Fletcher with bugs."

"He doesn't smile all that much, either."

"True." Leaning in, I gave him a quick kiss. "And I love your smile."

"Love yours, too. Bet I wouldn't see it at all if we got caught in a rainstorm while riding that thing. We'd be like drowned cats."

"I hadn't considered that. It's not very practical, is it?"

"Not that I can see."

I wasn't quite ready to give up on the thrill of having one. "Good gas mileage, maybe?"

"Drowned cat," he repeated.

"Maybe we're being too practical." And boring.

Hearing the door open, I looked back. Avery was walking in, Fletcher right on her heels. I couldn't be sure but I wouldn't have been surprised if she'd opened the door for herself. Fletcher was not as polite as Jeremy, not that Avery seemed to mind. She slid into the booth, sitting across from me.

"Hey, guys," she said, smiling brightly.

Dropping onto the bench seat, Fletcher immediately put his arm around her shoulders and acknowledged us with a nod. Fletcher Thomas was a guy of few words.

"What were you up to?" Avery asked.

I felt myself grow warm, knew I was blushing. "Nothing special."

Fletcher studied me, shifted his gaze to Jeremy, and hitched up a corner of his mouth. I figured he knew exactly what we'd been doing.

"We were down by the lake," Jeremy said, and I wondered if I'd wounded his pride, if he felt a need to prove something with Fletcher around.

"Skinny-dipping?" Fletcher asked, a devilish twinkle in his eyes.

"Absolutely not," I said with conviction. I gave Avery a pointed look meant to convey the question: *Have you skinny-dipped?*

Laughing, she rubbed his arm. "He's always trying to talk me into trying it."

"You don't know what you're missing," Fletcher assured us.

"Fish nibbling at things I don't want them nibbling at," Jeremy said.

I loved that he considered all the ramifications of his actions. Which was one of the reasons he'd make a good lawyer. And one of the reasons that he hadn't quite landed safely on second base yet. He put his hands under my shirt, but he never moved past my lower ribs. Limiting temptation and showing respect for me.

That's how he had explained it the night I thought we'd be going further, possibly even all the way. I'd told my mom that I was sleeping over at Avery's and instead had spent the entire night with Jeremy. We'd checked into a motel at the edge of town, walked into our room, and watched a roach crawl across the wall.

"This is not what I want for our first time," he'd told me.

It hadn't been what I wanted, either. We were both virgins . . . and too broke to afford anything nicer. So we'd left, driven to the lake, spent the night in his car talking about what our first time would be like. And he'd told me that he had too much respect for me not to make sure that it was special. That he knew I loved him and we didn't have to have sex to prove that.

I knew our first time was going to be awesome, but until then, all I could do was admire his control. I always knew exactly where we stood, what to expect. No surprises.

Although as my mom was fond of saying: "Life without surprises is kind of boring."

"Never found fish to be an issue," Fletcher said now, bringing my thoughts back to the present.

"You've really gone skinny-dipping?" I asked.

Fletcher lifted a broad shoulder, moved a saltshaker to the center of the table for no apparent reason. "Sure. You should try it sometime. Seriously."

I stared at the shaker he'd abandoned, moved it back where it belonged, before answering in a way that wouldn't make me seem like a prude. "We'll think about it. Now what do we want to eat?"

Avery and I told the guys what we wanted. They headed to the counter to place our orders. Leaning forward, I held Avery's blue gaze. "Don't take this wrong, but I'm still having a difficult time seeing you two together."

"Maybe you need glasses," she said, a teasing tone to her voice.

"What?"

"If you can't see us."

Avery only responded to the literal meaning of what I said when she was bothered by what I was trying to say, so I knew I'd hit on something that upset her. I probably wasn't the only one who thought she and Fletcher were an odd match. "I didn't mean that in a bad way," I assured her. "It's just that you're so opposite."

"Not as much as you think. But that's what makes it fun."

I looked toward the counter. I'd never seen Fletcher in anything except a black T-shirt that looked like it had shrunk in the wash. Even after our session in the car, Jeremy's light-blue shirt was barely wrinkled. "Do you think we're boring?"

"What? No." Avery touched my arm, brought my attention back to her. "What brought that on?"

"You've gone skinny-dipping, haven't you?"

"No." She took a sugar packet and tapped it repeatedly as though she was trying to stir up her answer. "Although I probably will before summer's over—or maybe once Fletcher and I get to Austin."

"You've changed since you got together with him," I said.

"A little, I guess. Don't you think you've changed since you started dating Jeremy?"

"Not really. We're the same as we were when it was just the three of us hanging together."

"You're cute together."

Inwardly I cringed. "Cute" sounded like we were in elementary school or something.

Two girls got in the line and immediately started talking to Fletcher. His shadowed jaw made him look older, more dangerous. He'd always drawn girls' attention. Jeremy, who had shaved before he picked me up, stood there trying not to look awkward, because they were ignoring him.

"What's wrong?" Avery asked.

"Those girls." I bit on my lower lip. "It's stupid, but it bothers me that they aren't talking to Jeremy. Like maybe they don't think they could be into him." I shook my head. "See, that is so shallow and stupid. I don't want to be jealous, but I wouldn't mind if girls were jealous of me." Because if they were, then I'd know that they knew I had a terrific guy. I didn't know why I needed that validation.

"I was," Avery said quickly. "Jealous of you. Before I had Fletcher. I know that's awful because you're my best friend, but for a long time I wished that Jeremy had wanted to be my boyfriend instead of yours. I mean, the three of us hung out together. What was wrong with me that he didn't choose me?"

"Nothing was wrong with you," I reassured her. Then I added, "But I didn't know you wanted him for a boyfriend."

"Now I can see that we wouldn't have been right

together, but I would have said yes in a heartbeat if he'd asked me out. He's so nice."

He was nice. But was he too nice?

The guys returned to the table. Avery dropped that bag of sugar. I snatched it up and placed it back into its holder, noticed a yellow packet mixed in with the blue ones, plucked it out, and inserted it in its proper place. Then I smiled at Jeremy—a little guiltily because we'd been talking about him—as he set a cheeseburger and shake in front of me, and a basket of fries between us.

"Thanks." He knew exactly how I liked my burger and he didn't mind ordering it medium well, with a slice of cheese on top and a slice on the bottom, pickle, and tomato that wasn't from the ends. Mustard on the bottom of the bun, mayo on the top, and the B. S. special sauce on top of the mayo. My mom always made me order my own burger. She was embarrassed that I couldn't just order a burger by calling out a number or saying *all the way*. But I was particular. What was wrong with that? I knew what I wanted.

Avery and Fletcher had cheeseburgers, too, but they were sharing a basket of onion rings. I carefully unwrapped my burger, peered beneath the top bun to see everything exactly as I liked it, and bit into it.

"So . . ." Avery said as she dipped an onion ring into ketchup. "You know Dot, the owner of the Shrimp Hut?"

The Shrimp Hut was the restaurant on the beach

where Avery worked on the weekends. "Yeah," I said.

"Her mom is having some surgery so she's going to be out of town for a few days next week and she asked me to house-sit, take care of her cat and dogs. The cool thing is, her house is on the beach. It has three bedrooms, and she said I could have company. Interested in joining us?"

Us? I looked at her, shifted my gaze to Fletcher, back to her. "The two of you?"

Grinning, she nodded.

"Your parents are okay with this?" I asked, stunned. Her dad was a cop who kept a pretty tight rein on things.

"I'm leaving for college in six weeks. They know they need to trust me. I'm officially curfew-less. They want me to let them know when I'll be home, but they know there is nothing I'm going to do right now that I won't do at college." She shrugged. "They're letting me grow up."

My mom hadn't given me a curfew in a while but I didn't know if she'd approve if she knew Jeremy was going to be there. I suppose I didn't have to tell her that he'd be there, although I'd felt so guilty about lying to her before that I'd confessed about our botched romantic night. Mom had just laughed and said, "Karma's a bitch." Now Karma was giving us a second chance with a bedroom on the beach. I couldn't hide my excitement about that as I looked at Jeremy. "What do you think?"

"Up to you."

He was always such a gentleman. Clearly he didn't want to push me into anything and would let it be my decision. Although I did wish I heard a little more enthusiasm in his voice. "Could be loads of fun. I just don't know if I can swing it with my mom."

"There's nothing you could do there that you can't do just as easily out by the lake," Fletcher pointed out.

I grimaced. "I don't exactly tell her we go to the lake. But you're right. I'll talk to her."

"Great!" Avery said. "We'll have a blast. It'll probably be two or three nights. Dot's still working out the details. I'll let you know when I have them."

"Sounds like a plan."

Beneath the table, I squeezed Jeremy's hand. We were getting an all-night-alone-in-a-bedroom-together do-over. This time I was determined we would round second base and head to third. I could hardly wait.

Chapter 2

JEREMY

As I walked through the door, I dropped my keys into a small bowl on a nearby narrow table that hugged the wall. I headed for the kitchen, not surprised when I heard, "You're a little late."

Stopping, I turned and faced my dad. No question whatsoever that we came from the same gene pool. Same blond hair, same boring brown eyes, same unimpressive height. "After the movie, we went to B.S. for a burger."

"Wish you kids wouldn't call it that."

My dad wished for a lot of things, mostly that he hadn't gotten my mom pregnant when they were eighteen. I'd heard numerous times about all the challenges they'd faced working, going to college part-time, taking care of me. Opportunities lost, dreams delayed.

"Sure that's all you did?" he asked in his best lawyerly

cross-examination voice.

"Movie and burger." What happened in between was none of his business even though I knew he thought it was. I'd had the responsibility lecture so many times that it was practically part of my DNA now. I pointed toward the kitchen. "I'm going to grab a water."

I tried to ignore the fact that my father was trailing behind me like a bloodhound on the scent of an escaped convict.

"This girl you're spending all your time with . . ."

Gritting my teeth, I grabbed a bottle of spring-fed water from the fridge, slammed the door closed, leaned against it, and unscrewed the cap. "Her name—again—is Kendall, and I'm not just *spending time* with her. She's my girlfriend."

"You're too young to be this serious about someone. You need to be exploring possibilities."

Strange advice coming from someone who had insisted I work at his law firm this summer, who had decided which universities I should apply to. "What possibilities? I love her. I'm happy with her. What more is there for me to look for?"

My dad glared. "I know you think I'm riding your ass for no good reason, but you're going to change. What you have now may not be what you want in a few years or even a few months."

"Talking from experience?" I didn't know why my parents were still together. They did nothing except pick at each other. I shoved myself away from the refrigerator and headed for the doorway.

"Don't take that attitude with me," he snapped.

I stopped only long enough to toss back at him, "Just because you're unhappy doesn't mean I am or will be. Kendall and I are perfect together. Get used to it."

I'd taken three steps when my dad barked, "Get a haircut."

I swung around to stare at him. "Seriously? That's how we're going to end this?"

"You're starting to look unkempt. Appearance is everything."

Appearance of a happy home, marriage, career. "Whatever."

Striding out, I suddenly wished that I owned that motorcycle Kendall had mentioned so I could go roaring away from here. But then again, that feeling was nothing new. I'd wanted to get out of here ever since I'd overheard my parents refer to me as the biggest mistake of their lives.

Chapter 3

KENDALL

Lunch?

Jeremy's text came in as I was leaning against a tree waiting for Drifter to finish sniffing around in search of the perfect spot to do his business. The German shepherd was so fussy. His owner, Sandy Miller, was out of town for a few days so I walked and fed him while she was away. He was fine being by himself at night. And it gave me a little spending money.

I texted back:

Jo-Jo's?

Jeremy:

C U there.

Smiling, I slipped my phone back into my shorts pocket. Drifter had come over and was looking up at me, his tail wagging fiercely. He was always so pleased with his accomplishments. Removing a plastic bag from the other pocket of my shorts, I proceeded to clean up his mess, tossed it in a nearby trash can, and carried on along the neighborhood trail.

Once I returned Drifter to his home, I headed off to meet Jeremy in my bright red Smart car.

He was already in a booth at Jo-Jo's Diner when I got there. Grinning, he slid off the bench and waited for me to join him. It was the manners thing his dad had drilled into him. When I got near, he kissed me on the cheek. Then we both settled into the booth.

We'd eaten at the family diner often enough that we didn't have to look at the menu. He ordered meat loaf and I went with fried chicken. While we were waiting, I reached across the table and held his hands. He was wearing a long-sleeved, buttoned, light-blue shirt and a dark blue tie. He'd loosened the tie. Made him look sexy, rebellious.

"Everything okay?" I asked.

He shrugged, smiled. "Missed you."

Warmth swirled through me. Even after all these months, sometimes it was difficult to believe that he loved me. His family had way more money than mine, lived in a larger house. His dad was a lawyer for Pete's sake, which just sounded fancy. They'd taken us to a high-end restaurant for Jeremy's birthday. He'd had to wear a sport coat. He'd looked great, but the evening was so formal and uncomfortable. I'd worried that I would use the wrong utensil or make a mistake in etiquette that would have everyone raising eyebrows at me. My mom and I liked to hang out at Cheez It Up, a pizza place with a rodent for a mascot and a carnival atmosphere. "How's work?"

"Same-o. Researching stuff."

"TV shows make it look so exciting to be a lawyer," I said. "What if you're bored because you really have no interest in the law?"

He looked out the window. "My dad would be disappointed. Sometimes I think he's trying to relive his life through me." He shook his head. "Sorry, just got into it with him last night. Guess some of the remnants of our *discussion* are lingering."

"Why didn't you say something when you texted good night?"

"I didn't want to bother you with it."

"Jeremy! I'm your girlfriend. We're supposed to share stuff."

"Not this."

I was a little hurt that he would keep something from me, because I assumed we shared everything. I'd been with him long enough to know he and his dad seldom had *discussions*. They were often at odds, but he rarely talked about it. I was surprised that he'd agreed to work with his dad this summer.

"Did the argument have anything to do with our going to the beach with Avery?" I asked.

"No, I didn't even go there. I don't have to get his

permission. I'm eighteen."

I stared at him, surprised but also impressed with his rebelliousness. He always got his parents' approval if we were doing something other than just hanging out. I wondered if Fletcher was rubbing off on him or if he was simply coming into his own.

The waitress came to our table. Jeremy and I unlocked hands and she set the food down.

"How's Drifter?" Jeremy asked, and I recognized that he wanted to move the discussion away from his dad. He'd met the dog when I cared for him before. See? The sharing thing.

"Doing good." I waved my drumstick around. "You know, I've been thinking that we could bring in some extra money pet-sitting while at A&M. It's not like high school, where we're in class all day. Our schedules will be more flexible."

"We?" he asked.

"Yeah, I figure we could do it together if you want. I even have a name for it. 'Pawsitively Pampered.' Positively spelled *P-A-W-S*, etc."

"You've given a lot of thought to it."

I shrugged. "I'm going to need some spending money. Don't want to depend on my mom for everything."

"Wish I didn't have to depend on my dad for anything.

I'll help you where I can, but I'm planning on getting a job that will give me more independence."

"Like what?" I asked.

"I don't know. But I'm going to start browsing the Aggie website for an on-campus job."

"I'll do that, too. It would be nice to have something firmed up before we got there. I can't believe it's only a few more weeks before we leave." We'd managed to get rooms in the same coed dorm. While we weren't sharing a room, at least we wouldn't be that far away from each other.

"It can't come soon enough."

"The beach vacation will be a nice break. Mom said I could go, so I'm all good." The advantage to being a high school graduate about to head off to college was that when I asked my mom if it was okay for me to spend a couple of nights at the beach, house-sitting with Avery, she didn't bat an eye when she said yes. But she did toss out one of her usual truisms: "Just remember that all actions have consequences."

I knew that she was referring to any actions with Jeremy, that she was aware he'd probably be there.

"It'll be fun," he said.

"And we'll get to share a bed."

Jeremy gave me a slow smile. "Yeah. Maybe it'll work out differently this time. Although it might be awkward with Avery and Fletcher there."

"Not if we're quiet," I said in a low voice. "And I can whisper."

He laughed. "At least my back shouldn't cramp."

Reaching across the table, I squeezed his hand. "I'm really looking forward to it."

"Yeah, me too."

I was also just a little bit nervous about the prospect of what all might happen when we were alone in a bedroom at the beach. It seemed like it had the potential to be so romantic. I decided I was going to pack candles, clean sheets—not that I thought those on the bed wouldn't be clean, but I just wanted to make sure. The more I thought about it, the more my palms began to grow damp. I needed a distraction.

"Hey, I'm working at the shelter this afternoon," I said. I volunteered at Second Chance, the local pet shelter, at least three times a week. "You know, if you can sneak away from the office."

"Not today. Besides, I need to get a haircut after work. My dad's been ragging on me about it. Just this morning he said I looked like I was a member of a rock band."

Jeremy looked more like a choirboy. His hair barely touched his ears. "Maybe you should grow it out for the rest of the summer. You know, continue the little rebellious streak you started by not asking your parents about the beach trip. I could really dig running my fingers through the longer strands."

He studied me over the rim of his glass as he took a sip of his sweet tea. "The law office is so conservative."

"But you're not actually a lawyer."

"True." He ran his finger up and down the condensation on the glass. "Think you'd like it long?"

"I'd love it long," I admitted. Jeremy was cute but I thought longer hair would make him hot. And if he didn't shave every day he'd look older. Like Fletcher. Course Fletcher *was* older.

"I didn't think my hair really mattered to you."

I lifted my shoulders. "I like it however you want it, but it doesn't hurt to change things up now and then." I wound some strands of my curly hair around my finger. "I'm thinking of cutting mine way short."

"I like it long."

"It's just so hard to take care of."

"Yeah, pulling it back in a ponytail is probably challenging," he said with a twinkle in his eyes.

I tossed a chip of ice at him. He ducked, laughed. I was so glad to hear him laugh. I hated when he was having a tough time dealing with his dad.

"I'm also thinking about adopting a dog," I confessed.

"Your mom would kill you."

I dropped my head back, groaned. "I know." I must

have inherited my love of dogs from my dad because my mom was not a fan. "But there's this little basset hound, Bogart. He's twelve, has arthritis in his hips, moves slowly. He's been there for three weeks. I don't think anyone is going to want him."

"Maybe you should give it a little more time."

"If you're not getting a haircut, maybe you could stop by the shelter, adopt him. Your mom is home all day." His mother didn't have a job. She was into serving on boards and committees for various charities around town, which I guessed was another sort of work.

"I don't think either of my parents would welcome a dog. And what about when I go off to college?"

"Do you have to be so practical?" I was really getting desperate to find a home for Bogart. Not that it was my job to place dogs. My job was to clean out their kennels, but still, I worried about them.

"Sorry, babe, but I know the dog would be miserable in my house."

Because Jeremy was miserable in his house. Or not in his house, but with his parents. They'd never really warmed up to me or made me feel welcome. They weren't rude or anything, but they were very distant. I was not at all bothered that we hardly ever spent any time at his place.

"I get that," I told him.

"Maybe Avery will take him."

"Maybe. I'll check with her."

"Or maybe when you get to the shelter, you'll find he's been adopted."

"That would be even better," I admitted.

But when I got to the shelter, Bogart was still in his kennel, curled in the corner. According to the forms that were filled out when he was brought in, his owner, Samuel Forrest, had died. I found that particularly sad. Not only had he lost someone he loved, but he'd lost his home.

He struggled to his feet, waddled over, and stuck his nose through one of the openings in the wired gate. I slipped my fingers through, rubbed his snout. Then, even though I had work to do, I opened the door, went in, and sat on the hard concrete. He crawled into my lap and I stroked his back.

"What am I going to do with you?" I asked with a sigh. We were a no-kill shelter so I knew he wouldn't be put down, but I hated thinking of his spending what little time he might have left in this small space. Removing a leash that was dangling over my shoulders, I hooked it to his collar. "Come on. Let's go out."

His tongue was lolling as I escorted him down the hallway. The other dogs went nuts barking, but their time would come. They'd all get to come out for a romp in the fenced-in area behind the shelter. When I got Bogart outside, I unhooked his leash. He just dropped down beside my feet.

I couldn't stay here with him. I had other dogs that I needed to bring out. Still I reached down and gave him an affectionate petting. He looked up, a plea in his eyes: *More, please.*

So I gave him a brisk rubbing over his back. He looked as though he were in heaven. "I'll be back," I told him reluctantly. He limped off to warm in the sun. My heart was breaking.

As I walked back inside, I pulled my phone from my shorts pocket and texted Avery.

Kendall:

At the shelter. Doesn't your brother want a dog?

Avery:

Course. He's a boy.

Kendall:

Come now. Have one for you.

Avery:

Not my decision.

Kendall:

Come look, anyway.

Avery:

K

I knew once I got her here that she would fall in love

with Bogart. Then she'd convince her parents that a dog was a good idea.

My step was a little lighter when I went to retrieve the chocolate lab whose owner had decided he had too many dogs. At least that was the reasoning he'd put on the intake form. I'd seen that reason countless times and I never understood it. Did the owner just look around one day and think, *I thought I had five dogs. Uh, I have six. One has to go.*

Didn't make sense.

I heard the beep of an incoming text and glanced at my cell phone to see a message from Jeremy.

Thinking of U. ☺

Smiling, I sent him back the same message. He was always texting me with little reminders about how much he loved and thought about me.

Chocolate was happy to see me, his entire body jerking back and forth with the enthusiasm of his wagging tail. He knew what it meant when I was holding the leash. When I opened the door, he jumped up, his paws landing heavily on the shoulders of my five-foot-four frame and nearly taking me down to the ground. He licked my neck and face. "Okay, okay." Here was another dog that I wished like crazy I could take home.

Heck, if I could, I'd take them all.

"Hey, Kendall," Terri, the shelter's director, said as

she walked in carrying what looked like a Lhasa apso mix.

"What a cutie!" I ran my fingers over his silken hair. He was beautiful, looked to be recently groomed.

"His name is Fargo. His owner just surrendered him because she can't take care of him anymore. It was hard on her. She went through half a box of tissues while she filled out the paperwork."

Difficult for the dog, too. He wouldn't be able to understand why he was here. But he had such a sweet face. "How old is he?"

"Four."

"Then he won't be here long," I assured her. The small, cute, young ones always went quickly.

"Hope not, but then I hope that for all of them." She walked off to get him situated in his temporary home, and I led Chocolate outside. Once I unhooked the leash, he bounded across the open expanse. I could see Bogart still sunning himself.

I brought out two more dogs before lifting Bogart into my arms to carry him inside. He could walk, just not that well, and I felt like loving on him a little. I'd just gotten him settled in and was moving on to take a golden to the play area when I heard the door to the reception area open and glanced back. Avery and her six-year-old brother walked in.

I grinned when Tyler immediately squatted down in front of the first kennel and pressed his hand to the door. He had so much energy and excitement that I knew he would make a wonderful friend for a dog. For Bogart.

I started striding toward them. "Hey!"

Avery smiled. "Looks like love at first sight here."

"You should look around," I told her. "Make sure."

"Oh, we will," she assured me. "We're not taking a Pyrenees home. My mom made it clear she'd veto anything too big."

"Avery, look!" Tyler cried out as he hopped over to the next kennel where a Jack Russell terrier was showing off by leaping onto the windowsill. "I want him."

"First of all, him is a her," she said patiently. "But we want something a little less rambunctious."

"What's ram . . . ?" He screwed up his face.

"Rambunctious means energetic. You run around enough for ten dogs."

"This one," he said, and dashed across to another cage. She just shook her head.

"We have a room where you can take a dog and play with him for a while, figure out if you mesh," I told her as we joined her brother outside another kennel.

She studied the sheet clipped to the door that provided all the stats we knew about the dog and some of our guesses. The dachshund had been a stray so we could only guess age, and as far as we could tell he wasn't housebroken. As though to prove the point, he lifted a leg—

Avery snatched her brother up out of the incoming stream. "Definitely want one that's housebroken," she said.

"There's a really sweet basset hound over here," I told her, and directed them toward Bogart.

Bogart struggled up and limped to the door. Sometimes I felt like the dogs knew exactly what was going on, that they were on display, that people were trying to determine whether or not to provide them with a home.

"What's wrong with him?" Tyler asked, squatting down until he was practically eye level. "Does he have an owie?"

"He has arthritis," I said. Tyler blinked at me. Right, he probably didn't know what arthritis was. "Yeah, he has an owie."

"Oh." He pouted out his lower lip in sympathy and turned back to Bogart.

I looked at Avery expectantly but she was shaking her head as she read his paperwork. "What's the life expectancy of a basset hound?" she asked really quietly.

I couldn't lie to her, no matter how badly I wanted him to have a home. "Ten to twelve."

She arched a brow. "That's going to give Tyler a really quick life lesson."

I grimaced. "I know." Since he'd been in the foster care system before Avery's parents adopted him, Tyler had enough life lessons under his belt already.

"I'm sorry," she said. "But we want something a little younger."

"No, it's my fault. I wasn't thinking. We did just get in a younger dog, adorable. Trained. His owner had to give him up."

I took them to where Terri had placed Fargo. Tyler laughed and clapped when he saw the Lhasa. Grinning, Avery took his paperwork and read it over.

"Oh, he seems perfect," she said.

"Do you want to take him to the playroom?" I asked.

"Absolutely."

I opened the door. Eagerly, Fargo raised up on his hind legs, placed his paws on my thighs. He was a smaller dog, with tan-and-white curling hair. I slipped the leash on him and led the way to one of our playrooms near the reception area. As soon as we were inside, I released my hold on the tether and he raced over to Tyler.

Tyler giggled, dropped down on the floor, and began to play with the dog.

"Well, that's a good sign," Avery said as she leaned against the wall, watching as her brother became engrossed in petting Fargo. "So I guess we're getting a dog."

"You won't regret it, I promise. Just give him some tender loving care."

"Dot said that was pretty much all I had to give her dogs while she was away. Tell me you'll be there to help."

"Yep. I got the all clear from my mom for going to the beach. And Jeremy is in."

"Great. We're going to have so much fun."

I hoped so. Pressing my back to the wall, I was close enough to Avery that I could whisper. "So just to be clear, when you mentioned the bedrooms—you and I aren't sharing one, right?"

She shifted her gaze over to me. "No. I figured Fletcher and me, you and Jeremy. Are you okay with that?"

"Oh, yeah, absolutely. I just wanted to make sure we were on the same page, or in this case, not in the same bed."

Turning, she rolled along the wall until only her shoulder was touching it. "That night when you told your mom you were spending the night at my house—"

"Nothing happened."

Avery furrowed her brow. "Nothing at all?"

"Very little. We kissed some, but mostly we sat out by the lake and served as a buffet for mosquitoes. I thought we'd do more. . . ." Avery was my best friend. I could tell her anything, but this was so personal. I felt the heat warm my face. "We chickened out."

"You weren't ready. There's nothing wrong with that."

"It's more like Jeremy wasn't ready. He's so cautious, wants to make sure we don't have any regrets."

"Again, nothing wrong—"

"Avery, look, he thinks I taste good!" Tyler crowed, interrupting our conversation. Fargo had settled on Tyler's lap and was licking his hand.

I knew even if Avery's brother had heard what we were saying, he wouldn't know what we were talking about. I knelt down. "Those are dog kisses," I told him.

He beamed. "He loves me."

I knew being loved was important to Tyler. Avery had shared with me some of the challenges of dealing with her brother's insecurities when he first came to live with her family. "I think he does, yes."

"Guess we found our dog," Avery said. "Will they hold him for us until Mom can come by and get him after work?"

"Absolutely. Come on, Tyler, we need to take him back to his pen."

"I want to keep him," he said, hugging Fargo fiercely.

"You will," I assured him, "but first we have to give him a chance to say good-bye to the other dogs. When your mom gets here later, he'll be ready to go. I bet you're big enough to walk him back to his pen."

He nodded. I knew at his age being big enough to do things was important, too. As we walked down the corridor, Avery leaned in and whispered, "Well played."

"You learn a lot taking care of dogs."

"You're going to make a good vet," she said.

"Hope so."

When we closed Fargo in his pen, he pawed at the door. I thought he was already in love with Tyler. When we passed by Bogart, my heart broke just a little because he didn't come to the door in anticipation. He stayed curled on the small bed set up for him in a corner, as though he knew he wasn't going anywhere.

Well, we'd just see about that.

Chapter 4

JEREMY

Need you to come by the shelter after work.

I had a feeling that Kendall's text didn't bode well. She didn't throw around the word *need* lightly. She liked being in control, depending on herself.

Although a part of me also wondered if her text was simply a diversion to keep me from getting a haircut. I'd been surprised when she mentioned growing it out. Not that I hadn't thought about it. I'd looked like a young conservative since I was four years old. My parents were all about appearances. Outward appearances, anyway. People driving through our neighborhood saw "upper class." They didn't see the insanity that occurred within the walls of our house.

I knew that I'd probably have another disagreement with my dad when he saw that I hadn't taken his firmly toned *suggestion* to get my hair cut, but Kendall's needs had precedent over his wants.

When I walked through the shelter doors, I waved at Terri who was standing behind the reception counter.

"Hey, Jeremy," she said. "Kendall's in the back."

"Thanks." I'd been here often enough that people knew me. I wasn't an official volunteer, but sometimes I came to help Kendall. She was a stickler for keeping all the cages clean, making sure all the dogs had equal attention. I'd left here covered in fur more than once.

I located her in the puppy room. She was holding a tiny pup, feeding it with a small bottle. I leaned against the doorjamb, crossed my arms over my chest, and just watched her. Her red hair was pulled back into a ponytail but several strands had escaped and were circling her face. Every now and then she would skew up her mouth and blow out a burst of air. The curls would fly around before falling back into place.

It was probably driving her crazy. She didn't like anything out of place.

But I thought it was sexy as hell. But then I thought everything about her was.

Looking up, she smiled the smile that had first kicked me in the gut. I'd been in the new school for all of a week, feeling out of place, missing my friends. Then she'd smiled at me in chem class when the teacher partnered us for a project, and after that I was pretty much a goner—although it had taken me several months to make my move.

"When did you get here?" she asked.

I sauntered over, pushed the loose strands behind her ear. "A few minutes ago. What's this guy's story?" I trailed a finger over his soft belly.

"There's four of them," she said, pointing to a small, gated area. "Someone found them under a bridge, abandoned. What is wrong with people?"

"They're idiots."

"You got that right." Setting the bottle aside, she lowered the puppy onto a mound of blankets where his siblings were sleeping.

"I'm not taking a puppy," I said, hardening my heart to the thought. I didn't know how she worked here and left all these dogs when her hours were done. It took everything within me not to cart them all home, and I wasn't nearly as dog crazy as she was.

"That's not what I needed you for. Come on."

We went out through the door into a corridor. Pens lined each side. Some dogs barked for attention. Some were quiet. Some ran around. Some were still. Kendall came to a stop in front of a door. On the other side was a brown-and-white-spotted dog with long flopping ears and sad, drooping eyes. *Uh-oh.*

"Bogart?" I asked, dreading where this was leading.

"Yeah."

"Kendall, I can't—"

"All I need you to do," she said, interrupting, "is sign the paperwork, pretend you're adopting him. Then I'll take him."

"You sign it."

"I have to be eighteen."

While I'd turned eighteen three months ago, she had fifty-four days to go. Not that I was counting, but I did have something special planned. Still, I wasn't comfortable with this deception. It felt like fraud. I'd spent too much time in my dad's law office obviously. "Have your mom come do the paperwork."

She shook her head. "She'll say no. She doesn't want a dog."

"So what are you going to do? Hide this one under your bed?"

"No, but once I have him at home, once she's met him—she's not going to make me bring him back."

"You don't think so?"

"I can handle Mom. I just need you to handle the paper-work."

I sighed. This was wrong on so many levels.

"You know what?" she said. "Never mind."

Oh, thank—

"I'll just have Fletcher do it."

It felt like a punch to the gut. I liked the guy but I didn't want him doing things for my girlfriend.

She took out her cell phone. I grabbed her wrist. She lifted her green eyes to me. I always felt like I was drowning when I looked into her eyes.

"You know he will," she said. "He has no problem bucking authority."

He was a tough guy, all right. Although not as tough as everyone thought, but he probably would sign the paperwork for her. He'd just think it was a lark. And really, wasn't the point to find good homes for these dogs? There was no better home for a dog than Kendall's.

"Okay, I'll do it." I didn't think that I could sound any less enthused.

Still, Kendall squealed, jumped up, wound her arms around my neck, and planted a kiss on me that had me staggering back against a Rottweiler's door. He charged and I thought I actually felt his teeth nipping at my backside. Lifting Kendall, I jerked to the side and out of reach.

She started laughing. "You were safe." Then she clapped her hands at the dog. "Jon Snow, down."

He crouched. Sometimes I thought she was the female version of the Dog Whisperer.

"Jon Snow?" I asked.

"Yeah, Terri has a thing for *Game of Thrones*. Names all the strays after one of the characters."

I chuckled. I guessed that was as good a place as any to get names.

She rose up on her toes and brushed her lips over mine. "Thank you."

"We'll see if you thank me when your mom grounds you for the rest of your life."

Chapter 5

KENDALL

I needed my mom to fall in love with Bogart at first sight because I wouldn't be able to take him to college with me. No pets were allowed in the dorm.

To cover my bases, I bought a big red bow and secured it around Bogart's neck so she'd understand he was a gift to her. But that didn't stop her from glowering at me as soon as Jeremy and I walked into the kitchen with Bogart. With her hands on her hips, she gave me a very formidable glare. Or she tried to. I could see her softening as Bogart stared up at her with his soulful eyes.

"He'll keep you company when I leave for school," I assured her. She was a freelance graphic designer, did most of her work from home. "I've been really worried about you getting lonely."

She arched a finely shaped brow. Her red hair was pulled back in a ponytail, and in spite of her age, she still had freckles that made her look adorable and too young to be scolding someone. "Yes, I'm sure my loneliness was a major factor here."

"Okay, not a major factor, but I did consider it. The thing is, Mom, he's near the end of his life expectancy. He mostly just lies around. I couldn't stand the thought of him dying in the shelter, possibly alone."

I was aware of Jeremy jerking his head around to look at me. I guessed he hadn't considered that aspect of adopting a senior. Some people adopted older dogs just so they could ensure they had a little bit of heaven here on Earth before they headed to the rainbow bridge. Of course, it was always possible that I was wrong and Bogart would be with us for a while. Life expectancy numbers were an average not a set expiration date.

"I knew it was a mistake to let you volunteer at a shelter," Mom said. "I guess I should be grateful you went so long without bringing one home." Then she narrowed her eyes at Jeremy. "What was your role in all this?"

He shifted uncomfortably. "I signed the paperwork."

"So legally he's yours?"

"Legally, yeah, but—" He shoved his hands into his pockets. "I'm worried about you getting lonely, too."

"If you're both that worried, get me a subscription to a dating service."

I laughed, then sobered when a red blush crept up Mom's cheeks. It had been five years since my dad had died, but still. "Are you serious?"

She didn't meet my eyes. "It *is* going to be really quiet around here when you two are gone. So, okay, Bogart can stay."

I gave her a hug. "Thanks, Mom. You won't be sorry."

"Dogs are man's best friends for a reason." She turned back to the stove. "Guess you'll need to go get him some stuff."

"We stopped at the pet store on our way home," I assured her.

She gave me a pointed look. "I suppose I shouldn't be surprised."

"Well, if you said no, I was going to take him to Grandma."

"Her cats wouldn't have been too happy about that."

She had three, but I figured Bogart was calm enough to get along with them.

Jeremy brought the items in from his car. We set the bowls in the utility room. Put the bed in my bedroom.

"I can't believe she said yes so easily," Jeremy said while I sprinkled a few chew toys around my room.

"He's going to win her over," I assured him.

When we got downstairs, Mom was tossing little chunks of meat that were supposed to go in the stroganoff to Bogart.

Yeah, everything was going to be fine. "So what can we do?" I asked.

"Why don't you make a salad? Jeremy, would you mind setting the table?"

He ate more meals with us than he did with his own parents. Mom had stopped treating him like a guest months ago. He knew his way around the kitchen and gathered up the plates while I got everything I needed out of the fridge.

I set it all on the counter, began slicing tomatoes, and tried to be as nonchalant as possible, although my heart was hammering as I considered my mom's earlier words. "So are you really thinking about dating?"

"Thinking about it." Mom laughed. "Then I start to get nervous. It's been twenty years since I dated your dad. I'm not even sure if I know how to do it anymore."

"It's probably like riding a bike, Mrs. J," Jeremy said as he came back in.

Mom smiled at him. "Probably. Guess I just need to take the plunge."

I tried to imagine my mom dating, having a guy in her life. So much would change and yet I didn't want her to be alone or lonely, either.

After dinner, Jeremy and I took Bogart for a walk along the running trail that snaked through my neighborhood. I didn't think I'd ever seen Bogart so happy as he scouted out the terrain. His limp was less pronounced. Maybe all he needed was to feel loved again. He had to be missing his original owner. I knew what it was to miss someone.

"I can't believe my mom is thinking about dating."

"It's been five years," Jeremy said.

I scowled, and he immediately looked contrite. "Sorry," he said. "I'm sure you're more aware of how much time has passed than I am."

My father had been involved in a freak car accident, driving beneath an overpass that was being repaired when it suddenly buckled—

I shook off the unsettling thoughts. I hated thinking about the randomness of it.

"I wish you'd known him," I said.

"Me too."

"He would have approved of us adopting Bogart. And your idea to put a big red bow on him was brilliant. How could my mom reject him after that? It softened her up."

"I think Bogart did that all on his own. I guess tonight you just want to hang around with him."

Looking over at Jeremy, I took his hand. "Yeah, if you don't mind."

"Seems wrong to abandon him after just breaking him out of the joint."

I laughed. "The shelter isn't exactly prison."

He slipped his arm around me, guided me off the path into a little clearing edged by trees. "I like it when you laugh. You look so sad at the shelter."

"I just wish I could rescue them all."

"I know. You have such a big heart. It's one of the things I love about you."

He lowered his lips to mine. One of the things I loved about Jeremy was his kiss. He always took his time and tasted of peppermint. I knew he carried a little stash in his pocket. He wanted to be ready for a kiss anytime, anywhere. So considerate, so—

"Get a room already," a deep voice bellowed.

Guiltily, we jumped apart. Avery and Fletcher were standing there, both of them grinning like lunatics as Fargo wriggled on the ground between them. I glared at Fletcher. "Not funny."

"I thought it was hilarious," Fletcher said. "It was like you thought you were doing something wrong."

"Maybe that's because you sounded like the PDA police."

"He's just practicing his baritone," Avery said, "for when he does become a cop."

"We didn't appreciate the interruption," Jeremy said.

Fletcher shrugged, not looking at all sorry.

I felt a tug on the leash. Bogart was inspecting Fargo's butt, Fargo was inspecting his. "Where's your brother?" I asked.

"He's not quite big enough for walking a dog," Avery said. "His chore is to feed him."

"Which was hilarious, since no one explained what that involved," Fletcher said. "He fed him from his plate at the table."

I smiled. I could see that, Tyler slipping the dog some food. I had a feeling there was going to be a lot of spoiling going on.

"So, did you just bring Bogart home for the night?" Avery asked.

"No, we"—I pointed between Jeremy and myself— "adopted him."

"Lucky dog," Avery said. "Glad we didn't take him when you asked us to."

"I think Kendall really wanted him," Jeremy said, slipping his arm around my shoulders.

I shrugged. "Sometimes you just connect with a dog." I'd connected with too many to count, but Bogart had needed me the most.

Jeremy crouched and held his hand out to Fargo, who

came over and licked it. "Cute dog. When did you get him?"

"Today," Avery said. "Kendall talked us into taking him."

"I didn't force you," I pointed out. "You chose him."

"I think he chose us," Avery said. "So far, though, he seems to be adjusting fine."

"He's a sissy dog," Fletcher grumbled.

Chuckling, Jeremy looked up. "What?"

"He's small, prances around."

"They've got a Rottweiler you could adopt," Jeremy said.

"No more dogs," Avery said. "One is enough."

Fletcher was living with her family for the summer. Another dog really wasn't an option.

"I like small dogs," Jeremy said, and I was glad that he was unlike Fletcher in that regard and didn't view any dogs as being sissies.

"We're going out for ice cream after our walk," Avery said. "Want to come with us?"

"We should probably stick close to home tonight," I said. "So Bogart gets a sense of security."

Avery furrowed her brow. "We don't have to stay with the dog all the time, do we?"

"No," I reassured her. "You have other people at your house. My mom isn't exactly a dog person. She's fine with him, but she won't love on him like I will."

"Who would?" she teased. "Okay, then we'll see y'all later."

They walked away, and I took Jeremy's hand. "Are you okay not going with them for ice cream?"

"Bogart comes first."

I hugged him tightly. "You're the best."

Twilight had settled in while we were talking, so Jeremy and I headed back home. Besides, I didn't think Bogart could do a long walk. I just wanted him to get out for a little exercise.

"So what about staying at the beach with Avery?" Jeremy asked.

"We should still be able to do that," I told him. "Bogart and Mom will have adjusted to each other by then."

"I still can't believe she didn't get mad about you bringing him home."

"I think she secretly wanted a dog. It's going to be lonely for her when I leave."

"Maybe she'll have a boyfriend by then."

I crinkled my brow. I wasn't ready for Mom to get a boyfriend. Dating was okay, but a boyfriend? I looked down at Bogart. Had she accepted him because there was something I was going to have to accept?

I shuddered with the thought.

Chapter 6

JEREMY

When I got home, the house was dark and funeral quiet. I figured my parents were out at one of the many fundraising functions they attended. I was proud of the fact that they were so involved in the community, but it also got a little lonely around here. If I weren't leaving for a college in a few weeks, I would seriously consider getting a dog.

I went into the kitchen, microwaved some popcorn, grabbed a bottle of lemon water, and headed into the den where the biggest TV known to man graced one wall. My dad always had to have the biggest, the best of everything. Sometimes they entertained, and he liked it when people gaped at everything we owned.

Not that I was complaining. Because of his obsession, I had all the latest gadgets.

I dropped onto the sofa, picked up the remote, and

searched through the on-demand possibilities until I found *Sherlock Holmes: A Game of Shadows*. I liked the way steampunk had been incorporated into the movie franchise. Munching on popcorn, I started up the movie.

I was about an hour into it when I heard voices from the front hall.

"You knew how important tonight was to me," Mom said. "Could you have looked any more bored?"

"What do you want from me, Marsha?" my dad asked. "I spent five thousand on silent auction items."

"I wanted you at my side as I greeted people."

"It was your moment. I was trying to let you bask in it."

"It was more like you were trying to escape it. And you wore that awful red tie."

"What's wrong with the tie?"

"It clashes with my dress."

"Drinking red wine clashes with your dress. How many times do I have to tell you that red stains your teeth? You looked like a vampire by the end of the night. Drink white."

"Maybe we should move to Denver so I can smoke pot. Would that make you happy?"

I turned up the volume on the TV so I couldn't hear them anymore. I didn't often side with my dad, but really what difference did a tie make? On the other hand, if Mom preferred red wine, who cared?

The lights in the room suddenly came on. I looked up as my mom glided toward me. The red shade of her hair was not to be found in nature. She wore it in a short style that served as a frame for her high cheekbones and blue eyes.

When she reached me, she picked up the remote and paused the TV. "What are you doing here?"

"I live here."

She gave me an indulgent smile as she gracefully lowered herself into a chair. "You know what I mean. It's early. You're usually out late with that girl you've been seeing."

I fought not to groan. "Kendall. Her name is Kendall."

"We should have her over for dinner sometime."

Yeah, listening to my parents pick at each other made for great entertainment. "We're both pretty busy. How was the fund-raiser?"

"Very successful, I think. It was for a women's abuse shelter. Now I can start working on a tea for literacy. We have a staggering percentage of people in this community who can't read English."

Talking to my mom was sometimes like being read a pamphlet. "If there's anything I can do . . ."

"I'll keep that in mind."

Which pretty much meant she wouldn't think of anything I could do to help. She wasn't good at delegating.

"Some friends and I are going to go to the beach for a

few days. Not sure exactly when—"

"That'll be fun," she said, boredom evident in her voice. She rose. "Night, sweetie."

My mom walked out without asking for any further details. Sometimes I thought she cared more about her fund-raisers than she did me. But then, if not for me, maybe she would have had a different life.

Chapter 7

KENDALL

When I walked into the shelter, I heard the dogs start yipping. A door separated the reception area from the kennels, but they could catch my scent, knew when I arrived. Or maybe I just wanted to believe that.

A guy with long, dark hair and a scraggly beard was standing at the counter talking to Terri. He looked to be about my age, but I didn't know him from school so he was probably a little older. He was wearing khaki shorts, Birkenstocks, and a brown T-shirt molded to his torso that read, YEAH, IT WAS ME. I LET THE DOGS OUT.

"Kendall," Terri said. "Meet Chase Harper. He's a new volunteer. Why don't you show him the ropes?"

"You mean, the leashes?" I teased. They both smiled. Bowing slightly, I extended an arm toward the door that led to the areas where the kennels were. We walked past the cat room where a dozen felines lounged about. They couldn't care less about us.

The dogs, though, went into a frenzy. Laughing, Chase crouched down in front of a metal grated door behind which a Chihuahua bounced and yipped. "Hey, sweet girl."

"It's best not to get too attached," I told him.

He peered up at me with brown eyes. "Yeah, I know. I've worked at shelters before, but it's hard sometimes to do what's best." Straightening, he gave me a once-over. "I bet you get attached."

"Sometimes," I admitted. I walked over to the wall where several leashes hung from a pegboard. "We use these to either take them for a walk or lead them out to the back." I grabbed one for myself, tossed him one.

I pointed to a clipboard. "We mark down when we take a dog out. We go by the kennel numbers."

"Impersonal."

"It's easier. The dogs frequently change, which is good. It's what we want. For them to be adopted." I studied the information on the sheet. "Looks like twenty-five and twenty-six are due for a trip out. Come on. I'll give you the grand tour and then we'll fetch the dogs."

We walked down the corridor. Enclosures were on either side. Each had a water bowl and a bed. Some had a dog. One had two dogs. That meant they'd had the same owner, who for some reason surrendered them.

"Man, I don't know how people can give up their pets," Chase said.

"Do you have one?" I asked.

"Swedish vallhund. Missed Dora like crazy when I was away at school. How about you?"

"Just adopted a basset hound."

"I knew you were the type to get attached."

I shrugged. "It's hard not to. My mom's simply grateful that I held out as long as I did and only brought one home."

We came to a door at the end of the corridor. "This is the puppy room."

We walked inside. Jade Johnson, another volunteer, was sitting in a rocker feeding one of the abandoned puppies with a bottle. In honor of graduating, she'd chopped off her hair, died it black, and gotten a nose ring.

"Well, hellllo," she said. "Looking for a puppy?"

"This is Chase," I told her. "He's a new volunteer."

"Great!"

I was pretty sure that her excitement had to do with him being in her orbit for more than today rather than the prospect of having more help around here. "Meet Jade. Another volunteer."

"You the Puppy Whisperer?" Chase asked.

"Something like that," she said. "I'll be happy to show you around when I'm finished here."

"I've got it," I told her.

He didn't know her well enough to know the smile she gave me was one of displeasure.

"If you decide you want another tour you know where to find me," she said.

She was such a flirt. I was just glad that she'd never set her sights on Jeremy. Not that I thought he would go for her type. He was as loyal as a golden retriever.

"I'll keep that in mind," Chase said.

As we walked by her, he reached down and petted the pup on the head. Jade beamed up at him, while the dog pretty much ignored him for the bottle.

I opened the door that led to another corridor of enclosures. Some of the dogs reacted. Some seemed to take the new guy in stride.

"I'll get twenty-five," I said. The collie mix eagerly came to me when I opened the door. I slipped on the leash. Glancing over my shoulder, I watched as Chase struggled with a highly energetic border collie.

"Down, boy, down!" he called out. When he finally got the leash on, he gave me a hard look. "Was that my initiation?"

I smiled. "No, your initiation will be cleaning out the kennels that have a mess in them. That's the new guy's job."

"No problem. I spent summers on my granddad's farm. Trust me. Cleaning up a dog mess is nothing compared to cleaning up after a horse."

I laughed. "I would think not."

We walked through a door to the outside and set the dogs loose.

"We just let them romp about for about fifteen or twenty minutes," I explained. "I can go in and get a couple more if you want to watch them."

"Yeah, I can do that."

"There are some balls in that container over there," I said, pointing out a plastic bin. "You know, if you want to play with them."

"Sure thing."

I retrieved four more dogs and sent them off to play with Chase. He was tossing a ball to one and a Frisbee to another. I stood on the porch watching him for a moment. He was definitely a dog lover.

Jade stepped outside and came to stand beside me. "He is so hot. I call dibs."

I stared at her. "On what?"

"On dating him."

I rolled my eyes. "I have a boyfriend. Jeremy Swanson. And he's pretty hot."

She scoffed. "No, he's cute. He's not smoking. I'm going to get third-degree burns kissing Chase and love every minute of it." Before I knew what she was going to do, she snatched the leashes from my fingers. "I'll help him bring the dogs back in."

She sauntered across the grass with such an exaggerated swing to her hips that I was surprised she didn't knock a bone out of joint. I went back inside and tried not to be bothered by her comment. Jeremy was hot, just not in a dark, dangerous kind of way like Chase. A girl would always feel secure with Jeremy.

That was a good thing. He was reliable. Safe.

I wanted safe, didn't I?

That thought nagged at me as I sat on the couch snuggled against Jeremy, with Bogart nestled on the floor near us. We were having a night in, binge-watching *The 100*. We'd done quite a bit of binge-watching since summer started. Always at my house.

My mom tended to leave us alone, as long as we didn't close ourselves into any rooms. Although tonight she was on a date. She was taking the plunge with a guy she'd met through a website that promised a perfect match. She was meeting him at a restaurant. I had to admit that I had mixed feelings. Happy for her, but apprehensive, wondering how our lives might change.

Jeremy was absently running his fingers up and down my arm. When he watched a TV show or movie, he was almost totally focused on the story. Usually I was, too.

But tonight I kept thinking about Jade's comment.

It wasn't that I wanted her coming after my guy, but I wouldn't have minded her showing a bit of interest in him. Jeremy and I had been friends before we'd started dating and I'd never heard of him asking another girl out. But what if he was with me because I'd been his only choice?

Jeremy stopped the episode before it could roll over into the next one. He shifted slightly, and I peered up at him. He trailed his finger over my cheek. "You seem distracted tonight."

I shrugged. "Thinking about my mom. It's weird for her to have a date. What if she really likes this guy? She wouldn't tell me his name or show me a picture of him. So I just don't know what to expect."

"Maybe she's just testing the waters and didn't want to get her—and your—hopes up."

I glanced back over at the TV. "What if she has sex with him?"

Jeremy laughed, then sobered when he realized I was seriously concerned. "She probably won't on the first date."

I moved so that I was almost sitting on him. He slid down until he was sprawled over the couch, and I was tucked up close to his side. "How many is the right number do you think?" I asked.

"Everyone is different."

Not really wanting to think about Mom anymore, I loosened one of the buttons on his shirt. "So how many dates have we had, do you think?"

He closed his hand around mine.

"What if your mom walks in on us?" he asked.

"What if she doesn't?"

"Do you have any idea how long she'll be gone?"

Shaking my head, I rolled over until I was on top of him. I skimmed my fingers through his hair. "You didn't get a haircut today."

"Nope. Maybe tomorrow." He grinned. "Or maybe I'll grow it out."

I rubbed my thumb along his jaw. "Maybe you shouldn't shave tomorrow."

"Why?"

"It'll make you look older."

"It'll also make my dad go ballistic. There's a dress code at the office."

"But it's like he's stifling your freedom to express yourself. You're not your father's clone. You didn't need his permission to go to the beach. Maybe you should rebel a little more."

He chuckled. "Rebelling within the confines of the family is one thing. To do it at the office is another. If I was going to rebel there, I'd do it by quitting."

"So do it."

"Yeah, right." He tucked my hair behind my ear. I loved the way he did it so his finger trailed lightly over my chin. "So what's with the hair, the shaving, the rebelling?"

Sighing, I nipped at his jaw. "I don't know. It's summer. It just seems like we should do something radical before we head off to college. Experiment a little." I kissed him. "You know, explore our independence."

He slipped his hands beneath the hem of my top, folded his hands around my waist. "Oh, yeah?" he asked in a raspy voice.

"Yeah." I planted my mouth on his, aware of him rolling us until we were on our sides facing each other. I wrapped one hand around his neck and used the other to nimbly free the buttons on his shirt. I flattened my palm against his chest, could feel his heart thudding.

I heard the front door open, shut. "Kendall!" my mom called out.

Jeremy jerked back, hovered at the edge of the cushion for a heartbeat before toppling over and landing with a thud on the floor. Bogart yelped and backed away as fast as he could. Quickly I sat up. "In here!"

Jeremy buttoned his shirt as he scrambled back onto the couch. He put his arm around me as he pressed PLAY on the TV and the next episode started up.

"Hey, guys," Mom said as she wandered in and sat in the slider rocker. Bogart crept over to her side, and without a thought—or so it seemed—she reached down and began petting him.

"How was the date?" I asked, although I had a feeling I knew the answer, considering that it wasn't even ten yet.

"Nice." She looked at the TV. "What are you watching?"

"*The 100.*"

"Mmm." I knew that meant nothing to her. She read romance novels. She didn't watch TV.

"Are you going to see him again?" I asked.

"I don't think so."

As though sensing that my mom had more to say, Jeremy stopped the TV. "Listen, I need to go." He stood up. "Good night, Mrs. J."

"Good night, Jeremy."

Holding his hand, I walked him to the front door. Turning, he kissed me. When he drew back, I tugged on his shirt. "Hope my mom didn't notice that your buttons are one off."

He grimaced. "Ah, man." Leaning down, he kissed me again. "See you tomorrow."

As he walked out, he began redoing his buttons. I loved this guy. He was so cute. When he was gone, I wandered back into the living room and curled up in the corner of the couch. "Want to talk about it?" I asked my mom.

"He wasn't your dad." She sighed. "I know that's unfair, but when I met your dad there was this instant electricity. From the get-go, he made me smile, made me happy to be with him. The guy tonight . . . I kept checking my watch."

I understood the electricity. I'd felt it with Jeremy. He was the new kid in town, and I'd decided to be bold and invite him to join Avery and me for lunch. After that, we'd become the terrific threesome, but always there was something a little more between Jeremy and me than friendship. "I'm sorry."

"Not your fault. He wasn't what I wanted or needed and I knew it five minutes after we met."

"So are you going to give someone else a try?"

"Oh, sure. In a couple of days. Meanwhile, want to share some ice cream with me?"

I smiled brightly. "Absolutely."

Three minutes later, we were sitting at the counter with a tub of chocolate-chip cookie-dough ice cream between us. I took a bite, let it slowly melt in my mouth.

"We've had so little time to talk lately," Mom said. "How are you doing?" While Avery was my best girlfriend, my mom was a close second. And she had many more life experiences.

"To be honest, I've been a little restless. Not unhappy exactly, but feeling like, I don't know, like I'm missing out on something. I don't know why."

She gave me a sympathetic smile. "You're on the cusp of adulthood. It's natural to question things: what you're going to do with your life, what you want that life to be."

"I guess that's it." But it seemed like it was more, like it was bigger than that. That it had to do with Jeremy and me, with us. That thought scared me. I didn't want to examine it too closely, so I didn't try to explain it to my mom because I wasn't sure I wanted the answer. Instead, pretending that her answer made me feel better, I dug in for some more ice cream.

Chapter 8

JEREMY

Avery lived a few doors down from Kendall. I always passed her house on my way out of the neighborhood. Tonight as I was driving by, I saw Fletcher sitting on the stairs that led into an apartment over the garage. Avery's parents were letting him use that room for the summer.

I saw him lift a bottle to his lips, saw no sign of Avery. I pulled to a stop at the curb just past their house and walked back. Fletcher and I weren't best buds. I'd barely known the guy before he got involved with Avery.

But I was feeling a little out of whack since seeing Kendall. I couldn't explain it but things didn't seem quite right between us. Not that I thought Fletcher was a Dr. Phil or anything, but he'd had a rep for being a player before Avery convinced him that she was worth leaving all that behind.

I crossed over the driveway and started up the steps. The light above the garage illuminated him enough for me to see his eyes widen slightly. I didn't blame him. We never hung out together without the girls being around. "Hey, man," I said.

"What's up?"

"I just left Kendall. Saw you sitting here. Where's Avery?"

"Got called into work. Some private party or something at the Shrimp Hut. They needed extra hands."

"Nice for her, money-wise."

"Yeah." He carried the brown bottle to his lips, tipped it up.

"Got an extra one of those?" I asked. "I could use a beer."

He studied me a full minute before saying, "It's root beer."

That surprised me, but at the same time I was relieved. "Okay then, never mind."

"You do remember that Avery's dad is a cop, right?"

I chuckled. "Yeah." There were moments when Fletcher really didn't live up to his rep for getting into trouble.

"So how's the lawyer business?" he asked.

"I don't know." I pointed to a step. "Mind if I sit?"

Shaking his head, he chuckled. "You are too polite."

"I'll take that as a no, you don't mind." I dropped down

beside him. I'd had manners drummed into me at an early age. Manners and never appearing slovenly. There isn't a single photo of me with a hair out of place. When we visited my grandparents at Christmas, I had to sit in a chair until the family photo was taken. No roughhousing with my cousins, no snitching fudge or cookies. Heaven forbid I get a crumb on my white shirt.

Maybe Kendall was right. Maybe I should grow out my hair, shave less frequently. I was eighteen. What could my dad do about it? Oh, right. Cut off my funds for college.

"You're so lucky to have your own place," I said, leaning forward and planting my elbows on my thighs.

"Can't argue with that."

I glanced over my shoulder. "You and Avery—never really saw that coming."

"She makes me a better person." He held up a hand. "Now I'm getting into soul-baring territory and I won't go there. Want to come in and watch giant crocs terrorize people? There's a *Lake Placid* marathon tonight."

I laughed. "Nah. I don't know why I stopped. I just . . ." I really didn't know what it was. "I was a little surprised to hear that you wanted to be a cop. Does it have to do with your dad going to prison?"

Slowly he shook his head. "Mostly it has to do with Avery's dad taking me in, providing me with a place. Not just the apartment here, but a place in the family. I never had that before."

I wasn't sure if I did, either. Sure, I had both my parents but we never did anything together. Kendall had only her mom but there was way more love in her house than in mine. I liked hanging out over there. And I knew no matter what Kendall did, her mom respected and accepted her. If I bucked my dad, there would be hell to pay, and yet I couldn't seem to stop thinking about what Kendall had said. I didn't know if Fletcher would get it, considering the non-relationship he had with his dad, but I didn't know anyone else who had changed so much in such a short time. "Okay, I don't know if this will make any sense, but as long as I can remember I've been on the path to becoming a lawyer, following in my dad's footsteps, which is odd because I'm nothing like him."

"So you're rethinking it?"

"Maybe. Kendall said something tonight about experimenting—"

"Sure she wasn't referring to sexual positions?"

I glared at him. "You're a lot of help." I really didn't know why I'd stopped here. I had other male friends but we mostly played video games together. As for knowing other girls—once Kendall pulled me into her orbit I didn't develop any other female friendships. She and Avery were

71

enough, although I couldn't see myself talking to Avery about this since it involved Kendall. I figured Avery shared everything with Kendall and vice versa. I was pretty sure it was a girl thing.

Fletcher shrugged. "If you don't want to be a lawyer, don't be a lawyer."

Everything was so black and white for this guy.

"Lawyer is my trajectory. I've never even thought about doing anything else. Not to mention my parents would be devastated."

"Parents should be devastated when their kid dies, not when he changes his major."

"You don't know my parents."

"Avery thought she knew her parents' expectations. She was wrong."

"Well, I'm not. Trust me."

He took another long, slow sip of the root beer. I was regretting not taking one. "So you just sit out here until Avery gets home?" I asked.

"Pretty much."

"Exciting."

He grinned. "The *exciting* happens when she gets home."

She had really gotten to this guy, although I had to admit that I was glad he was nuts about her. I liked Avery a lot. I'd always enjoyed hanging around with her and

Kendall before Kendall and I got serious.

"Well, guess I'd better go," I said, and shoved myself to my feet.

"Everything okay with you?" he asked as though it suddenly occurred to him that it would be polite to ask.

I started down the steps and tossed over my shoulder, "Yeah, everything's fine."

Now, if only I could believe it.

Chapter 9

KENDALL

I was hosing down one of the kennels when Darla Bernard, another of the volunteers, stopped and leaned against the wired wall of the enclosure. All the enclosures had a drain in the center to make washing them down easier. Even the most housebroken dog sometimes had an accident if he couldn't get outside.

"Have you seen Jade making a fool of herself with Chase?" she asked as she chewed gum. "She is all over that guy."

"She thinks he's hot," I said, although it was probably an unnecessary comment.

"He is totally, but jeez, give him some breathing room."

"Wanting to make a pass at him yourself?" I teased.

She blushed. "I won't deny that I've thought about it. How about you?"

"I have a boyfriend." Who had visited on occasion, with whom she had seen me more than once. Why was Jeremy so forgettable?

"Anyone I know?"

I turned off the hose. "Jeremy Swanson."

Wrinkling her brow, she looked up at the ceiling like she expected to see his portrait painted there or something. "Oh, yeah, I remember him. Didn't know you two were together."

"Since spring break."

"Huh. Well, anyway, Terri wants to see you when you're done cleaning the pen."

She could have led with that, because I was finished. I put the hose away and headed to the reception area, wondering if someone was surrendering a dog, but then Darla could have taken care of that.

I stopped walking when a text came in from Jeremy.

Miss U. ☹

It shouldn't have made me smile, but it did.

Miss U 2.

Then I shoved the door open and went through into the reception room. Chase was there, arms folded on the counter as he talked with Terri. She brightened when she saw me. "Just the person whose opinion I wanted," she said.

"Yeah? What's up?" I asked.

"They're going to start breaking ground to build the

new wing next week," Terri said.

"Great!" She'd been working on fund-raisers and approaching businesses for support for a couple of years now, so we'd have room to house more dogs.

"So we really need this year's Bark in the Park event to bring in more money than ever," she said. She coordinated the annual event that was held in a park downtown. People were encouraged to bring their pets and to adopt pets. We displayed a lot of our dogs. So did a couple of the other shelters. "Chase was telling me about a fund-raiser he was involved in at his college. I was thinking we could incorporate it. He calls it a 'gun show.'"

I furrowed my brow. "What have guns got to do with dogs?"

Chase held up his bent arms, made fists, and displayed a very nice set of biceps. "These guns."

"Wow! I'm impressed, but how does that bring in money?" I asked.

"Studs, such as myself, display our guns, and people vote with their dollars for the best set. All the money goes to the shelter."

"And people really make donations just to see muscles?" I asked.

"You bet. I brought in six hundred and seventy-three dollars. Pretty cool, huh?"

"It sounds like something different, something fun,"

Terri said. "And there's no monetary investment on our part. We just have to find a few guys willing to show off their physique. Think your boyfriend would be interested?"

At least someone remembered I had a boyfriend. What was more, she thought he might bring in some bucks for the shelter. I just didn't know if Jeremy would be willing to flaunt his stuff. "I can ask."

"What do you think of the idea overall?" Terri asked.

"Seems a little sexist."

Chase grinned. "Hey, it's no different than a beauty pageant and it's for a good cause, not a tiara."

And he'd no doubt have girls flocking around him, which was probably his ultimate goal in suggesting this. But he was right that it was for a good cause. Convincing Jeremy of that, though, was something else entirely.

That night we met Avery and Fletcher at Joe's Pizzeria. They had the best salad bar and pizza buffet in town. Avery and I focused on the salad while the guys loaded up on a variety of slices. Fletcher picked up the jar of Parmesan, sprinkled the flaky cheese on a slice, and set the jar off to the side.

"So something interesting happened at the shelter today," I began, putting the jar of Parmesan back in the center where it belonged.

"All the dogs got adopted?" Jeremy asked.

"I wish. Wouldn't that be great? But no, we're preparing for our annual Bark in the Park fund-raiser, and we're adding a new element this year. A gun show." I didn't know why I grimaced, maybe because all three looked at me like I'd lost my mind. "It's not what you think." Then I went on to explain how it worked. I ended with, "So are you guys willing to show your guns?"

Fletcher shrugged. "Sure."

The way his T-shirt hugged him, he was pretty much showing off his build now. I looked at Jeremy. He didn't appear quite as eager. It was probably the lawyer in him, looking for loopholes, wanting to read the small print. He was the only person I knew who actually read licensing agreements. "So what? We just stand there?" he asked.

"Pretty much, I think. And, you know, show off the guns."

"Shirtless?"

"Not necessarily. I think it's whatever you're comfortable with." Although I could certainly see Chase removing his shirt if he got competitive.

"I guess it seems harmless," he said.

"And it's for a good cause," I reminded him. Reaching over, I stroked his arm. "I bet you'd bring in a lot of money."

"Only if you're saving your dollars and vote for me."

"Of course I'm going to vote for you."

"Okay, then, as long as I'm assured of making a couple of bucks so I don't look like an idiot, I'm in."

Smiling brightly, I squeezed his hand. "Yay! And you'll make more than a couple. I promise."

"Guess I'd better start saving my dollars for Fletcher's jar," Avery said with a challenge in her eye.

"Might need to make it fives," I countered, "if you want any chance of Fletcher beating Jeremy."

"Oh, yeah? Maybe I'll make it twenties."

"Still won't be enough."

"Whoa!" Jeremy exclaimed. "You girls might need to take this down a notch."

"It's just a little friendly competition," Avery assured him.

"That's right," I confirmed. "But it's game on."

Fletcher laughed. "Do you know how competitive Avery is?"

"Of course, I know," I assured him. "We've been best friends forever."

"May the hunkiest boyfriend win," she said. She tapped knuckles with Fletcher. While I'd never been able to beat her at grades, this was different. This was a chance for Jeremy, who no one seemed to notice, to shine and stand out.

"By the way," Avery said, "I know it's kinda short notice but Thursday is when I'll start house-sitting. Dot will be back Sunday. Are you guys still in?"

"I am," I said, and looked at Jeremy.

"Should be able to get a day off from work," he said.

"Would you mind driving?" she asked. "Don't think we really need two cars."

"Sure, no problem."

"We're going to have so much fun."

When Jeremy and I got to my house, we slipped into the backyard and stretched out on a lounge chair on the patio. I was pretty sure Mom knew we were home—she had to have heard the car drive up—but she never seemed to have a problem with us staying outside smooching.

Course we weren't going to take it any further than kissing here, but then we never did. I pushed back a little bit, just so I could look into Jeremy's face. Not that I could see it all that well in the shadows. "Thank you for being one of the gunslingers," I said.

"Oh, my God." He laughed. "Is that what they're going to call us?"

"Maybe. I just thought of it. I think it's cute."

"I don't know, Kendall. Being on display, it's really not my thing."

"But it's for such a good cause." I kissed his chin. "And it'll be fun."

"You and Avery seemed really serious about the competition."

"I have complete confidence in your ability to whip Fletcher's butt."

"I love your faith in me, although it might be misguided here. Have you really looked at the guy? He's ripped."

I wasn't blind, but neither did I want to undermine his confidence. "If you're worried about beating him, you could hit the gym."

He scooped my hair behind my ear. "Probably not a bad idea. I really don't want to make a fool of myself out there."

"You could never do that." I settled my mouth over his, and he pressed his hands to my back, flattening me against him.

I liked the way it felt when we were together like this. I unbuttoned two of his buttons, felt his hand slip under my shirt to skim my bare skin along the small of my back. One of my sandals plopped softly to the ground, and I ran my foot along his calf.

I had to admit that I'd had reservations about the gun show when Terri first mentioned it, but I was excited now that Jeremy was going to participate. I would have to start saving up my pet-sitting money, because I really wanted him to win. All the girls who volunteered at the shelter wouldn't forget him then.

Chapter 10

JEREMY

As I stood at the copier, duplicating some documents my dad needed for a meeting, I could see a faint reflection of myself in the window. Combing my fingers through my hair, I admitted that I liked it being a little bit longer. The office had a small gym that I'd used that morning before I reported for work. I'd never been the popular guy in school, not like Fletcher. I hadn't realized it bothered me until this competition came up. Kendall's faith in me made me want to win—for her. And maybe a little for myself.

The copier shut off. I straightened my tie, made sure my shirt was tucked tightly into my Dockers, and gathered up the documents. Then I headed to my dad's office.

He was sitting behind his desk, his glasses perched on the end of his nose. As I walked in, he looked up, waved a hand to the side like a king greeting his minion. We'd agreed that at the office I wasn't to be treated like his son, that work was separate from home. "Just set them on the credenza," he said.

After doing that, I came to stand in front of his desk. He'd gone back to studying whatever needed to be scrutinized. "Sir?"

This time when he looked up, his brow was furrowed. "Check with my secretary. She'll tell you what else needs to be done."

"Actually, I already know my next task, but I needed to ask for some time off."

"Time off?" he asked as though it was a foreign concept. Considering he put in about seventy hours a week, it probably was. I admired his work ethic, but we had very little time together for father-son things.

"Yes, sir. I need Friday off."

"Why?"

Obviously Mom hadn't told him about my going to the beach for a few nights. Not surprising since that would have involved actually talking to him.

"I'm going to the beach for a few days with some friends."

"That girl you're seeing?"

The anger shot through me, but I just ground my back teeth together to keep my tone even. "Kendall. Yes. And Avery and Fletcher. We're house-sitting for—"

"No." He went back to studying the documents on his desk.

Blinking, I shook my head. "What?"

He leaned back. "You can't have time off. Work needs to be done around here."

"Other interns get time off."

"Other interns aren't my son."

"Thought we agreed we wouldn't play the father-son card at the office," I reminded him.

"Fine. When we get home, ask me if you can go to the beach and I'll tell you no. So you won't need the time off."

"Mom's okay with it. Besides, you can't stop me from going. I'm eighteen."

Taking off his glasses, he tossed them onto the pile of papers. "Which is exactly why I'm saying no. Staying at the beach with a girl is a disaster waiting to happen."

"How do you figure that?"

"I was young once. I know about temptation, and I know how your life can be thrown off track by one mistake. No more parties, no more thinking just about yourself. You have to grow up and take responsibility. I'm doing this for you, so you don't have regrets."

All the words that followed *mistake* seemed to come at me from the end of a long tunnel. I was the mistake, the reason he had regrets.

"As far as this office is concerned," he continued, "you

may not have time off to go play house with this girl. As for the rest of it, we'll discuss it at home." He picked up his glasses, settled them on the bridge of his nose. "And get a haircut during your lunch hour."

I stared in disbelief as he returned his attention to some case.

"I quit." The words were out before I'd considered all the ramifications, but I knew they were the only ones I could say.

Dad looked up, gave me a condescending grin. "This is precisely what I'm talking about. You're acting without thought, which is exactly what you're going to do with this girl at the beach—"

"Kendall," I interrupted. "Her name is Kendall. I love her. And while it is none of your freaking business, we haven't had sex. But when we do, again it's none of your freaking business. But I'm not quitting because of her." Not entirely true. I hated that he failed to recognize how important she was to me. "I'm quitting because you're not treating me like every other intern here. Anyone else could have a day off. And I don't hear you telling anyone else to get a haircut. I'll notify HR about my resignation on my way out of here."

I spun on my heel.

"Jeremy." My dad punctuated my name like it was a command. I turned back to find him standing behind his desk. "If you want to throw away this opportunity, this stepping-stone to a respectable career, I won't try to stop you. It could prove to be a good life lesson, so I won't kick you out of the house or take away your college fund, but that's the extent of my generosity. If you want spending money, you'll need to get another job elsewhere."

"Don't worry. I've got it covered." Another lie, because I had no idea where I could get another job this late in the summer.

Chapter 11

KENDALL

"You do realize we're only going to be gone for three nights," Jeremy said as he studied my collection of luggage in the front entryway.

I had a small suitcase for my clothes and personal items; a ginormous tote bag stuffed with beach accessories; a cooler with our favorite drinks; a large, handled sack of snacks; and a box of miscellaneous items that didn't easily fit into one of the other categories. "I know, but I just wanted to make sure we had everything we needed."

"Because they don't have stores at the beach?"

"Because they're able to hold people hostage with their prices. It's better to take everything rather than have to buy it there."

Jeremy picked up the cooler. "Good thing we're not

traveling on a motorcycle or you wouldn't be able to bring all this stuff."

I swatted playfully at his arm before reaching for my suitcase and rolling it to his car. "I would have changed my organizing strategy."

He opened the trunk. Inside was one large backpack.

"That's all you brought?" I asked.

"Yep. Pretty much all I need at the beach is shorts and swim trunks." Placing his hand on my neck, leaning in, he gave me a lingering kiss. "I knew you'd take care of everything else."

I knew everything else didn't include condoms. He and I had talked about birth control early on in our relationship, and he always carried some just in case. It was just another indication of how considerate he was, although I was really hoping we'd put them to use this weekend.

"Wait until you see everything I have planned for our little vacation," I said. "You are going to be amazed."

"You always amaze me."

I gave him another quick kiss, as whatever restlessness I'd been feeling drifted away. He always managed to make me feel special and appreciated.

"I was afraid your dad wouldn't let you have any time off," I told him as we walked back to the house for the last of the items.

"It's only one day."

When we finished loading up everything, he slammed the trunk lid closed.

We drove down to Avery's house. She and Fletcher were waiting in the driveway, with a couple of tote bags and a cooler. Jeremy and I got out of the car and greeted them.

"I picked up some munchies," Avery began as Jeremy popped the trunk. When she saw everything inside it, she laughed and looked at me. "I should have known you would, too."

"Just a few things," I said.

"Can never have too much food or too many drinks," Fletcher said.

"That's true," Avery said. "Dot said we were welcome to eat whatever was in her pantry and fridge, but I didn't want to take advantage. Although she has some steaks that are in danger of spoiling, so we need to eat those."

Fletcher slammed the trunk. "Think we're ready."

We all climbed into the car, and Jeremy took off.

I couldn't help but think how nice it was going to be to sleep in the same bed with him, to have him hold me all night. To snuggle beneath the blankets. I could hardly wait.

The house was set on stilts and was, literally, right on the beach. Nothing blocked our view of the ocean. We walked up the stairs, and Avery unlocked the door. The dogs immediately greeted us. The cat, lounging on an ottoman near a window, couldn't be bothered.

Laughing, I knelt and rubbed the fur of a golden retriever, and a chow that was mixed with something small and sweet. I knew it was a chow only because of its blue tongue. "Hey, ladies," I said, letting them sniff and lick me.

"You are so much better with dogs than I am," Avery said as she stood off to the side and watched. "The golden is Pooh Bear, the chow, Duchess."

"They're sweethearts," I said.

"Let's check out the place, decide on our rooms, and the guys can haul our stuff in. We're not allowed to use the master bedroom, but Dot said there were two guest rooms."

The house was fairly simple. The front door opened into a large living room, a long counter separating it from the kitchen. We walked down a short hallway with a master bedroom and a guest bathroom on one side. Across from them were the two guest rooms. One with a queen-sized bed. One with two singles.

"Which room do you want?" Avery asked, as disheartened as I was by the sleeping choices. She was letting me determine the arrangements because she was the hostess, and I needed to decide if I was going to be gracious and take the one with—

"We'll take the two beds," Jeremy said as he edged past us with my suitcase and tote in tow.

It was typical of nice, considerate Jeremy to make the unselfish offer. Still I was disappointed and just a little hurt that he hadn't jumped at the chance to share a bed with me. I walked into the room and wondered if it would be inappropriate to do a little rearranging: maybe move the nightstand that stood between the beds so we could shove them together. Maybe it wasn't worth the effort, though. It was only three nights.

But at least we'd be sleeping in the same room. That could be romantic. Listening to him breathing through the night. I didn't even know if he snored.

While the guys brought everything inside, I helped Avery put some things away and set aside what we would have for dinner. While she started arranging all the makings for sandwiches, I fed the dogs, attached their leashes, and took them out to do their business. The yard around the house wasn't fenced in. It was mostly sand with a few sprigs of grass, but the dogs were used to the shifting turf. Jeremy followed me out.

"Are you okay that I said we'd take the two beds?" Jeremy asked.

I forced myself to smile. "Sure."

He put his arm around me and I leaned against him. "Besides," I continued, "they're both taller than us, so they'll be more comfortable in the bigger bed."

"You looked disappointed, like you thought we were missing an opportunity."

Turning, I gazed up into his eyes. "I thought something more might happen, but I also thought the house would be bigger." I twisted my face in a way that made him grin. "Not gonna be a lot of privacy here."

He cupped my face between his hands. "No, there won't be." He stroked my cheeks. "I want it to be really special when things between us go further."

"I'll be with you. How can it not be special?"

"How did I get so lucky?" he asked before he lowered his mouth to mine.

I moved until I was pressed against him. The chow jumped up on me, flopped down, jumped up again. The golden was nudging my other hip.

"Okay, okay," I said with a laugh as Jeremy and I broke apart. "I get it. You want more attention."

I handed the golden off to Jeremy and he began lavishly petting the dog. Watching him while I stroked the chow, I felt this tightness in my chest. He was such a good guy. I didn't know why I was feeling so dissatisfied. Maybe I just wanted him to sweep me up into his arms, give in to our passion.

We took the dogs inside, washed our hands, then grabbed a plate and made a sandwich from everything

Avery had set out for dinner.

"It's not fancy," she said as she was preparing her own plate, "but it just seems like if we're going to be beach bums, we should be lazy."

"Works for me," Fletcher said.

We sat in Adirondack chairs on the front balcony. We had a clear view of the rolling surf. The beach before us was public, but since it was late in the day, not many people were still out. A few were playing volleyball. The ocean roared, salty brine scented the breeze. The setting sun was painting the sky in a wash of oranges, purples, blues.

"I could get used to this," I said.

"I know. Isn't it great?" Avery asked. "I really don't have any plans for us to do much while we're here. I figure tomorrow we'll spend some time down there sunning."

"That's definitely on the schedule," I told her.

"The schedule?" she asked. "What schedule?"

"I prepared an itinerary for the weekend. Tonight's Monopoly. Tomorrow night is cards. I brought everything. We'll sun in the morning before it gets too hot. In the afternoon we'll read. I'll post the schedule on the refrigerator."

"Kendall, I think we should just chill," she said.

"But we're on vacation."

"Exactly. I want days without scheduling."

"Taking care of dogs, you're going to need a schedule. You should probably take them for a walk later this evening," I said, trying not to take offense that she wasn't thankful for all the planning I'd put into the next three days.

"Works for me," Avery said.

We waited until the sun had set and the beach was completely vacated. I walked Pooh Bear while Avery led Duchess. The guys had stayed behind with the excuse of cleaning up after supper. Not that there was anything really to clean up. I figured they just knew that Avery and I wanted some time together.

Wearing flip-flops, we walked along the water's edge. The dogs trotted along beside us, stopping every now and then to sniff at something.

"Guess you figured out that I invited you because you have way more patience with dogs than I do," Avery said.

"Hey, whatever gets me to the beach."

"Sorry about the two beds," Avery said.

"Not a problem. I'm pretty sure nothing was going to happen, anyway." Especially since Jeremy didn't seem to hesitate to take the twin beds.

"Is everything okay?"

"Yeah, I just—" Pooh Bear pulled on the leash. I let her lead us over to the dunes. We stood there while the dogs explored.

"You just?" Avery prodded.

"I want something a little different from what I have."

There. I'd spilled it, had actually said it out loud and it kind of scared me that the words were now being carried on the breeze. I looked back to make sure that Jeremy wasn't behind me, that he hadn't heard me.

"Are you thinking of breaking up with Jeremy?" Avery asked. "You seem so perfect together."

"No, not thinking of breaking up. I adore him. But he's so cautious. *We're* so cautious. You and Fletcher can't seem to keep your hands off each other. Jeremy and I never embrace the passion. It's like we're afraid, worried about consequences."

"That's good, though. You don't want to make rash decisions."

How could I explain what was missing? "I want more romance. Running instead of walking into each other's arms. Doing something spur-of-the-moment before I've had time to analyze it, to put it on a schedule."

She touched my arm. "I hurt your feelings about the schedule."

"No. Maybe a little. But that has nothing to do with Jeremy and me. I'm more upset that he was totally okay with two beds. I thought this weekend would be a chance for us to go a little further than we have."

"We'll take the two beds."

"No, it's not even that anymore. It's just what it signified. He's too nice."

She gave me an indulgent smile. "Kendall, that's not really something to complain about."

"I know. It's totally messed up. I'm hoping that being part of the gun show will cause him to break out of this shell of politeness, will unleash this tough competitiveness that will make him strut his stuff more."

"His stuff?"

"There's a new guy at the shelter. Chase. Jade was all over him. And she said that Jeremy wasn't hot. It bothers me that she doesn't realize what a catch Jeremy is."

"I don't think you should worry about what Jade thinks."

"I know, but it's more than that. It's like at the B. S. when he and Fletcher were standing in line to place our order—girls talked to Fletcher. They don't talk to Jeremy."

She groaned. "Fletcher knows so many girls. He's hung out with so many girls."

"Jeremy just hung out with us," I said, even though I didn't think it mattered how many girls either of them hung out with. Hands down, Fletcher was a chick magnet.

"Which is good, right? It's nice that he isn't a player."

"It is, but I guess I wouldn't mind if people *thought* he was a player."

"You want people to be jealous of what you have?" she asked.

"Sorta. Is that wrong of me? I just think we could be a little more exciting."

"I think you need to be careful what you wish for."

"That sounds like something my mom would say."

"Probably because it's true."

Chapter 12

JEREMY

Standing on the balcony, resting my forearms on the railing, I watched as Kendall walked along the shoreline with Avery. She'd pulled her red hair back so it wouldn't get tangled in the breeze. The thing was that I loved it loose, loved the way it flowed around her. I'd even be willing to comb out the tangles.

"They're not going to get here any faster if you watch them," Fletcher said.

I glanced back at him. He was sitting on a chair, sipping a root beer. The guy seemed to be addicted to the beverage. Not a bad addiction to have, I guess.

"Maybe we should go down and meet them," I suggested.

"Sure." He set the bottle aside and stood. "Let's go."

We stomped down the wooden stairs. It was so peaceful here. Just the roar of the ocean. The breeze keeping the mosquitoes away. The scent of salt and brine.

"You didn't have any trouble getting time off from the auto shop?" I asked.

"Nah. I didn't really have any time off accumulated so I'll put in extra hours the next couple of weeks. You?"

"I had to quit my job."

He stopped walking and stared at me. "For a day off?"

"Partly. There were other factors. Mostly my dad being a jerk." I shoved my hands into my shorts pockets. "But don't say anything to Kendall. She's been looking forward to this weekend so much that I didn't want to ruin it for her." Although I may have done that, anyway, when I suggested we take the room with the two beds. She had a lousy poker face.

"Had to be hard working for your old man," Fletcher said.

"His expectations weren't mine. I got tired of it." I wasn't going to tell him that my dad wouldn't even call my girlfriend by her name. "Don't suppose they're hiring at Smiley's." It was the auto shop in town where Fletcher worked.

"You know anything about cars?"

It made me feel unmanly to admit it, but I couldn't lie. "I know where the gas goes."

Fletcher laughed.

"I'm serious. My dad is not one to get his hands greasy. We've never had bonding moments of looking under the hood of a car. Tire goes flat, we call Triple-A."

"That'll make it a little tough to convince Smiley to take you on."

"Appreciate the honest assessment. I just want to find something fast so my dad can't hold it over me that I'm not working."

"Can you hammer a nail? I heard Tommy Simms's dad is hiring."

"Oh, yeah? I know Tommy. Maybe I'll talk to him."

"Couldn't hurt," Fletcher said, and he started walking again.

I was liking the idea. Working construction could be a good thing on a couple of levels. Hauling lumber around would help beef me up.

I fell into step beside Fletcher. "So what do you really think about this gun show thing?"

"As long as Avery doesn't mind, I'm okay showing off some muscle. And it's for a great cause. Although, since I like you, I'll go ahead and tell you that there is no way you're going to win," Fletcher said.

I knew the guy was doing his usual overconfident, swaggering, I-am-totally-cool thing, but still it stung that he didn't see me as any competition at all. With Kendall's comments lately, now I was wondering if there was more to this contest than raising money for the shelter. Was she dissatisfied with me?

I shook off the thought. I wasn't going to start reading things into this contest. But my pride had me saying, "You might be surprised."

"Smiley's is going to sponsor me."

"Sponsor you?"

"Yeah. Smiley overheard me telling one of the other mechanics—Eric—about it. Eric's a buff guy. I thought he might be interested. Smiley said he'll sponsor us. Two hundred and fifty bucks each, so that's what I'm starting with."

"Maybe I'll get a sponsor, too." Although I wasn't sure who I'd ask. My dad wasn't going to support something that had his son flexing muscles. My mom, maybe. She was always making donations to charities. I didn't have to give her the details.

"I really think that's the only way they're going to make this work," Fletcher said. "Otherwise, it's just ego-tistical guys showing off."

I wasn't sure how much I was going to be showing off. Fletcher had height, muscle, and age on his side. The guy looked tough, like he'd be the last one standing on one of those survivor reality shows. Me, I'd find a cave somewhere and figure out how to access the internet so I could order pizza.

We caught up with Kendall and Avery as they were walking up the path.

"We were just heading back," Avery said.

"It's getting dark," Fletcher said, moving in and slipping his arm around her.

"It's not there yet," she said. "Besides I brought a flashlight."

I took Kendall's hand. "I bet you did, too."

"Of course."

I leaned low. "Why don't you give Fletcher the leash to your dog? We'll go for a walk."

"Okay." She turned to Fletcher and extended the leash. "Do you mind? Jeremy and I are going to take a stroll."

Without hesitating, he took Duchess.

"We'll keep the lights on," Avery said.

"We probably won't be long," Kendall said.

We trudged along the path until we reached the open beach. A half-moon was coming up.

"It's so peaceful out here," she said.

"I like it."

"Why the walk?" she asked.

"I wanted to be alone with you."

"You'll be alone with me all night."

"Yeah, but I'll be asleep."

"This will be the first time that we sleep together," she said, slipping beneath my arm, placing her hand on my chest.

"I know you're disappointed about the two beds, but it didn't seem right for us to take the queen when we wouldn't even be here if Avery hadn't invited us."

"I know. You made the right call. Totally."

I put my arm around her, drew her in, always amazed that even when we were this close together we could walk without tripping over each other's feet.

"I have to admit I'm a little nervous," she said.

"Why? We already decided that nothing was going to happen other than sleep."

"I know." She bounced her head against my shoulder. "But you might see me with my mouth open or drooling or maybe I snore."

I grinned. "I bet even your drool is cute."

"Yuck! No." Easing away from me, she walked to the water's edge. "I sleep with a mouth guard but I didn't bring it because it is so not sexy."

"So do I."

She spun around. "Really?"

"Yeah, I clench my teeth when I sleep. I think most people do."

"Did you bring it?" she asked.

"No. That whole not-sexy thing."

She laughed lightly. "We've been dating for months and I didn't know about the mouth guard. What else don't I know?"

I looked out over the ocean. Even as the darkness was moving in, I could see the whitecaps rolling into shore. "I snore when I'm on my back so if I snore, just nudge me onto my side."

She stepped up to me, put her hands on my waist, and tipped her head back. "We sound like a couple of old people discussing our mouth guards and snoring."

Stepping back, she reached down and grabbed the hem of her shirt and dragged it over her head. My heart kicked against my ribs. We'd definitely left boring behind. "What are you doing?" I asked.

She shimmied out of her shorts. "Going for a dip in the ocean."

"Skinny-dipping?"

Her grin flashed in the moonlight. "More like underwear-dipping. Who knows who can see us out here? Come on!"

Then she was running through the waves, splashing as she went. I pulled my T-shirt over my head, shucked my shorts, and kicked off my flip-flops.

And went after her.

Chapter 13

KENDALL

Jeremy and I had gotten so boring. I wanted some excitement. I wanted us to grow, experiment, live life. We'd gotten predictable. And no one would predict this.

Swimming in the ocean at night in my underwear had never been on my bucket list, because it wasn't something I'd ever even considered doing. Which was why I'd decided to do it. It was daring, bold, so not me. It was also a little scary. But it was thrilling to step out of my comfort zone and so far survive.

I hadn't been sure if Jeremy would follow me in, but there he was lifting me into his arms. I wound my legs around his waist as the waves buffeted against us.

"You're crazy," he said. "There could be sharks out here."

"What are the odds?" Before he could recite them—because he probably knew, geek that he was—I wound my arms more tightly around his neck and plastered my mouth to his.

We'd gone swimming in a pool together. I knew what his chest felt like when it was slick with water, but this was somehow different, seemed a little more forbidden. We were in a public area. That no people were around at that moment was beside the point. We hadn't come out here to go swimming, and yet here we were waist deep in the water swirling around us.

Breaking off the kiss, I laughed and reached my arms toward the sky. "Why does this seem so much more fun than swimming during the day?"

"Maybe because you're not in a bathing suit," he said, and pressed a kiss to my chest.

"Almost. If my underwear had polka dots, no one would know."

"You'd never wear anything with polka dots."

"True." I looked out over the ocean. A short distance away, there were no waves. Moonlight glinted off the still water.

"Want to go farther out?" he asked.

I shook my head, suddenly not all that comfortable with what we were doing and where we were. If we got caught in an undercurrent, who would rescue us? This wasn't one of the activities I'd planned for the weekend. I'd had enough change and boldness for now. "It seems kind of ominous. Does it make me a chicken not to want to stay out here any longer?"

His hands drifted away and I clutched him tighter. "Carry me out. I think I stepped on a crab earlier."

He put his arms around me. "There was a crab? Why didn't you tell me?"

"He's probably gone."

"Probably." He started walking, hopped to the side. "I think he was there."

"Then don't drop me."

"This was your idea. You should be carrying me." He lengthened his stride.

I kissed his neck, his ear, his temple. "My hero."

When the water was swirling around his ankles, I told him he could put me down. I sat in the wet sand and let the water wash over my legs. He dropped down beside me.

"I'm a little disappointed," I told him. "I got scared too quick."

"You got smart. You can't see what's in the water. But you can say you swam in the surf at night. It'll be our secret that you only did it for two minutes."

"I didn't hear you try to convince me to stay."

"Where you go, I go."

I saw a shadow slicing through the water. "Is that a fin?"

"Probably a dolphin."

"What if it's a shark?"

"We're safe on land." He stood up, reached down, and offered me his hand. I slipped mine into it, welcomed the strength as he pulled me to my feet.

I pressed my hands to his chest. "You know, you really are in good shape. The shirts you wear, they hide it. You should buy your T-shirts a size smaller."

He traced his finger along my bra strap. "I can do that."

I shivered, but not from his touch. Even though it was warm out, the breeze was starting to feel cool.

"Here." Jeremy got up, snatched up his T-shirt, and shook it out. Then he handed it to me. "It'll be warmer than your top."

He was right. I slipped it on. Then I dragged on my shorts and slipped into my flip-flops. He'd put on his shorts.

Holding hands, we began walking toward the beach house; I wished that I hadn't chickened out so quickly. So much for being wild and passionate. We climbed up the stairs and went inside.

Avery and Fletcher were sitting on the couch, watching a movie about a giant python.

"Is your hair wet?" Avery asked.

"Yeah, we went swimming. I'm going to grab a quick shower."

I went to our bedroom and dug around in my bag until I found panties, jersey shorts, and a tank. Then I headed into the bathroom.

Fifteen minutes later, I was sitting on the loveseat waiting for Jeremy to finish his shower. When he joined me, he smelled so good. I snuggled against him; his arm came around me. Only one lamp was on, and even with a ginormous snake devouring people, with the roar of the ocean echoing around us, it was really romantic. I wished we had the entire place to ourselves.

On the other hand, we did have a bedroom to ourselves.

I gave an exaggerated yawn. "Can't believe how tired I am. Just something about being on the beach wears me out."

Avery gave me a look that said, *Really?* Then she said, "What about Monopoly?"

She would bring that up, even though she'd shown no interest earlier. "I'm too wiped out for that."

"Okay, then. Just make yourself at home and go to bed whenever."

"Think I will." I stood up. Jeremy stayed where he was. I glared at him.

"Oh," he said in surprise. "Yeah, I'm really tuckered out after that swim." He got up.

I took his hand. "Night, guys," I said to Avery and Fletcher. "See you in the morning."

"Sleep as late you want," Avery said. "We've got nothing to do all day."

I gave her a pointed look. "Take out the dogs, feed them."

"Oh, right, yeah. Guess this isn't a complete vacation."

While I knew it was her responsibility, I wouldn't be here if she hadn't invited us. "I'll take care of it. What time do they usually go out? Do you know?"

"Seven. Crack of dawn. But I'll take care of it. You should enjoy your time here."

"We are enjoying it. We'll get up with the dogs."

"Okay, I won't argue. Thanks."

"Argue," Jeremy groused teasingly.

I pulled him toward the hallway. "We've got it."

When we entered our bedroom, he closed the door, and I started to feel a little bit nervous again. We were actually going to sleep in the same room. We'd studied in my bedroom—with the door open. But we'd never slept in it.

I stepped away from him and rubbed my hands on my shorts. I could still hear the ocean. It was a soothing lullaby.

I sat on the bed nearer to the window. "I'll take this one."

"So will I," Jeremy said.

I know my eyes widened as he sat beside me. "I figured we'd make out for a while," I told him, "but as for sleeping—"

"I want to sleep with you."

"Should we move the beds together?"

"I checked out that possibility earlier after my shower, but because of the headboards, they're not going to fit together perfectly. There's going to be a gap in the middle."

"We could put the mattresses on the floor."

"Or we can just scrunch up."

I smiled. "Scrunching sounds good."

After reaching over and turning off the lamp, Jeremy rolled me onto my back and stretched out beside me, his mouth covering mine as though he knew exactly how I'd be positioned, as though he'd thought about it a lot.

This was so much better than a car.

I heard a door close in the hallway and stiffened. Jeremy lifted up slightly.

"I guess they've gone to bed, too," I whispered.

"Sounds like."

We heard a bed squeak.

"Glad we came to bed first," I said.

"Me too," he responded, before settling back down and drawing me in against his side.

"This is nice," I said, resting my hand on his chest.

Even if this was all we did, it was nice to be held, to be together.

"Until we get up at the crack of dawn with the dogs."

"You don't have to."

He skimmed his fingers along my arm. "I'm teasing. I'm taking the dogs out with you."

"They're sweet girls."

I heard a scratching on the door.

"Where do they sleep?" Jeremy asked.

"I saw dog beds in the master bedroom." Still, I scrambled out of bed, turned on the lamp, and walked to the door.

As soon as I opened it, both dogs trotted in. The golden jumped onto the bed with Jeremy and settled down. The chow hopped onto the other bed, circled twice before curling up.

I put my hands on my hips. "Ladies, there's not enough room for all of us."

Jeremy laughed as he petted the golden. "We can't get a break."

I sat down on the edge of the other bed and stroked the chow. "I can get them out of here, but they're probably missing Dot, so I hate to shut them out. I could bring their beds in here."

"Think they've claimed their beds," he said. "What about the cat?"

"Cats don't miss anyone."

Then as though he needed to prove me wrong, the cat sauntered in, leaped onto the bed with the chow, and curled up on the pillow.

Jeremy chuckled. "What now, Pet Whisperer?"

I sighed. "We make the best of it."

With a great deal of goading, we got the golden to the other bed, which caused the chow to abandon its spot and move over to the free bed.

"At least she's small," Jeremy said as he climbed back into bed.

I turned off the light and snuggled up against him, felt Duchess settle across our feet where they were intertwined.

"Not how I thought tonight would go," I admitted.

"You're sleeping in my arms," he said. "That's a win."

Yes, it is, I thought as I snuggled closer to him.

Chapter 14

JEREMY

I woke slowly, lethargically, with the sun barely peering into the room. I fought not to move, not to disturb Kendall. She was snuggled against me, her nose buried in my chest. Her eyelashes rested on her cheeks.

Even in sleep she had a little furrow between her brows, and I figured she was trying to organize her dreams or something. I'd known that she'd created an itinerary for our vacation. She wasn't a fan of surprises. Respecting that, I'd never given her one, but now I wondered if maybe that was part of the reason she seemed discontented. I was predictable. We were predictable.

Knowing my mom wasn't happy, I wanted to be the complete opposite of my dad. I wanted Kendall to be happy.

I probably should have picked the bigger bed. But then

it probably wouldn't have mattered. We were so close together that we weren't using all of this one.

Slowly she opened her eyes. Her mouth curled up. "Hey."

Her voice was raspy with sleep, and the sound of it shot straight to my gut. Placing my hand against her throat, I tilted her head up slightly and kissed her. She released a soft sigh. I loved the way she always managed to sigh when we kissed.

I could stay here forever. Holding her, kissing her. I usually wasn't a fan of the morning, was a grump until I'd had my first cup of coffee, but Kendall made me glad to be awake. She was better than any dark roast. I became lost in her, lost in the sensations. She was breathing heavily, her breath warming my ear—

Wait. I broke off the kiss, glanced back, and was greeted with dog breath. "Whoa!" I covered my mouth and nose. "Dog, go lap up some mouthwash or something."

Kendall laughed. "Pooh Bear, down."

I released a puff of air as the golden leaped onto the bed, straddling me to nudge at Kendall's shoulder. The dog weighed a ton. Kendall shimmied away from me and got up. The golden jumped from the bed.

"Think she needs to go out," Kendall said as she clipped up her hair.

"I'll come with you." Guess putting on our shoes was a signal because both dogs rushed to the door and slammed against it.

"I'll meet you by the front door," Kendall said as she let them out and followed them into the hallway.

I finished putting on my sandals. When I caught up with them, she already had them leashed. I took the bigger dog. She strained against the leash as we went down the stairs, and immediately did her business once we hit the sand.

"The sun's just coming up," Kendall said. "Why don't we take a short walk along the beach?"

"Sure." I took her hand. "Even though I shouldn't reward them for interfering with my moves this morning."

"It was nice waking up next to you," she said. "I wish we were sharing an apartment at college. I don't know why I thought we should get the full college experience by spending at least a year in the dorm."

She'd researched all the dorms and analyzed the campus map before deciding which one we should request for our residence. While we couldn't share a room, we'd still be near each other. "We'll have enough adjustments without trying to set up an apartment," I said.

"I hope we have roommates who don't hang around much."

"We'll make it work." We left the dunes and walked

over the packed sand to the water's edge. The sun's glow was casting the sea in gold. The sky was streaked with deep blue, orange, and pink.

"So pretty," Kendall said.

"Like you."

She looked at me. "You've never told me I was pretty."

"Haven't I?"

She shook her head. "No, I would have remembered. I mean, I didn't think you thought I was a troll or anything, but I don't really think of myself as pretty."

"You are. You and your seventeen freckles."

With a laugh, she covered her face and peered at me through her fingers. "You counted them?"

"This morning while you were sleeping."

"I hate my freckles."

"They're cute."

"You can say that because you don't have any."

"I can say it because it's true." I put my hands on her waist, drew her in—

And jerked her to the side when Pooh Bear went after a sandpiper and reached the end of her tether. I firmly set my feet so she couldn't go any farther.

Kendall rubbed her hand along my shadowed jaw. "I'm liking this."

"Glad you like it. I forgot to pack a razor."

"Didn't you make a list?"

"Nope. Decided to wing it, take my chances. Be wild."

"Of all the different ways to be wild, you decided to let loose with your packing?"

"What can I say? I live for danger."

Her laughter echoed over the surf. I loved making her laugh.

She tiptoed her fingers over my jaw again. "You should consider going with this look for the gun show. It's pretty sexy."

Was I not sexy before? I didn't think that's what she'd meant, but still it bothered me. Lately I was noticing lots of little flaws in myself and I had to wonder if she'd noticed them, too. Maybe it was my dad's constant harping making me second-guess everything. I really couldn't wait to get to college.

Kendall tugged on Duchess's leash. "We should probably get back."

As we headed for the beach house, I was beginning to wish that I hadn't agreed to participate in the gun show. It was all supposed to be in good fun, but I wondered if I'd have anyone other than Kendall donate even a penny on my behalf.

Chapter 15

KENDALL

We returned to find Avery and Fletcher preparing breakfast. I put out food and fresh water for the dogs, then sat at the counter and helped myself to the bacon, biscuits, and scrambled eggs. For some reason, everything tasted better. Maybe the salty air cleared the palate.

"So, I know we just want to chill," I began, "but I think we probably should head to the beach as soon as we've eaten so we can claim a spot before it starts to get crowded. Jeremy and I could wander on down if no one else wants to go out this early." I couldn't quite let go of the schedule I'd made for the weekend.

"We'll all go," Avery said. "There's a little storage room beneath the stairs where Dot keeps some umbrellas and lounge chairs that we can use."

"We expecting rain?" Fletcher asked.

Laughing, Avery gave him a playful push. "No. They're big beach umbrellas for providing some shade."

"Why do we need shade?"

"Because not all of us tan like you do."

Fletcher had dark hair and looked like he lived most of his life in the sun. Came from riding his motorcycle, I guessed. Avery was fair-skinned with blond hair, while I was freckle city if I wasn't careful. Jeremy's hair was sandy-blond; the bristles along his jaw—which I was really loving—were darker than his hair. In spite of his coloring, he did tend to tan. Maybe it had something to do with his brown eyes.

When we finished breakfast and cleaned up the kitchen, we changed into our bathing suits, stuffed towels and essentials into my huge beach bag, grabbed the umbrellas and a small ice chest filled with drinks, leashed up the girls, and headed out to claim our spot.

We drove a couple of spikes into the ground and secured the leashes to them so the girls could wander around but not bother anyone. Avery and Fletcher set up under one umbrella, Jeremy and I beneath the other.

I settled onto one of the lounge chairs. "You might want to lie in the sun for a while," I told Jeremy. "Even out your tan a little."

He gave me a blank look.

"You know, for the competition," I explained.

"Didn't think we had to take our shirts off."

"You don't but, you know"—I rubbed his arm—"bronze is sexy."

"And prone to cancer."

"I'm just saying a little bit of sun wouldn't hurt." I nodded toward Fletcher who was already stretched out on a lounge chair and sipping a root beer. He was tanned to perfection. I lowered my voice and arched a brow. "If you want to give him a run for his money, that is."

"Yeah, I do. He already thinks he has me beat."

"You'll show him."

He grinned. "I'll try." He dragged off his loose T-shirt. He really did have a nice physique. He just didn't show it off the way Fletcher, or even Chase, did. For a moment, I simply enjoyed watching the way his muscles rippled as he slathered on lotion. Then I scooted toward him. "I'll do it."

Taking the tube, I leisurely spread the sunscreen over his back. "See? I had an ulterior motive," I whispered near his ear.

He laughed. "I know your motive. Funds for the shelter."

"This, too." He was so firm. Not an ounce of fat. I ran my hands over his shoulders and back.

"That feels good," he said. He twisted around. "Let me return the favor."

I drew my knees up to my chest, wrapped my arms

around my legs, and pressed my cheek to my knees. I'd clipped up my hair so Jeremy had easier access to my back. He took his time. The long, slow movements were luxurious.

"Maybe we should give each other massages later," I suggested.

"Was it on your to-do list for the weekend?" he asked.

"No, but since we're not using my itinerary . . ." I shrugged.

"Does that bother you?"

"A little. How can we relax if we're constantly worrying about what we're doing next?"

He kissed my bare shoulder. "Don't worry. It'll all work out."

I sighed. "I guess I should be more spontaneous."

"You were last night. That was fun."

"For all of two minutes."

"It was a great two minutes."

Turning my head back, I managed to capture his mouth for a short kiss. "Thanks. You always make me feel like I'm not totally obsessive."

I took the tube from him, wiped off some lotion that had oozed out when he'd capped it, and tucked it into its place in the side of my tote. I handed Jeremy his book— he usually read books with *clockwork* or *iron* in the title. I didn't really get steampunk, but that was okay because

Jeremy wasn't a fan of romance, which I read voraciously. I loved that they always had a happy ending. I pulled out my latest Meg Cabot book.

More people began arriving. Some with surfboards headed out into the waves. I spotted a couple on a Jet Ski. In the distance, a speedboat sliced through the water and a guy dangling from a parasail lifted up. Other people were lying around. Some kids were building a sand castle. A group of five—three guys and two girls—claimed the volleyball net near the sandy area where we'd set up. They tossed the ball back and forth among themselves for a while.

Then one of the girls wandered over to Fletcher and thrust out a hip in what I guessed she thought was a provocative pose.

"Want to join our game?" she asked, like Avery wasn't sitting right beside him.

"No, thanks," he said.

"But we need someone on our team."

He waved his hand. "Lot of people around."

I thought she'd ask Jeremy next. Instead, she trudged away. I huffed.

"What?" Jeremy asked.

"I can't believe how girls notice him."

"He's six three. He could spike the ball without even jumping, so of course they asked him."

"You're tall."

"Five eleven. Not that tall."

"Tall enough that they should have asked you," I said.

"If they asked, I would have declined, so what's the point?"

The point was that they should have paid attention to him. That I didn't like that he was ignored. If they weren't impressed with him, who was going to notice him at the gun show? But I couldn't tell him that without hurting his feelings, undermining his confidence. "You're right. I just thought it was rude."

"Maybe they could just tell that I was taken."

Maybe. Fletcher did have that lone-wolf vibe.

"Do you think we're boring?" I asked.

"What? No. Why would you think that?"

"We're never noticed. We never do anything exciting or different."

"Last night we swam with the sharks."

I sat up and swung my legs over the side of the chair. "You said it was a dolphin."

He shrugged. "Could have been a shark."

I looked out over the water. Was it still there? The odds were it was a dolphin. What did it matter? I was dissatisfied and I didn't know why. "Yeah, let's tell people it was a shark."

"Done."

I settled back down and tried to bury myself in my story but I kept getting distracted by shouts from the volleyball players or the squeals of little kids running into the waves or the roar of the ocean itself. My gaze would wander from the words to all the activities surrounding me. The breeze brought tiny particles of sand and the fragrance of sunscreen. It was growing warm, warmer. . . .

I didn't realize I'd drifted off until I felt a nudge on my shoulder. I opened my eyes. Jeremy was sitting on the edge of my lounge chair holding a blue snow cone. "Where did you get that?" I asked.

"Went for a walk. There's a stand just down the beach a bit."

I swung my legs to the side and sat up. "You should have woken me up."

"I wanted to surprise you."

Nudging my shoulder against his, I took the snow cone. "Thank you." I bit off a section of crushed ice. "Mmm. Coconut. My favorite."

"I know."

I handed it back to him, watched as he took a bite. Then I pressed my cold mouth to his. It felt funny until my lips grew warm. "You're the best boyfriend ever."

I took another bite, glanced around. "Where are Avery and Fletcher?"

"They headed back to the house to fix lunch."

And had packed up all their stuff, taken it and the dogs with them. I didn't blame them. It was really getting hot out here. "Guess we should head back, too."

We finished off the snow cone first, then gathered up our stuff and trudged back to the beach house. Tomato soup and grilled cheese sandwiches were waiting for us. I wolfed mine down. I hadn't realized how hungry I was or that it was already the middle of the afternoon.

"So I know this may sound silly," I began, "but this is my vacation for the summer. I was thinking of going souvenir shopping this afternoon. Anyone up for that?"

Fletcher looked like he was trying to blend in with the woodwork. I had a feeling he was not one for browsing shops. Avery looked at him, then looked at me. "I was thinking of napping."

The sun could zap your strength but I'd already gotten in my nap.

"I'll go," Jeremy said.

I knew he was just doing it to be a good boyfriend. I shook my head. "Never mind. It was just a thought."

"You don't want to be with me?" he asked.

His question took me totally by surprise. Where had that come from? "No. I mean, yes, no." I shook my head. "Of course I want to be with you, but I know you're not into shopping."

"I'm into hanging with you, so that works out. Besides,

what else do we have planned for this afternoon?"

According to my itinerary, this afternoon I'd planned to gather seashells that we could use for craft projects, but even as I thought it I realized how totally unexciting that sounded. Not to mention, no one really cared about my itinerary. "Okay, then, yeah. Let's go."

Avery said she and Fletcher would clean up. Jeremy and I were in charge of supper.

Leaving the dogs behind, Jeremy and I walked along the hard-packed sandy road. Tall grass and dunes on one side separated it from the public beach. I'd grabbed my wide-brimmed hat and tossed on a lacy top to shelter me from the sun. Jeremy had put his T-shirt back on and added a baseball cap.

Seagulls squawked and swooped down. The sky was an incredible blue, hardly a cloud in sight. And my boyfriend was holding my hand.

"Guess you know what we're fixing for supper," he said as we walked past a grocery store.

"I brought a box of rice and beans because it was easy to transport, but now it seems boring."

I felt his gaze land on me. "You're really worried about being boring."

I shrugged. "Didn't you think things would change after we graduated from high school? That there would be this big moment of wonder, discovery, and expansion?"

"I figure that will happen in a few more weeks when we head off to college."

"I guess I'm just impatient, but I do know I don't want beans and rice."

"How about some danger?"

I looked over at him. "Excuse me?"

"Cooking with fire, down on the beach at sunset. Hot dogs, roasting marshmallows."

I grinned. "I like that."

"We'll stop at the grocery store on the way back."

I leaned against his arm. "We're a good team."

"The best."

We reached the souvenir shop. The large, weathered wooden building was almost completely open on one side. We went up the steps, walking past barrels that contained seashells for sale. For anyone who was too lazy to bend down and pick one up off the beach, I guessed.

"So what are you looking for?" Jeremy asked.

"Just browsing really."

"I see a cooler at the back. I'm going to grab something to drink."

"Okay." He wandered off and I walked over to a rack of T-shirts. I found a muscle shirt that was kind of stretchy. I wondered if I should buy it for Jeremy for the gun show. Maybe. I'd think about it.

I walked by a carousel stand that had small license

plates displayed on it, the kind kids bought to go on their bikes. Each one had a different name. I noticed WARREN was next to ADAM. How had that happened?

I moved WARREN to reveal ALICE. People were so careless when they put things back. I put WARREN in his place, noticed another out of place. . . .

"What are you doing?" Jeremy asked.

"These are all out of order."

"Kendall, babe, that's not your job."

"It'll just take me second."

He took the plate I was holding and slipped it into place so MARY was now hiding NANCY.

"But, Jeremy, if a girl named Nancy is looking for a license plate she's just going to see two Marys. She's not—"

"You need to let this go." Folding his hand around mine, he began leading me outside.

"It's chaos and it's supposed to be orderly."

"It doesn't matter. It's just a cheap souvenir."

"It might matter to someone."

Stopping, he faced me. "Go fix it."

"It'll just take me a second."

Took me more like a hundred and twenty, but he was sitting on the steps waiting for me, drinking a cherry-flavored water, when I was finished. I crouched beside him. "I know I should have been able to walk away. . . ."

"It's okay." He extended his bottle. Taking it, I gulped

down some water before handing it back. He finished it off and tossed it into a nearby garbage can. He shoved himself to his feet. "Come on, let's go grocery shopping."

Taking his hand, I couldn't help but think that I was so lucky to have him.

Chapter 16

JEREMY

I didn't know why Kendall needed to have so much order in her life. I figured some of it might have to do with her father's death. It had to be hard growing up without your dad—even if your dad tended to be a jerk like mine. In spite of everything, I did love him. Just didn't like him a whole lot.

Although based on things Kendall said, I knew she had liked her dad. A lot. She really missed him. So I tried to be understanding when it came to her need to control everything, because she hadn't had any control over his dying.

As Kendall and I went through the tiny grocery store, a couple of times I noticed her reaching to straighten something, then pulling her hand back. We quickly grabbed what we needed—including roasting skewers that had a picture of people near a campfire—and headed back to the beach house.

We waited until near dusk before hauling everything down to the beach. Fletcher and I gathered driftwood and built a fire. After, Kendall and I sat on a blanket with her back to my chest, my arms around her as the sun set. It was pretty amazing. As night fell, a quiet hush seemed to come with it. Only a few people remained. I didn't figure they'd be staying much longer, but they weren't bothering us.

After skewering the wieners, we held them just beyond the reach of the dancing flames.

"This was such a good idea," Avery said. She examined her wiener, then slid it into a bun and took a bite. "There's just something about roasting hot dogs over a campfire that makes them taste better."

"It's the danger," I said. "The fire. It's why guys like to cook outside using a grill. The kitchen is too tame."

"And yet so many chefs are guys," Avery pointed out.

"But you've seen the knives they wield, right?" I asked.

She laughed. "Yeah, some of them are pretty wicked looking."

When everyone had their fill of hot dogs, Kendall broke out our dessert. "This reminds me a little of Girl Scout camp," she said as she skewered a marshmallow.

"So should we start telling creepy stories?" Avery asked.

"No," Kendall said as she plucked the gooey mess from the skewer and popped it into her mouth. "I won't be able to sleep."

I slipped my arm around her. "I'll protect you."

She gave an exaggerated shudder. "You'll try, but the guy is always the first to go."

"Nah," Fletcher said. "The guy is usually the danger, the one you least expect."

"Oh, thanks," Kendall said. "No more marshmallows for you."

He shrugged. "No biggie. I've got my root beer."

"Doesn't anything upset you?" Kendall asked.

"Not the small stuff."

I'd really only gotten to know Fletcher after he started dating Avery. He was a year older than us, but in some ways he was a lot older than that. I'd only recently learned he'd had a really rough life. That was the thing about people. You didn't always know what was going on in their lives. I thought Kendall shared everything with me—but then she probably thought I did the same with her. She was probably going to be upset when she learned that I'd quit working at my dad's office, which was why I wasn't going to tell her until after our time here. I just wanted a few days without any hassles.

When most of the marshmallows were gone, Kendall packed everything away and then settled in against me again. I put my arms around her and set my chin on her shoulder.

"You can really see the stars out here," she said.

"Fletcher and I come out here a lot at night," Avery said. "It's just a great place to unwind. We're really going to miss it when we go off to school."

They were going to Austin. Kendall and I were going to College Station.

"I'm going to miss *you*," Kendall said.

"Same goes," Avery told her. "We should plan a trip for winter break. Maybe go skiing."

"That sounds like fun," Kendall said. She glanced back at me. "Don't you think?"

"Absolutely." Not that my dad was going to fund a trip away with my girlfriend. But I'd cross that bridge later.

"Oh, I forgot to tell you," Avery began. "Dot called. Her mom did really well following the surgery. She'll be checking her out of the hospital and bringing her back here tomorrow, so this is our last night."

"I'm glad for her mom," Kendall said, "but I have to admit to being a little disappointed. I'm not ready to leave."

"I know." Avery shrugged. "But what can we do? They won't be here until the afternoon, but it is kind of a bummer."

With Avery's news, we settled into a quiet stillness,

watching the flames growing smaller as they devoured the wood.

"Okay," Avery said after a few interminable minutes where there was only the crackling of the fire and the chirping of insects. "We need to spice things up. How about a preview of the gun show?" She nudged Fletcher hard enough that he nearly toppled over.

"You're kidding, right?" he asked.

"No. Show us what you got."

He looked at me, and I saw the challenge in his eyes. This guy was really going to take this seriously.

"I think we should wait to reveal what we've got until the appropriate time," I said. "I don't want to broadcast any secret weapons I might have."

With a laugh, Kendall snuggled against me. "Good strategy."

"I think you're just chicken," Fletcher said, and struck an exaggerated bodybuilder pose, which looked even more ridiculous because he was sitting on a beach towel covered in daisies.

"Think what you want. I'm not going to be goaded into giving anything away."

With two fingers he pointed to his eyes, pointed to me, pointed back to his eyes. "I'll be watching you."

I almost puffed out my chest. If a guy like Fletcher thought I was competition—

Who was I kidding? He had at least four inches and twenty pounds on me. Not to mention chicks like Volleyball Girl drooling over him. I didn't stand a chance. Sometimes I hated my realistic, pragmatic outlook on life.

When the fire burned itself out and cooled, Fletcher and I covered it with sand. We gathered everything up and began trudging back to the house.

"I call dibs on the shower first," Kendall announced.

"First one back gets the shower," Avery said, and she started running.

With a shriek Kendall raced after her.

"Not fair!" I called out as I shifted the cooler I was hauling.

Beside me, Fletcher laughed, then grew quiet. "So you know that I was just messing with you earlier? I don't really care who wins this thing, although Avery might care and if she does, then I do."

"Yeah, well, I might surprise you and offer you some real competition."

"I guess we won't be the only ones, right?"

"Probably not, but I have no idea who else might be involved."

"Doesn't matter. We'll kick butt and take names."

Had to admit it salvaged my pride to think that he thought I could at least do that.

Chapter 17

KENDALL

Because Avery was an astonishing six feet tall and had long legs, she beat me to the house. Laughing, she dropped down onto the steps. "Go on. You can shower first."

"Thanks." I hesitated. "And thanks for inviting us. It's been great."

"I remember when earlier in the summer you and Jeremy weren't getting much time alone." She arched a brow, and I knew what she was asking.

"We're still not doing much more than kissing." I sat beside her. "How about you and Fletcher?"

She lifted a shoulder. "A little more than kissing, but we're taking it slow. I don't think there's anything wrong with that."

"You're right. There's not." But still I wanted to make the most of tonight.

After I showered, while Jeremy was in the bathroom getting off all the sand, I shut out the pets for the night and set the four candles I'd brought around the room—two on the dresser, one on the nightstand, one on a short shelf that contained books and assorted shells. Lighting them, I inhaled the jasmine scent. So romantic. I turned down the covers on one bed. Then I switched off the lights.

I sat on the edge of the bed and waited. I was wearing a soft cotton tank and shorts that weren't particularly sexy, but I didn't want to be the one making all the moves. I just wanted to hint that I was ready for Jeremy to make some.

I heard Avery and Fletcher moving about in the next room. I really wished this house had thicker walls. Then they went quiet and all I could hear was the blood rushing between my ears. Footsteps in the hallway. The door opened—

The dogs rushed in ahead of Jeremy and leaped on me, causing me to fall back on the bed. "No!"

"Sorry," he said with a laugh, trying to get the dogs off me.

"It's okay." I managed to scramble out of the bed. I called the dogs over to the other one, and with several commands to "Stay!" I was able to get them settled where they'd been the night before.

When I straightened, I saw Jeremy looking around. His gaze landed on me. "Wow!"

Suddenly I felt really self-conscious. "I wanted to do something special since it's our last night."

He shut the door, walked over to me, and braced his hands on either side of my face. "I like it."

He pressed his lips to mine. Somehow we fell onto the bed, without breaking off the kiss. I loved the way it felt when we were together like this. I slipped my hands beneath his T-shirt, felt the ripple of his muscles. Yeah, he had a few surprises awaiting Fletcher when they faced each other. My mind flashed to Fletcher doing his exaggerated poses. While I felt guilty that my thoughts traveled to unromantic places while Jeremy was kissing me, I couldn't seem to shake the image of Fletcher wearing black jeans and a black T-shirt. It was pretty much all he wore. Maybe he didn't know how to coordinate clothes. Or maybe it was just that he knew he looked really good in them. Even this morning when we'd been on the beach, he hadn't been wearing swim trunks. Although Jeremy was now wearing gym shorts, earlier in the evening, he'd been wearing cargo shorts.

"What would you think of wearing jeans?" I asked against Jeremy's neck as I rained kisses over it.

"What?"

"For the gun show. Tight jeans are sexier than cargo shorts any day of the week."

"Are we really talking about my wardrobe right now?" he asked.

I knew the timing was wrong, but it seemed a little late to backtrack since I'd broken the mood. Once we finished this discussion, my thoughts would clear and I could focus on Jeremy. Easing away, I tugged on his shirt. "It's just on my mind since Fletcher was challenging you earlier. I saw a muscle shirt at the souvenir shop that we might want to pick up tomorrow before we leave. It would hug your body the way I do. It was gray but maybe we could find it in red. I love you in red."

"Anything else?"

I thought he sounded just a little irritated, except that Jeremy never got irritated. "Well, since you're asking, how about black sneakers instead of white?"

"What color should my socks be?"

"Might want to go with black there, too."

"Boxers or briefs?"

"Probably boxer briefs, don't you think?"

Gently he pushed away from me and sat up. "What I think is that you have major control issues—"

"No, I don't."

"Kendall, every time someone moves an item on the

table, you put it back where it was. You rearranged souvenirs."

"If things have a place, they should be put back in their place."

"You tried to discourage Avery from getting involved with Fletcher."

"Because she's my friend and I care about her. And he didn't seem right for her at the time. I got that wrong."

He twisted around until I could see him better. "You've encouraged me to grow out my hair, not shave, beef up, and now change my clothes."

"I thought you wanted to beat Fletcher." I'd just been trying to help but I could see now that maybe I'd taken it a bit too far. We just seemed so boring, and I guess I saw an opportunity for Jeremy to be different, for us to be different.

"But you make me feel like you think I don't have a chance in hell as I am," he said.

I felt like he'd punched me. That wasn't at all what I'd wanted to do. I placed my hand on his back, felt him stiffen. "That's not what I meant. Don't take it so personal."

"Little hard not to when you seem to be finding fault with everything."

"Just forget everything I said. You're perfect."

"Yeah, well, I'm not really feeling that way right now.

I'm going to sleep on the couch." He got up and headed for the door.

"What? No. You can't do that."

"Actually, I can."

"Jeremy, don't leave in a huff. You're not the sort who leaves in a huff."

He looked back over his shoulder. "Well, maybe tonight I'm *experimenting*, trying to be different."

He walked out. The door closed with an ominous click that seemed to echo louder than if he'd slammed it. The dogs leaped onto my bed. I wrapped my arms around them and hugged them tightly, trying to figure out what had just happened.

Chapter 18

JEREMY

I sat hunched on the outside steps. There was no reason to settle on the couch yet because I wasn't going to be able to go to sleep, anyway.

I had a clear view of the ocean, the moonlight reflecting off it, the whitecaps rolling in. I let the crash of the surf wash over me. I had to admit that maybe I'd overreacted a little to Kendall's latest suggestion. What did it matter what I wore?

But I guess with all the hints and suggestions she'd been making lately, I was starting to doubt whether she was really attracted to me, if she was content. I knew I wasn't the most exciting guy in the world, especially when I was standing next to Fletcher. I liked him, but the guy was a chick magnet and I wasn't at all. Then this stupid gun show had come along. . . .

I'd drop out, except then I'd feel like a total loser. And Kendall would be disappointed that I wasn't doing something that might bring in some bucks for the shelter. I hadn't thought I'd do too badly. I wasn't totally out of shape, but I hadn't been working out since graduation. I was no longer on the high school baseball team, hadn't gotten a baseball scholarship, so, yeah, I'd slacked off in the exercise department. So I could probably use some beefing up.

And the truth was, I did want to look good for Kendall.

I didn't turn around when I heard the door open and the soft patter of bare feet. I was very much aware of Kendall lowering herself beside me.

"Jeremy, I am so sorry that I've been so obsessed with how you should look at the competition."

"No, I overreacted. My dad is always trying to shape me into his mold, and the suggestions you've been making lately—I thought maybe you were trying to shape me, too."

"I don't want you to change."

Except for trading in my car for a motorcycle, then changing my hair, stubble, physique, clothes. The outer stuff that wasn't really the measure of a person unless that person lived in my family. We were judged by everything. I looked over at her. "But you wouldn't mind me being a little different."

"I don't want you to change," she repeated.

"Too late now, you put the idea in my head. Guess we

ought to go buy that muscle shirt tomorrow."

She laughed, but I heard tears in her voice when she said, "I love you, Jeremy."

She was the last person in the world I wanted to make cry. I felt like such a jerk. "You're going to love me more when you get a load of the hot Jeremy."

"I don't know if it's possible to love you more."

"I just want you to be happy." And I meant it. Nothing, no one mattered more to me.

"I am."

"But you'll be happier if I collect the most money for this fund-raiser."

"I don't know if *happier* is the right word, but I'd find some satisfaction in it," she admitted. "Chase thinks he's top dog. I'm pretty sure that's why he suggested this idea, just to prove he's a stud muffin."

I furrowed my brow. "Wait a minute. Who's Chase?"

She shrugged. "This new guy at the shelter. He's a couple of years older and all the girls act like he's God's gift. They flirt so outrageously with him. No work is getting done. So I'm looking forward to you giving him a run for his money." She beamed at me. "And giving Fletcher a run for his as well."

Why had I thought she didn't have faith in me? I really needed to get my dad out of my head, had to stop viewing every suggestion Kendall made as though it came from the same place as my dad's criticisms.

Standing, I took her hand, drew her to her feet, and led her back to our bedroom. The dogs looked up, seemed to think all was okay, and settled back in on the bed they were sharing. I pulled Kendall down onto the other and held her close.

With my thumb, I stroked her cheek. "I love you. I want to win this. I want to win it for you."

"I love you, too, whether you win or not."

Then she pressed her lips to mine, and I took the kiss deeper. I wished we didn't have to leave tomorrow. I wished I didn't have to get back to the real world of finding a job and getting my dad off my back. I wished I didn't have all these doubts about the way she viewed me.

I'd never been the popular guy in school. Hadn't realized until now that it bothered me that I'd never stood out. I wanted her to be proud of me.

And I would do whatever it took to make that happen.

KENDALL

"Hot studs," Jade said. "And I am not talking about the nails being hammered into the wood."

I didn't think she was. I was wishing I were still at the beach when I arrived at the shelter on Tuesday. I'd needed a little more time to get things right with Jeremy. He said we were okay, but things still seemed a little off-kilter. I tried to shake it off. Right now I needed to worry about the dogs.

I'd just let one of the strays—Jaime Lannister—that had come in over the weekend out into the fenced yard to romp around for a bit. From there, I could see that a lot of progress had already been made on the new addition to the shelter. Cement had been poured, and the frame was up.

Darla, who preferred hosing down the kennels to being

outside because of her fair skin, surprised me by stepping outside with a dog and unhooking its leash.

"Oh, wow," she said, "there is just something about a rolled-up sleeve that makes my heart palpitate."

I nearly strangled on the laugh I tried to swallow back. "Down, girl."

She knocked her shoulder against mine. "There is one guy over there, a blond. Tall, slender, but his sleeves are rolled up, and I'm telling you—"

"I've already got dibs on him," Jade said.

"You can't call dibs on every guy you see," Darla said. "You called dibs on Chase."

"Well, now I'm going with Thor."

"Thor?" I didn't hold back my laughter with that.

"Close enough," Jade said. "There are a lot of hotties over there. Pick another one."

"I shouldn't have pointed him out," Darla said.

"Which one is he?" I asked, curious, but at a glance it looked like there were maybe two dozen guys at work.

"That one over there, helping to hold a board in place," Darla said.

I followed the direction of her finger. My breath caught. It couldn't be. Mostly I could see his back and a little bit of his side, but I'd know that profile anywhere. "I'll be back," I said.

My mind reeling, I walked through the shelter. Once I

got outside, I headed to the construction area. They'd finished with that board. The guy was reaching for another.

"Jeremy?"

Looking up, he gave me an almost shy, definitely guilty grin. "Hey."

"What are you doing here?"

He glanced back. "Hey, Mac, I'm taking ten!"

The guy who I assumed was the foreman waved a hand. "Over here," Jeremy said, and led me to the back of the fenced area, so we were away from where all the work was happening. Immediately a couple of dogs rushed over and began sniffing around. He put a couple of fingers through the diamond opening, let the dogs lick him.

"Jeremy?" I prodded. "What is going on?"

He removed his hard hat, plowed his fingers through his lengthening hair, and settled the hat back into place. He sighed. "I quit my job at my dad's law office."

"Why? When? What happened?"

"My dad and I have been butting heads for a while, and I'd just had enough. I hated working for him, listening to his opinion on things, pretending I agreed because it was easier than creating waves."

"When did you quit?"

"Before we went to the beach."

I felt awful. He'd been dealing with this on his own. "Why didn't you tell me?"

"Because I didn't want to ruin our time at the beach. There was nothing you could do. It was done."

"But you must have needed to talk."

"No. I was good with the decision. Real good with it."

"What about college? What about—"

He touched his fingers to my lips. "I know you have a lot of questions."

Understatement.

"But I have to get back to work. I'll tell you everything tonight."

"Come over for dinner. Mom has another date."

"You're going to cook?"

"I actually know how to prepare a few things." Lifting up on my toes, I gave him a quick kiss. "See you later." I started to walk away. Stopped. Looked back. "By the way, Darla and Jade both think you're hot. Jade nicknamed you 'Thor.'"

"Oh, yeah?" It looked like he puffed out his chest a bit. He definitely appeared pleased as a wide grin spread across his face. He looked toward the porch. They were both standing there. If they weren't volunteers, they'd get fired. "Tell them that I think they're hot, too."

"No way. I'm not encouraging flirtation." But they were right. Something about the rolled-up sleeves was just downright hot.

When I got back to the area where the kennels were,

I discovered Darla and Jade hovering near the doorway.

"Sorry, girls, he's taken," I said, and kept walking.

"Lucky girl," Darla said. "Anyone we know?"

I swung around and grinned. "Me. That's Jeremy Swanson."

"I thought he was a geek," Jade said, her brow furrowed so deeply that the stud in her eyebrow jutted up.

"He's into computers and stuff. Doesn't mean he can't be hot."

"You go, girl," Darla said.

"And he's one of the gunslingers." I spun on my heel and headed off to take care of the dogs. These girls weren't going to forget about my boyfriend anytime soon.

Chapter 20

JEREMY

Fletcher had been right about Mr. Simms looking for short-term workers. I hadn't realized until he hired me that the job would be helping to build the new annex to the animal shelter. I'd hoped that Kendall would be too busy with the dogs to notice that I was here. I'd planned to tell her about my job situation tonight, but I guessed her knowing now was no big deal.

A bigger deal was watching her talk to some guy in the dog run area. Seeing as he'd brought out a couple of dogs and set them loose to romp around within the fenced zone, I didn't think he was here to adopt.

On top of that, I'd seen him kissing one of the female volunteers earlier, off to the side of the building away from any windows. So the workers inside the shelter might not have seen him, but those of us building the new wing had certainly gotten an eyeful.

He must be that guy, Chase, Kendall had mentioned.

I didn't know him, had never spoken to him, but I didn't like him.

I didn't normally judge people. I pretty much was a live-and-let-live kind of guy but when I saw him talking to Kendall my gut clenched. She gave him such big smiles and laughed at things he said. For some reason, I found it most difficult to deal with knowing that he could make her laugh.

That was my job.

To make her laugh, to keep her happy.

I leisurely tied a folded-up bandanna around my head to absorb the sweat. It gave me time to watch them. I'd never seen her give so much attention to another guy. In high school, she'd talked to guys in the hallway but it was mostly in passing. She was always waiting for me or we were together.

"Total bummer, man," Tommy Simms said.

I jerked my attention to him. "What?"

"That was your girl, wasn't it?"

"She's still my girl."

"Oh." He squirted a bottle of water over his head, didn't move when the droplets fell onto his shoulders. "I thought maybe she was with him now."

"They just work together."

"Okay."

"What does that mean?" I didn't like the way he said it: like I was totally clueless.

"They've been talking for, like, ten minutes."

"Probably about the dogs. Kendall starts talking about dogs and she loses track of time."

"Lot of funny stuff being said about dogs."

I rubbed the back of my neck. Just to confirm my suspicion, I asked, "You wouldn't happen to know who he is, would you?"

"Yeah, man. Chase Harper. Graduated a couple of years ago. Hung out with my brother."

So that *was* Chase, originator of the gun show idea. Even his muscles had muscles. No wonder Kendall had suggested I beef up.

"The guy is a total babe magnet," Tommy added.

Yeah, I could see that, and it looked like Kendall was being pulled toward him.

Every muscle, muscles I didn't know I possessed, muscles I was pretty sure I didn't possess, ached as I got out of the car at Kendall's. They'd started hurting as soon as I got home. They'd stopped bothering me while I was in the hot shower, but once I was out of it, they'd started protesting again. I was pretty sure that I was not going to be able to move tomorrow. I was eighteen years old. I should not be so out of shape. But apparently I was.

It took everything in me not to hobble to the front door, not to groan when Kendall opened it and threw her arms around me.

"I'm so glad you're here!" she exclaimed.

I was glad I was here, too, because it meant I wasn't dead yet. I wasn't quite sure I'd be able to say the same by the morning.

"I'm starving," I said.

Releasing her hold, she smiled brightly. "I bet you are. I can't believe you didn't tell me everything that was going on."

I shrugged. I wasn't exactly sure why I hadn't told her. We'd always shared everything. "I was stepping out of my comfort zone. Guess I wanted to make sure I wasn't going to retreat back to it before I said anything."

"How do you like working construction?" she asked as I followed her to the kitchen.

"I actually like it. Not enough to want to do it for the rest of my life, but I'm glad to be out of my dad's law office." I sat on a stool at the counter. Thank goodness, it looked like everything was done, so I wouldn't have to do any moving for a while. Still, I asked, "Anything I can do to help?"

"Nope."

She pulled a tray of garlic toast out of the oven, the

aroma wafting toward me, popped a couple of slices onto two plates, and brought them to the counter. The stools were usually set up side to side but she moved one onto the other side of the counter so she could face me. Made it easier to talk. Made it harder for me to hide any grimaces when I moved.

"So why did you do this?" she asked.

Because I was tired of my dad hinting that you were going to ruin my life. Not that I was going to tell her that. My dad was being a jerk. No reason to hurt her feelings.

"I didn't like what I was doing," I said as I scooped out some spaghetti and meatballs from a bowl, then dug in. I didn't know if I'd ever been this hungry in my entire life.

"So you're not going to be a lawyer?"

I swallowed, took a gulp of cold sweet tea. "Yeah, I'll still be a lawyer. Just not in my dad's law firm. Besides, being a lawyer is different from being a gofer."

"But wouldn't it look good on your résumé?"

"It'll be years before I need a résumé, and I'll have an internship somewhere before that." Or at least that was the plan.

She twisted spaghetti onto a fork, let it fall off. I knew she was recalibrating our life. She didn't like changes to plans. She liked everything structured. It was one of her cute little quirks.

156

"Why construction?" she suddenly asked.

"Little late in the summer for finding a job so I couldn't be too picky, and I definitely wanted something quick so my dad couldn't hang my not working over my head. Fletcher mentioned that he'd heard that Mr. Simms was hiring, so I talked to Tommy. He put in a good word for me. Pay isn't bad, considering I have no skills but am learning as I go." I grinned, finding some solace in the fact that my facial muscles didn't hurt. "I also figured it would be a great way to beef up. Hauling stuff all day is bound to improve the guns. And the best benefit of all? It puts me close to the shelter and you."

I'd expected her to laugh, or at least smile, not look more worried. "You didn't do this for me. . . ."

"I did it for me," I assured her, although maybe part of it was for her, too.

She was still stirring her spaghetti. "I just always saw you working in an office."

"I will eventually. This is just part of your we-need-to-explore-and-be-adventurous-this-summer mantra. Change a little. You were right."

This time when she twirled spaghetti onto her fork, she ate it, so I figured we were good. Her initial reaction had worried me a little. I'd started to wonder if she was going to be like my dad, who only thought I had worth as long as I was investing in a law career. He hadn't bothered to hide his disappointment in me. The men in our family did not wield hammers.

"Your dad's okay with it?"

"Not even the tiniest bit, but at least he didn't kick me out or cut off the college fund."

Reaching across, she placed her hand over mine. "I have to admit to being impressed that you've taken this stand. It took guts. I'm proud of you. And I'll see you a little more. Maybe you can take your breaks when I'm at the shelter."

"When I can, sure. Although—" I stabbed a meatball. "You didn't seem to be lacking for company today."

"What do you mean?"

I met and held her gaze. "I saw you laughing an awful lot with Chase."

Did I imagine her looking guilty? "Oh, that. He was just telling me some stuff about his dog. It has this thing it does that he calls a 'guilty shuffle' whenever it's caught doing something it shouldn't—like chewing up his sneakers."

"I got the impression when you talked about him before that you didn't like him."

"He's nice enough. He's just a little too cocky and thinks he has this competition nailed." She furrowed her brow. "How did you know it was him, anyway?"

I lifted a shoulder, regretted it as soon as I did it when the muscles protested. Fought back the grimace. "Tommy knows him."

"Tommy Simms? We should have him in the gun show, too. I'll ask him tomorrow."

She really had a one-track mind when it came to the shelter. Although I completely understood, because animals were so important to her.

"How long will it take to finish the wing?" she asked.

"From what I understand, the rest of the summer."

"It's going to be so nice when we can handle more dogs." She squeezed my hand. "You'll be part of that, of making a difference."

"I'm making a difference with that fund-raiser."

"That, too."

With her fork, Kendall broke off a bit of meatball and tossed it to Bogart. The dog snatched it out of the air. Then he settled down, chin on the floor, as though that small action had tuckered him out. I was tempted to join him. I didn't know if I'd ever been so tired.

"So, your mom's date? Same guy?" I asked.

"No, someone different. He took her to the Shrimp Hut. If Avery were working tonight, I'd have her text me a photo of them."

"You haven't seen him?"

"Nope. Mom wouldn't even tell me his name. Think

she was afraid I'd Google him."

"Has to be hard for her to date after so long."

She started playing with her food again. "I miss him sometimes, you know?"

"You probably always will."

She nodded. "But some days it's more than others. It's going to be hard on Mom when I leave."

"But it'll be good for her and you," I said, even though I didn't know if that was true. I had no experience with psychology.

"Was today scary for you?" she asked, her green eyes filled with earnestness.

"Actually I started working yesterday. It was a little strange. Totally different environment, but I like it."

"I still can't believe you didn't tell me."

"I didn't want you to worry about it."

"I wish your dad saw you like I do."

"You mean as hot stuff?" I asked.

She laughed lightly. "No! I just wish he had more faith in you."

Sometimes I did, too.

She dropped her fork into her bowl. "I'm done." Then she reached for my empty bowl.

"I'll help you clean up." I slid off the stool, moaned a little as the muscles rebelled.

Her eyes widened. "You okay?"

"Just sore."

"Want a massage?"

"That's a lot of trouble."

She put her hands on her hips. "What else are we going to do tonight? You're obviously not up for walking Bogart."

"It's not that bad."

She gave me a pointed look.

Okay, so it was that bad. I sighed. "Be gentle."

She gave me a seductive smile that almost banished all the aches. "I think I'm about to have you exactly where I want you."

Chapter 21

KENDALL

We went to my bedroom. As long as we kept the door open, I knew Mom wouldn't mind.

Jeremy took off his sandals and his shirt—the buttoned kind that I was used to him wearing. It was short sleeved, and I wished it had been long sleeved so he could have rolled them up. I knew it was crazy, because he'd only been working at his new job for two days, but I could have sworn his muscles looked firmer. With a groan, he stretched out facedown on the bed. I went into my bathroom and located some lotion, grabbed a towel, and returned to my room. Bogart had followed us up and was resting on the floor, his droopy eyes on Jeremy as though he understood his pain. Dogs were supposed to be intuitive about stuff like that.

I poured a little lotion along the dip in his back, along

his spine. He jumped a little.

"That's cold."

"It'll be warm in just a minute." I'd caressed him before, applied sunscreen, but I'd never tire of having the opportunity to just admire the expanse of his bare back. He was cradling his head on his hands, with his face turned to the side. He was watching me. Leaning down, I kissed his cheek. "Relax."

He took a deep breath. "Yeah, okay."

I skimmed my hands from the waistband of his khaki shorts all the way up to the nape of his neck. He released a long, slow moan.

"Nice," he murmured.

Yes, he was indeed nice, very nice. I was feeling slightly superior to Jade and Darla because I was seeing what they hadn't; I was touching what they never would.

"I got a little jealous today," I admitted quietly while I slowly stroked his shoulders.

"Yeah?"

"You don't have to sound so pleased."

"I just never really thought I was the kind of guy that girls got jealous over."

"Of course you are." Even if Jade and Darla hadn't remembered him from before. I wasn't going to tell him that. I gently kneaded his muscles. Ran my hands down his arms, back up and over his shoulders.

"You don't have to be jealous," he said. "You're it for me."

I nipped at his ear. "Same goes."

I skimmed my hands over the broad expanse of his back. Had I ever realized how broad he was? He really needed to wear smaller T-shirts. The kind that looked like he'd been melted into them.

"Have you ever thought about getting a tattoo?"

"Mmm-huh," he murmured sleepily.

"What would you get?" I asked.

"Dunno. A wolf maybe."

"Where?"

"Back, left shoulder."

I pressed a kiss there. "Anywhere else?"

"Right shoulder. A tiger."

I kissed his right shoulder.

"Neck," he muttered.

I nuzzled his neck. "Where else?"

"Every . . . where."

The last of the word trailed off. Lifting my head, I peered at him. His eyes were closed, his face totally relaxed. A tiny little snore sounded. He was obviously not only sore, but exhausted.

Very carefully I eased off the bed and moved to the chair at my desk. I studied him. I was probably the only one who would notice that his hair was a shade longer. He hadn't shaved before coming over. The shadow over his face made him look a little older. The khaki shorts were the old Jeremy. It was a little like I was looking at what I'd had and what he was going to change into.

I wondered if the khaki would eventually go away. I wondered if I'd even recognize him. I shook my head at the stupid thought. Of course I would. The outside might be changing, but inside he'd be the same.

Wouldn't he?

The light in the hallway hitting my eyes woke me up. I was on my bed, lying on my side, Jeremy's arm around me, his bare chest to my back. I blinked at the shadowy apparition standing in my doorway. I nearly screamed before I realized it was Mom.

Gingerly I eased off the bed and padded over to her. "I know this looks bad," I whispered, "but I was giving him a massage—" Okay, that might not sound any better.

I stepped out into the hallway so I wouldn't disturb him and gave her a quick explanation about his new job and the toll it was taking on him. The entire time she just gave me this secretive-looking smile.

"Kendall," she finally said, "I trust you. In less than a month, you're going off to college. I won't know precisely what you're doing or whom you're doing it with. But I expect you to be the smart girl you've always been."

"I will be," I told her. Nodded. "I am." Then I realized how dark it was. While I didn't know the exact hour, I was pretty sure it was late. "You enjoyed your date."

"I did, yes."

"Are you going to tell me his name?"

"Sam Morris."

"Of the car dealership?"

She nodded.

"You met him online?"

"No, actually I've known him for a while. We crossed paths at the produce section of the grocery store the other night. . . . One thing led to another and he asked me out."

"Are you going to see him again?"

"I think so, yes. He's a widower, so he gets me."

Just like Jeremy got me. "I'm glad. You deserve to be happy again."

"Well, let's not order the wedding cake just yet." She ruffled my hair and nodded toward my bedroom. "His parents might be looking for him."

"I'll nudge him awake."

"Night, sweetie."

There was a dreaminess to her walk as she carried on down the hall. It made me smile, reminded me of how I'd felt the night that Jeremy had first kissed me. I walked back into my room and sat on the edge of the bed. "Hey, you," I whispered.

Jeremy squinted up at me. "I'm awake. Woke up while you were talking to your mom but decided to play possum so I didn't disturb you."

"Sam Morris," I told him. "Can you believe it? He has to be years older than she is."

"Just because he has white hair doesn't mean he's old." He sat up. "Maybe you can suggest he dye it."

"Funny. He is good looking," I said. Tall, slender.

"Maybe you should ask him to be one of your gun-slingers," Jeremy suggested as he pulled his shirt on and buttoned it.

I tucked my legs beneath me. "Huh. Someone to appeal to the older crowd."

He paused, looked at me. "I was kidding."

"I'm not. It's all about raising money for the shelter. Some diversity in ages could make a difference."

"Do you really want to put a guy your mom is dating up there for people to gawk at?"

I hadn't thought of that. Maybe I didn't want to see him in a T-shirt flexing his muscles. On the other hand—

"I asked you to do it."

"True enough."

Standing, he took my hand. "Walk me out."

167

We didn't say anything as we went down the stairs and headed outside. When we got to his car, he leaned back against the door, put his hands on my hips, and brought me in for a searing kiss. It was like we hadn't kissed all summer. Or maybe he needed fortification before he headed home.

He pressed his forehead to mine. "Could have been doing that all night instead of sleeping."

"You needed the rest. We'll make it up tomorrow night."

"Count on it."

He got in the car. I watched him drive away, his speed a little faster than usual. I didn't know why that bothered me.

The pressed-trousers-and-buttoned-shirt Jeremy never would have bucked his father, never would have left the law firm. This jeans-and-rolled-up-sleeves-at-work Jeremy—he was hot. He was what I wanted. Wasn't he?

Chapter 22

JEREMY

Kendall might not have any interest in Chase, but I was pretty sure the guy was very much interested in her. He always seemed to be in the dog play area whenever she was. He always spoke to her, always made her laugh. Once I saw him fold his hand over her shoulder, and I nearly bit the nail I was holding between my teeth in two. I really didn't like this guy. I especially didn't like the attention he was giving my girl.

Three days in, and I'd had enough.

After work, I found myself knocking on Fletcher's door. When he opened it, he seemed as surprised to see me as I was to be there.

"What's up?" he asked.

"Was wondering if you happened to have an extra root beer you'd be willing to part with."

He gave me a once-over. "Sure. Come on in."

"I'm not disturbing anything?"

He grinned. "Dude, I wouldn't have invited you in if you were. Avery's helping her mom cook dinner so I've got a few minutes before I need to get over there."

I followed him into his apartment. It was a single room with a sitting area, bed, and dresser.

"Take a load off," he said as he reached into a mini-fridge and pulled out two brown bottles.

Dropping onto the couch, I took the bottle he offered me and drank deep. "Thanks."

Sitting in a chair, he put his feet on the coffee table, studied me, waited. I wasn't really sure why I'd come to see him. Yes, I was.

"So you were right about Simms Construction. I got a job helping with the work on the animal shelter."

"That's good, right?"

"Oh, yeah. It's just that . . ." Leaning forward, I dangled the bottle between my fingers. This was hard. "I see this guy, Chase, flirting with Kendall when she's taking the dogs outside."

"Dude, she's crazy about you. You don't have anything to worry about."

I wasn't exactly worried—or maybe I was. I just knew that I didn't like it. "This gun show we're doing? It was Chase's idea. I'm pretty sure he thinks he's going to win.

I'd rather he didn't. I thought maybe you should take the competition a little more seriously and whip his butt."

"Why not you?"

"You've got a good three inches in height on me."

"Height's got nothing to do with it. It's all about the abs. They're the first things a girl's eyes go to."

"I don't have any abs."

"We won't know that until we dig for them. You played baseball this spring, right? So you're in pretty good shape. Start doing a lot of crunches. I mean, a lot of crunches. Those abs will seem to come out of nowhere. Then during the competition, do a little shirt lift, and the girls will go absolutely crazy." Pointing his bottle toward me, he arched an eyebrow. "Don't ask me how I know that's true."

"You really think that's all it'll take? Sit-ups?"

"Add some curls for your forearms. You know, lift weight, put it down. Up. Down. Old-school exercising can do it."

I narrowed my eyes at him. "Is this what you're doing?"

"You know it."

"You could have mentioned this when we were at the beach house."

"I wanted to win for Avery. Wasn't going to lose my advantage. But now it's more important for us both to beat this guy."

I regretted a little that I hadn't become friends with

Fletcher sooner. He might be a tough guy, but he was a good tough guy.

"Don't say anything to Avery because she'll tell Kendall, and I don't want her to know what I'm doing."

"She'll probably notice when you're making out."

"That's fine. I just don't want her to know until she notices."

He grinned again. "The things we do for chicks, right?"

Right. This was for me, too, but I didn't want to lose Kendall. And suddenly I was afraid that if I didn't change— if I didn't at least beat Chase—that I might.

KENDALL

I was starting to see Jeremy more while I was doing my volunteer work at the shelter than I did in the evenings. The couple of nights during the week that he did come over, we made out a little, but mostly we watched TV. While he was getting accustomed to the strenuous work, the heat still took a toll, so he was usually tired, content to just hold me on the couch.

I'd get to the shelter around lunchtime, stopping first at the B. S. to pick up some burgers. Jeremy would take his break when I arrived. We'd sit under a tree and visit, while watching the dogs romping in the fenced area. We'd talk about leaving for college, the things we thought we should take with us, what we thought it would be like. The classes we wanted to share. The distraction of waiting to hear if we got the on-campus jobs we'd applied for.

Saturday, after I got out of the car at the shelter, I grabbed a wicker basket out of the backseat. I'd decided to do something special and make the lunch myself. My grandmother's chicken salad sandwiches and Jeremy's favorite dessert: double fudge brownies.

As I walked toward the construction site, I spotted him talking with Jade. He was wearing a red tank top that revealed his clearly defined muscles and his bronzed skin. His face was shadowed with stubble. He looked older, tougher . . . sexier.

I couldn't deny that at that moment I didn't think he'd ever looked hotter. I wanted to wrap my arms around his waist and plant a kiss on him. Shallow, I know, to be so mesmerized by the transformation from buttoned shirts to tight cotton. But I wanted to skim my hands over his arms and shoulders, feel the firmness of those muscles that hadn't been there at the beginning of summer.

I wanted to do exactly what Jade was doing.

I stopped in my tracks as she took her fingers on a little journey along his biceps. I hadn't noticed how close they were standing. She'd be able to feel the heat shimmering off him. She was giving him a seductive smile that was filled with wicked promises.

He was smiling back.

My chest tightened at the sight of their obvious

flirtation, and I was fighting to draw in the hot, humid Texas air. He'd never grinned at me like that, like he was considering doing naughty things with me. I had the fleeting thought that I wanted to leave, that I didn't want to see this. I'd wanted to make other girls jealous. I hadn't wanted to be the one who became jealous.

Jeremy saw me. His smile grew and he waved. His apparent gladness at seeing me loosened the knot in my chest so I could at least breathe again. Squaring my shoulders, I walked over.

"Hey," he said.

"Hey," I repeated, my brain not really functioning yet.

Jade gave me a once-over as though she were sizing me up for a wrestling match. Then she looked back at Jeremy and did this stupid little thing where she touched the tip of her tongue to her upper lip. "See you later."

She walked off with an exaggerated roll to her hips.

"I wonder how she keeps her balance," I mused.

"Practice, probably."

I turned to face him. "Do you find that kind of walk sexy?"

"I hadn't really thought about it, but now that you mention it—not really." He grinned. "So what'd you bring?"

"A surprise."

Most of the workers were taking their break now. Jeremy led me over to our tree. He didn't have a tree with

Jade. We sat in the shade. I opened the basket and handed him a sandwich. He examined it, grinned.

"Your grandmother's chicken salad?" he asked.

"Yeah, except I made it. Something's missing. I think she may have a secret ingredient that she didn't write down."

He took a huge bite, chewed. "Tastes the same to me."

"Thanks." Nibbling on my sandwich, I didn't agree with his assessment. I'd eaten way more of my gran's chicken salad than he had. I swallowed, having difficulty getting the food past the lump in my throat. I opened a Coke, took a long sip. Better. "So, uh, what were you and Jade talking about?"

"Oh, Scooter Gibson's having a party tonight at his parents' lake house. They're out of town. She wanted to make sure we knew about it."

Yeah, I was pretty sure she couldn't have cared less if I knew about it.

"I was thinking we'd go," he said as he finished off his sandwich.

"We haven't seen each other much lately," I pointed out.

"Which is why I thought we'd go."

"But I was thinking just you and I would do something."

"We haven't done anything with anyone else since I started working this job. I'm beginning to feel like an old married person or something."

I knew he hadn't said that to be hurtful. It wasn't in Jeremy's nature to be hurtful, but I liked when it was just us.

"I figured you'd jump at the chance to do something different. You're the one who said we were getting boring, should shake things up."

My quick burst of laughter sounded more like I was choking. "I did say that, didn't I?"

"Yeah. Ask Avery and Fletch to go with us."

Fletch? Some of the cool kids at school had called Fletcher that, but Jeremy never had before. It seemed odd, and yet, it didn't.

"Okay, I'll text her before I check in for my shift."

"You can do it now," he said, just before starting in on another sandwich.

"This is our time."

"We're only eating. That way we'll know if we're picking them up or not."

Our time together was so precious that I wanted to be selfish with it. Still I pulled out my cell phone and sent Avery a quick text about the party. A couple of seconds later, her response came back.

"She says they're in."

"Cool. Fletch doesn't drink. He's designated driver."

I stared at Jeremy for a minute. He didn't drink, either.

Well, one beer when we arrived at parties with booze and no parents. He was always completely sober by the time we left, even if I was a bit tipsy. Although maybe he'd never drunk more because he was always the driver.

He reached into the basket and brought out a foil-wrapped item. Opened it. Grinned. "Brownies!" Leaning over, he brushed a kiss over my cheek. "Thanks."

That was the Jeremy I knew, the one who never took anything for granted. I tugged on his shirt. "This is new."

"Gets hot out here, and I got to thinking about what you said about a little tan helping win the contest. The tank we got when we were at the beach, I'm saving for the competition."

"I like it." I considered touching his arm, but then I thought about Jade doing the same thing. I didn't want to be like her.

Jeremy finished off his brownie. "I need to get back to work."

"I'll see you tonight then."

"Yep." He pushed himself up and sauntered off.

There was something different—a toughness—about his walk, the way he moved. Stronger, more confident.

I didn't know why it made me feel less confident about us.

Chapter 24

JEREMY

When we arrived at the party, Fletch and I left the girls by the pool and went to get drinks. We'd been to a party here before graduation so we were pretty familiar with the setup. The hard liquor was in the kitchen. Beer was in ice coolers near the deck that ran along the back of the house. As we neared, I caught sight of Chase. He was holding Jade in his arms, lifting her up and down like she was a set of barbells and he was doing a workout. People standing around were counting off the reps.

"That's him," I said to Fletch.

"Who?"

"Chase. Over there with Jade."

"Impressive."

I scowled at him. "You're not supposed to be impressed. You're supposed to be pissed. He's such a show-off."

We reached the coolers. I opened one, grabbed a beer, twisted the cap, and took a long, slow swallow.

"We can beat him," Fletch said.

"I don't know. I've been doing the crunches until they almost kill me, and I'm starting to see some definition but realistically—look at that guy."

"But he's showing off everything he's got. We're more subtle. That's better. And we'll have a secret weapon."

I finished off the bottle, tossed it into a nearby trash can, and reached for another. "Oh, yeah? Fill me in on that."

"This guy who brought his car into the shop is a personal trainer. Totally buff guy. So we got to talking about tricks of the trade and he said if we add just a dash of grape seed oil to our abs, biceps, shoulders, it'll really make them pop."

I felt this wave of appreciation. "You could have kept that to yourself, given yourself an edge."

"Probably would have if I was having to watch this guy flirt with Avery. Although it looks like maybe he's moved on to Jade."

The counting came to an end with a round of cheers and applause. Chase bowed, then he and Jade wandered off.

"Maybe." I downed more beer.

"Shouldn't you take it easy with that?" Fletch asked.

"You're designated driver." I dug my keys out of my jeans pocket and tossed them to him. "I'm in the mood to party, especially now that we have a secret weapon."

When the bottle was empty, I did a free throw move to get it into the trash can. I grabbed three more beers. "Let's get back to the girls."

We were halfway there when Jade was suddenly standing in front of me. "Hey, handsome."

No one had ever referred to me as handsome. Cute, maybe. But not handsome. I vaguely wondered where Chase was. Then I was struck with this crazy thought that she had abandoned him so she was free to come over to speak with me. I dug the possibility that she might have tossed him aside in favor of me. Served him right for flirting with my girl. More surprising, however, was the realization that Jade didn't even seem to notice that Fletch was standing beside me. I was used to him getting the attention when we were together. I had to admit that I liked being noticed. I liked it a lot.

KENDALL

"Can you believe they broke up?"

Tamara Dailey, who had barely given Avery and me the time of day while we were in high school, was suddenly acting like we were best buds. As soon as the guys had walked off to get us something to drink, Tamara—one of the biggest gossips in high school—had rushed over like she'd just heard Channing Tatum was going to make an appearance at our sides. But her news was more sobering: Amber Montgomery and John Ramirez had called it quits.

"They've been together, like, forever," Tamara said. "Since freshman year."

"He's going to Stanford, isn't he?" Avery asked. She knew all the smart people.

"Yep," Tamara said. "And Amber is going to the junior college."

"It's hard to have a long-distance relationship," I said.

"But they don't know that yet. He hasn't left."

"Well, maybe they just decided it was best."

"But if they can't stick it out, what does that mean for the rest of us?" Tamara asked.

I wasn't a big fan of spreading tales about other people, so I decided to call out Tamara on her unnecessary dramatics. "I forget. Who are you with?" I asked.

She jutted out her chin. "No one, but now I don't know if there is any point in getting together with someone."

With that pronouncement, she marched off.

Avery released a small laugh. "Wow. Talk about sweeping generalizations."

"They were together a long time, though."

Avery shrugged. "Our world starts to expand after high school. We have new experiences, meet new people. Not everything stays the same."

Boy, that was true. Uncomfortable, I shifted from one foot to the other. "Maybe we shouldn't have come."

She furrowed her brow. "Why?"

Because it was Jade's idea. "I don't know. Just one of those things that didn't stay the same. It's louder, a little wilder."

"Seems the same to me."

"What seems the same?" Fletcher asked as he handed us each a beer.

"Scooter's party. It doesn't seem as though it's changed much since we were here just before graduation," Avery said.

He grinned. "You got plastered that night."

"I did not. Well, maybe a little."

Fletcher had given her a ride home, and that was the start of them getting together.

"Where's Jeremy?" I asked.

"He got waylaid." Fletcher jerked his head back over his shoulder.

I followed the direction of his motion. Jeremy was standing at the edge of the pool talking with Jade and her usual partner in crime, Melody Long.

"What's he doing with them?" Avery asked.

"Jade has the hots for him," I answered.

"Really?"

I glared at her. "Why do you find that so odd? He's the complete package."

"Well, yeah, I know, I just always thought Jade went with guys who looked dangerous."

Had she not taken a good look at Jeremy tonight? Probably not. Her focus was completely on Fletcher. While mine was on Jeremy. He was wearing a gray T-shirt tucked into jeans that hadn't been pressed. Both were a snug fit that didn't leave any doubt that his body was firming up as he worked on the construction crew. He hadn't shaved. His hair looked as though he'd just run his fingers through it—or someone had. I didn't want to consider that it looked a little more mussed than it had when he picked me up. Surely it was because the breeze was ruffling it. He wouldn't let another girl—

I shook my head. He wouldn't.

"I'll be back," Fletcher said, and he wandered off to talk with a couple of guys. I wondered if he thought I needed a few private moments with Avery.

"Is everything okay with you guys?" she asked.

"Yes." But I didn't sound sure enough to convince a jury. I'd gone with Jeremy once to watch his dad in action in the courtroom, and Jeremy had snuck over to my side to narrate everything the lawyers and judge did. I missed those moments we shared. I capitulated. "Not really. I think I'm losing him."

She looked at me as though I'd just announced that I'd spotted a spaceship landing. "Why would you think that?"

"He doesn't text me anymore."

She gave me a blank look. I realized Fletcher would not be the texting sort, so she probably didn't know what I was referring to. I'd convinced myself the lack of texts was because he was so busy at the construction site that he didn't have time, and then I was with him on his breaks. . . .

"Jeremy used to text me during the day—just quick little messages so I'd know he was thinking of me. He hasn't done that since we were at the beach. And now look at him with them."

Her brow furrowed. "They're just talking."

It was more than that. Jade and Melody were in his personal space and he was standing his ground, letting them in. They were in bathing suits, all that bare skin just inches from him, and he wasn't uncomfortable with it. If he was, he would have backed up.

Because Avery was my best friend, because I trusted her, I knew I could tell her the truth, and she wouldn't judge me. Or if she did, she'd do it kindly. "I've been asking him to change."

She blinked. "To change what?"

In my head, it all sounded so stupid now. "His clothes, his hair, his . . . I don't know. He's always so nice. He never seems to get attention."

"Is that what this gun show thing is all about?"

"Sorta. I guess. Yes. He was a geek. Not that there's anything wrong with being a geek. I thought I wanted him to not be so geekish. But now I'm wishing I had my geek back."

As I watched him flex his muscles, I realized that it might be too late for that. Both Jade and Melody pinched and prodded his arms like they were trying to decide if he was fruit ripe for plucking. I downed half my beer before handing it off to Avery. "I'll be back."

I marched toward them, sidestepping a couple of weaving guys, darting out of the way when someone in the pool splashed water at me. I finally reached them and came to a stop. "Hey."

"Hey," Jeremy said, smiling brightly, a little too brightly. "I was just telling them about the gun show."

I didn't see the point. Jade already knew about it.

"Looked like maybe you were demonstrating the gun show," I said. "Why would they donate to the shelter if they've already seen it?"

"Oh, we'll donate," Melody said. "Don't you worry about that." She clucked and winked at Jeremy. "Catch you later."

They walked off.

"What did she mean by that?" I asked.

Jeremy shook his head. "I'm not really sure. I didn't catch most of what they were saying." He placed a bottle to his lips, tipped his head back, and gulped several times. Then he gave me a speculative once-over. "Are you jealous?"

"I just don't like to see girls pawing at you."

"They weren't pawing."

Not technically maybe.

He slung his arm around my shoulders, staggered into me a little. "I don't remember these parties being so much fun."

I was glad one of us was having a good time. No, I wasn't. I didn't want him having fun with other girls. He never gave other girls the time of day. What was going on?

"You need another drink," he said.

"No, I'm good."

He tilted his head like an inquisitive dog. "You don't seem good."

"Maybe we should go."

"We just got here. Come on." With his arm around my shoulders, he led me toward the house.

I slipped my arm around his waist, slid my hand into his back jeans pocket. It was silly for me to let Jade and Melody upset me. This was a chance to spend time with Jeremy. That's all I wanted. To be with him.

Very few lights were on inside the house, but I could see shadows moving in front of the floor-to-ceiling windows that provided a wonderful view of the lake.

We went up the stairs to the deck. People were lounging around. Some were kissing. I thought one guy was sleeping or maybe he was passed out. It didn't matter. None of these people mattered. Only Jeremy did.

He slid the door open and we walked into the kitchen. A blender was whirring. A guy we knew from high school was standing near it.

"Hey, Marc, we'll have one of those," Jeremy said as he tossed his beer bottle into a trash can before reaching down to a cooler and grabbing another bottle.

"How many have you had?" I asked, because it wasn't like Jeremy to throw orders around. Normally he would ask if we could have something. He was always extremely polite.

"Not keeping count," Jeremy said.

"Shouldn't you be?"

"I'm not driving. Just here to have fun."

Only this wasn't fun. It was like being with someone I didn't know. Just then he smiled at me, placed the flat of his palm on the small of my back, and gave me a sweet, but quick, kiss. This was Jeremy. I realized I was just feeling insecure because of the attention he'd given Jade and Melody. They were the flirts. Not Jeremy.

Marc poured the pink mixture into a plastic cup and handed it to me.

"Thanks," I said.

The last time we were at a party here, I hadn't come into the house because it was make-out central. I figured we'd leave after we got our drinks, but Jeremy put his arm around my shoulders again and guided me through a darkened dining room into a huge dimly lit living room. Music was thrumming. Candles were burning, providing the only light.

As my eyes adjusted, I saw shadows writhing on the sofas and chairs. Some people were sprawled over huge pillows. The temperature of the room was stifling. It was like all the air had been sucked out of it.

Rising up on my toes, I spoke loudly into Jeremy's ear. "Why are we here?"

"Thought you wanted to explore things. Not be boring."

"Not this, not like this."

"Why not? I'm getting mixed messages, Kendall. You want something different, but when I offer it you don't want it."

"This isn't different. It's more like awkward."

"I'm not feeling awkward." I watched as he gulped down the beer, then set the bottle in the middle of a potted fern.

"Jeremy, are you drunk?"

"No." He said it fast and harsh, like he was offended. "I'm having a good time. We can make out by the pool."

I didn't think I'd be up for that, either, but I didn't say anything because I just wanted to get out of the house. Taking my hand, he led me back the way we'd come. In the kitchen, he snatched another beer.

He staggered down the steps, nearly missed the last one, and laughed. He slung his arm around me. "Do you think I'm handsome?"

"Of course I do."

"I think you're pretty. We should tell each other things like that." He gave me a goofy grin. "I'm going to win the gun show. I have a secret weapon."

"What is it?"

He waved his finger back and forth in front of my nose, and I realized he'd had a lot to drink. A lot. And that wasn't like him, either.

"I can't tell you."

He began leading me toward the pool, although he was leaning heavily on me and his steps weren't quite so sure. He drank as we went, then tossed the empty beer bottle onto the grass. That was so not Jeremy.

"I'm thinking we need to go," I said.

"Thought we wanted to have fun." He stopped walking and pointed to my plastic cup. "Are you going to drink that?"

"I don't think so."

He took it from me and gulped down the drink. The cup went the way of the bottle before it. I glanced around. I needed to find Fletcher.

"Jeremy, we need to leave."

"Why? It's just starting to get interesting."

"You've had a lot to drink."

"And you haven't had enough. You need to relax, Kendall. Enjoy the moment."

How could I when this wasn't us? During the last party, we'd had a couple of drinks, but mostly we'd danced and kissed a little in the shadows. We'd focused on each other. Tonight I felt alone, even though there were so many people around and so many things going on.

There was a high-pitched yell. Jeremy released his hold on me, turned—

Someone slammed into him and catapulted him into the pool, then followed him in. They both came up laughing and sputtering. The girl combed her fingers through her short, black hair.

Jade.

"Told you I'd get you into the pool before the night was over!" she yelled.

Jeremy laughed again, but it didn't sound like his laugh. It was like some stranger or an alien had taken ahold of him.

Melody cannonballed into the pool and was soon bobbing beside them.

I stared in disbelief as the two girls began climbing all over my boyfriend. All I could see were arms and legs. Jade and Melody were wearing two-piece bathing suits. Their bared skin flashed in the Japanese lanterns that were hung around the pool. Their shrieks and laughter echoed toward me. They weren't the only ones in the pool, but they were the only ones I could really see and hear.

Or at least, I would have sworn that they were the ones I was hearing.

Jeremy finally broke away and swam to the edge of the

pool. He hauled himself up and sat on the edge. He dragged his T-shirt over his head, wadded it up, wrung it out.

In stunned fascination I watched the muscles ripple over his torso and arms. Over his abs. Where had those come from? I knew he was in shape because of baseball. I'd seen his bare torso at the beach and when I gave him the massage. It seemed impossible that he could have changed so much in such a short time, so maybe it was just the way the shadows and light played over him but it looked like he was now sporting a six-pack.

"Come on, Jeremy," Jade whined, bouncing up and down in the water. "I got you into the pool. You have to stay for a while."

Where was a shark when I needed one?

Jeremy plowed his hands through his hair. I couldn't believe how sexy that action was. Apparently Jade and Melody thought so, too, because they each grabbed a leg and before I knew it, he was back in the pool.

"That's your guy, right?"

I turned at the deep, familiar voice and looked at Chase. "What are you doing here?"

"Jade told me about the party. Thought maybe she was into me, but looks like I got that wrong."

"I think you got it right. She's probably just messing with Jeremy while waiting for you. You should let her know you're here."

"Oh, she knows. She was spending time with me until lover boy over there showed up. Then it was time for a pitching change. She couldn't get to him fast enough."

"Well, he's not going to stay with her."

"You don't think?"

I glanced back at the pool in time to see him lift her up and toss her playfully away. Melody was climbing on his back like she thought he was going to give her a piggyback ride. "This is crazy."

"Want me to chuck you in there so you can defend what's yours?" Chase asked.

I was wearing my favorite sandals. Besides I wasn't sure I'd come out ahead. The very notion of me getting into a brawl with them—of me having to defend what was mine—was ridiculous. "No."

Jeremy dumped Melody off his shoulders, again swam to the edge of the pool. But this time when he hauled himself out, he didn't sit at the edge. He grabbed his bundled-up T-shirt and staggered away.

He looked around. I waved. He spotted me and wove toward me. "The world is spinning," he slurred.

"I think you had too much to drink."

"Not that much." He took a deep breath, opened his eyes wide. Then he narrowed them at Chase. "Seen you at the shelter, but we haven't really met."

"I'm Chase."

"I'm Kendall's boyfriend." He jabbed his finger into Chase's chest. "You need to remember that."

"Maybe *you* need to remember that," Chase said. "You were the one in the pool letting Jade climb all over you like you were a jungle gym."

Looking confused, he shook his head. "I've seen you flirting with my girl. You'd better stop. 'Cuz you're not going to win."

"Win what?"

"Anything."

"Dude, you're not making any sense."

"You just—"

"Hey, Jeremy," Fletcher said, putting his arm around Jeremy as though he thought he might fall down without some support. "Think we need to go."

"Yeah, man. Don't tell him."

"I won't."

Fletcher started to lead Jeremy away. I turned to Chase. "I'm so sorry."

"No need to apologize to me for his actions. They're not your fault."

But I sort of wondered if they were. "I'll see you at the shelter."

"Count on it."

I caught up with Avery and followed along as Fletcher supported Jeremy to the car.

"What happened to him?" Avery asked.

"I think he drank too much too fast. He had two beers and some alcoholic drink in about ten minutes."

"He had a few beers before that," Fletcher called back.

He unceremoniously dumped Jeremy into the backseat. I'd recently learned that Fletcher's dad got drunk a lot so I knew he didn't have a lot of tolerance for those who abused alcohol. Jeremy could not work the seat belt so I reached over and did it for him.

He gave me a really goofy grin. "You should have come into the pool."

"I think there were enough people in the pool."

"It was fun."

My gut clenched. I didn't want him having fun with Jade. Or with Melody for that matter.

He didn't say anything else. By the time Fletcher pulled into my driveway, Jeremy was asleep.

Not exactly the way I'd planned for tonight to go.

"I'll take care of him," Fletcher said.

"Thanks." I said that to be polite, because at that moment, I really wasn't sure that I cared.

As I walked into the house, I wondered what had happened to the Jeremy I loved.

Chapter 26

JEREMY

A little construction crew had taken up residence inside my head and was pounding sledgehammers against the front of my skull. I thought if I didn't move maybe they would go away. But they didn't. They just slammed harder.

Squinting, I cracked open my eyes. Faint morning light was easing between the slats and around the edge of the blinds at the windows. The room looked familiar but I couldn't quite place it. The idea that something was terribly wrong ratcheted through me. I shouldn't be here. It shouldn't be morning.

"Here, drink this."

Shifting my gaze, I saw Fletch sitting in a chair near the bed, extending a glass of what looked to be tomato juice toward me. My stomach rebelled at the mention of drinking anything, and I thought I might hurl.

"No," I croaked.

"It'll make you feel better."

I started to shake my head and pain ricocheted through it. "What happened?"

"You got drunk, passed out on the way home, and I hauled you up here. Seriously, this will help."

I rose up on an elbow, took the glass, and drank the most foul-tasting stuff I'd ever had in my mouth. I gagged.

"Drink it all, one big gulp. Hold your breath. Makes the going down easier."

"What is it?"

"Something my old man would have me fix for him when he went on a bender."

I held my breath and swallowed it down, then handed the empty glass back to him. "Do I want to know what's in it?"

"Probably not," he said.

But I was beginning to feel a little better. My queasy stomach was settling. The construction crew in my head seemed to have gone on break, although I felt sluggish. Slowly I pushed myself into a sitting position and swung my legs over the side of the bed. Placing my elbows on my thighs, I buried my face in my hands. I realized I was wearing sweatpants and a T-shirt that were a little big on me. "Do I want to know everything that happened?"

"Probably not," he repeated.

I peered at him through my spread fingers. "But you're going to tell me."

"Do you remember being in the pool with Jade and Melody?"

I groaned. Yeah, I remembered that. I'd never been the kind of guy that girls went crazy about. Before we moved here, I was a bit of a geek. I'd studied in school, enjoyed playing with computers and video games. I hung out with guy friends. Didn't have girlfriends. Or many friends that were girls.

When we moved here, I met Kendall and Avery. I liked them. They let me hang out with them. I fell for Kendall. But having girls I barely knew giving me attention was insane. Talking to me, fine. Pushing me into the pool and wanting to get into some sort of water fight was nuts. Although if I were honest, I'd really liked the attention. I'd liked that maybe they thought I was funny or cute or interesting. Last night I'd actually thought that I might win that contest, that I might raise the most money for the shelter. That I would beat this Chase guy that was always hanging around Kendall.

Oh, crap. That Chase guy.

"Did I get into a fight with Chase?" I knew that I'd wanted to. I'd wanted to punch him. I didn't know what it was about him that irritated me so much.

"Nah, just poked him in the chest and told him you had

a secret weapon and were going to win. Didn't make a lot of sense, although I figured you were talking about the oil."

"Ah, man." I scrubbed my hands up and down my face.

"I've never seen you drunk like that. You didn't seem like yourself all night. What's going on with you?"

"I don't know. Some things that Kendall has said lately . . ." I shook my head. I was not going to tell him that I was feeling insecure in my relationship with her. She kept saying she wanted us to change, and it felt like we were. But the changes were taking us away from each other. "I take it these are your clothes."

"Yeah, you came to as I was getting you up here. Somehow you managed to change into dry clothes, then you flopped on the bed and were out."

"Thanks for giving me a place to crash." I stood up. "Where are my clothes?"

"Drying in the bathroom."

"I really appreciate this."

"Not a problem."

That was a lie. It was a huge problem. And I knew it.

After I changed back into my clothes, I thanked Fletch again and left. My car was waiting for me in the driveway. Climbing in, I knew I needed to get home, but I wanted to see Kendall first. I drove over to her house and rang her doorbell. When she answered, she looked tired and sad. I felt like a total jerk. "I'm sorry about last night."

"Do you like her? Do you like Jade?"

"No! Not like that. She's fun, but that's all. She wanted me to get into the pool, but I told her no. She said I would before the night was over. So that's what all that was about. It didn't mean anything." I shifted uncomfortably on the porch. "What about Chase?"

"He's just a guy I work with at the shelter."

"But you spend so much time talking to him."

"Because he's there, and he's interesting."

"Thought you thought he was a tool."

"At least he doesn't go around punching guys in the chest. What was wrong with you last night?"

I cringed. "I drank too much, too fast."

"It seemed like it was more than that."

"You wanted me to change."

"Not into a jerk."

I deserved that. I also knew things weren't right between us. That they hadn't been for a while.

"I wish I'd never asked you to do the gun show," she said.

"It started before that. You were hinting that you wanted something different. You weren't happy with me the way I was." Just like my parents. No matter what I did, it wasn't good enough for them. "I don't want to hurt you, Kendall, but I don't know who we are anymore."

"I don't know, either, Jeremy." She sounded sad,

resigned. I hated where this was going. But I also hated feeling like I couldn't do anything right. That nothing I did was enough. "I don't like that you're flirting with other girls."

"I don't like that you're laughing with other guys."

"Maybe we should take a break."

The construction crew in my head moved to my chest and took a sledgehammer to my heart. I wanted to tell her that was a bad idea. But we weren't who we'd been at the beginning of summer. I didn't know who we were anymore. I nodded. "Yeah, I think you're right."

"Okay then." She backed up a step. Waited.

I waited, too, although I wasn't sure what we were waiting for. Finally she turned on her heel and went inside.

I headed for the car, wondering how what should have been the best summer of my life had turned into the worst.

Chapter 27

KENDALL

I texted Avery:

Can U come over?

Avery:

BRT

I managed not to run into my mom before I got to my room. Avery joined me there a few minutes later, although by then my eyes were red and swollen, my nose stuffed, and a mountain of used tissues was piled on my bed.

"What happened?" she asked.

"We broke up," I forced out in a nasally twang, finding it difficult to breathe.

"Oh, Kendall, no." She crossed over to the bed, climbed onto it, and put her arms around me. Burying my head on her shoulder, I seemed only capable of nodding. "Because of last night?"

I nodded again, shrugged, and drew back. "Because of a lot of things. Like I told you. I asked him to change. And he did. He's never gotten drunk before. He *wanted* to get drunk. And he's never ignored me. He liked Jade and Melody pawing at him. I don't think he's ever had attention like that before. It kinda went to his head. I don't like that he liked it."

She looked at her hands, like she was trying to make sure she still had all her fingers.

"What?" I asked.

She lifted her gaze to me. "You really seemed to like talking with Chase. Maybe Jeremy didn't like that, either."

"Are you excusing his behavior?"

"No, I'm saying a relationship takes two. You were pushing him to change. Maybe he needed to feel accepted and Jade and Melody were all-too willing to provide that acceptance. I'm not saying it was right or what you did was wrong. But maybe there is a way for you to get back together if you really love him."

I shook my head. "I don't know, Avery. In my head, I can't stop seeing him in the pool with them. I don't know who he is anymore."

"Then maybe this is for the best."

It wasn't. It was the worst. I hurt all over. It was a struggle to keep breathing. All I wanted to do was cry. I couldn't imagine my life without Jeremy.

It was awful not to get a single text from him all day. When I went to bed that night, I stared at my phone, willing a good-night text to appear. Just one word to give me hope that everything between us wasn't completely and absolutely over.

But the phone stayed quiet. All I heard were my sobs.

I didn't usually volunteer to work at the shelter on Monday. But Terri had asked me to come in around two to help her design the layout for the Bark in the Park event and figure out our volunteer needs. She appreciated my organizational abilities. Or at least that's what I told myself. I didn't want to admit that it was probably my need to control things that had her asking for my help. Once I knew what we wanted, I'd obsess about making sure everything ran as it should.

I was dreading going. I hadn't seen or heard from Jeremy since he left my house yesterday. With no word from him this morning, our breakup was seeming more real. But even so, I felt like a ton of bricks had landed on my chest and was crushing me when I saw him taking a break, sitting under *our* tree, talking with Jade. Although mostly she was doing the talking. He was nodding and grinning. Grinning, like he was enjoying being with her.

It was our tree!

Hoping they didn't see me, I hurried into the shelter.

Chase was standing behind the counter, watching a couple filling out some paperwork. The woman was holding a miniature poodle.

Chase smiled. "Hey. Terri's waiting for you in her office."

"Thanks." I started to walk on but he crooked his finger and urged me nearer. The couple was occupied, so I eased up to the counter.

"I saw Jade out at the construction site earlier. Everything okay after the other night?" he asked.

I just shook my head.

He gave me a sympathetic look, which made me feel like a total loser. So I forced on a brave smile before heading to Terri's office. The door was open. She looked up when I walked in. She smiled. "Hi!" Then she sobered. "You okay?"

I shook off my morose musings, hated that I was so easy to read. "Oh, yeah. So what have we got?"

"Pull up a chair and I'll show you."

On her computer was a layout of the park. "We'll make use of this area here, along the main path through the park. Set up various stations. We'll figure out what we want at the stations, how many people we'll need to man each, who should manage each."

I pointed to the entrance to the park. "We should probably set up the adoption station there."

"That's what I was thinking. I'll be there all day. I was hoping you'd take the morning shift when we'll have more dogs on hand. You have a real talent for keeping them calm and showing them off."

I felt myself blush. "Thanks. I love helping them find their forever homes. Of course I'll work the morning shift."

"Great. Where do you think we should put the gun show?"

A couple of days ago, I would have said that I wanted it across from us so I'd be near Jeremy, so I could watch him. "Farther up the trail, I think. So they don't distract from the adoption."

She grinned. "Yeah, the way Jade has been talking about it, I have a feeling she is definitely going to make sure they're noticed."

"Jade?" I echoed.

"She asked to be in charge of that station."

Of course she did.

I commented halfheartedly as we discussed where to set up watering stations for the dogs, refreshment areas for the adults, face painting, a magician, and other entertainments for the kids. I loved this event, but I kept picturing Jeremy with Jade.

It was nearly two hours before Terri and I were finished. We had our layout, our volunteer needs mapped out. We created a sign-up sheet for the volunteers.

I went to pin it on the bulletin board in the small break room, crossing my fingers that Jade would not be there. Thankfully the place was empty except for Darla, who was sitting at a table, feet propped on a chair while she read.

She lowered the book, looked at me. "What's that?"

"Sign-up sheet for Bark in the Park."

"Awesome." She got up, wandered over, took a pen from a nearby desk, and signed up for setup and a shift at the gun show. "So who do you think is going to win?"

Forty-eight hours ago, I would have said Jeremy. "Chase, of course." Maybe Fletcher.

"You're not a very loyal girlfriend."

"I'm not a girlfriend anymore."

"Oh. Sorry."

"Not your fault."

I walked into the hallway and nearly rammed into Chase. I released a self-conscious laugh. "Sorry."

"That's okay," he said. "I've got no problem with a cute girl running into me."

"I'm not feeling very cute today."

"Did you and your boyfriend break up?"

Tears flooded my eyes. Stung. I hated feeling so weak. Roughly I swiped them away. "Yeah. But I'm okay."

"No, you're not."

Sniffing, I shook my head. "But I will be."

"I've had some breakups. They're a bitch. I'm here if you need me."

I was touched, but I also knew that at that moment he wasn't what I needed. "Thanks."

"When you're ready, maybe we can go out."

I didn't know what to say to that. "Maybe."

When I got outside, no one was sitting under the tree any longer. I didn't see Jade anywhere. Jeremy was on the roof, helping to put shingles in place. His blond head was bent; he was focused on the task.

Part of me wanted him to see me, part of me didn't.

I turned on my heel, headed for my car, and pulled out my cell phone. I sent a text to Avery.

Got time for ice cream?

I Scream was one of our favorite hangouts. Avery and I had some of our most important discussions over an assortment of flavors, toppings, whipped cream, and cherries. I poked at my banana split while she dug into her sundae.

"I think Jeremy is with Jade," I blurted.

She stilled, her eyes wide. Slowly she pulled the spoon from her mouth. "That's crazy! You only just broke up yesterday. Why would you think that?"

"I saw him talking with her this morning."

Her brow furrowed. "Where?"

"The shelter. I had to go in to help plan the fund-raiser.

Neither of them knew I was going to be in. They were sitting together under a tree."

"Did they see you?"

I shook my head. "No."

She reached across the table and squeezed my hand. "Oh, Kendall, I'm so sorry. I know this has to hurt."

I shook my head. "I can hardly breathe."

"I can't believe he'd be interested in her."

"You're just saying that because you're my bestie. But Jade is fun, exciting, uninhibited. She doesn't care about saltshakers."

She released a small burst of laughter. "What does that mean?"

"I require order, lists, plans. At the beach? I straightened up the displays when we went to the souvenir shop. Jeremy understood my need for control. Jade is spontaneous. Without any planning, she pushed Jeremy into the pool. I'd check the labels on his clothes first to make sure the chlorine wouldn't bleach them out."

"You're not that bad."

"You're tolerant because you love me." Jeremy had as well and I'd blown it. "But I wanted us to change, to be different. He changed. I didn't."

"I really think you're being too hard on yourself."

Maybe, maybe not. I ate some whipped cream. It had no taste. Suddenly nothing had any taste. "I don't know if

I can keep volunteering at the shelter. It hurts so much to see him, and I want to lock Jade in one of the pens."

"You can't let them stop you from doing something you love."

"You're right. I know that. And I don't want to give up on the Bark in the Park fund-raiser. This could be our best year." I dug my spoon into my ice cream. "It's funny. I think Jeremy actually stands a good chance of winning."

She grinned. "No way. Fletcher has this hands down."

I wished I could hate Jeremy. I wished I could root for Fletcher. But the truth was, I hoped Jeremy would win, because then maybe I wouldn't feel so badly that it had cost us so much.

Chapter 28

JEREMY

". . . forty-eight, forty-nine, fifty." As I called out the final number, did the last crunch, I flopped back, breathing heavily. Beside me, Fletch did the same.

It was Thursday, and we were in his apartment getting in our daily reps. I was astonished to discover that when I looked in a mirror, I could see a definition to my abs that hadn't been there before. I should have been pleased. Instead, I wasn't sure I was going to go through with this gun show.

I wished I hadn't quit my dad's law firm. Wished I hadn't started working construction. Wished I didn't have to watch Kendall with Chase on the days she volunteered at the shelter. They laughed and talked while letting the dogs out.

Jade would visit with me on her breaks. She was nice

enough. But she wasn't Kendall.

"Don't suppose Avery's mentioned how Kendall's doing," I said when my breathing slowed. It had been only a few days, but it seemed an eternity since she and I had been together.

"It's tough but she's hanging in there."

I knew Fletch wasn't the type to ask how I was doing. I wouldn't have answered anyway, because the truth was that I didn't know. Mostly I was numb. I stared at the ceiling. "Jade asked me to go to some party with her Saturday. Probably going to do it."

"You like her?"

"She's fun." I could use some fun. And she seemed to accept me as I was. She wasn't making subtle suggestions that I should change things about myself. "It'll be weird, though."

"How so?"

Sitting up, I grabbed a bottle of water, unscrewed the cap, and gulped down a good portion of the contents before recapping it. "I've only ever dated Kendall." I looked over at him. "I'm actually a little nervous. You dated a bunch of girls. Any tips?"

He shoved himself up. "Didn't really date before Avery. Just hung out with a lot of girls. How'd you start dating Kendall?"

I released a strangled laugh. "It just happened naturally.

We were friends, palled around. One night we were going to a movie, Avery was sick, so it was just Kendall and me. During the movie, she laughed at something. I can't even remember what it was now. I just remember looking over at her and knowing there was nothing I wanted to do more than kiss her at that moment. I've always loved her laugh. Now she shares it with Chase. I really want to beat that guy, but maybe I should just withdraw from the whole stupid thing."

"Because you think you'll lose?"

"No, because it's important to Kendall. I know she'll be at the event, taking care of things. I don't want my being there to make it hard for her. On the other hand, if I bring in some money for the shelter that would make her happy." I scrubbed my hands up and down my face. "I know it's crazy. We're not together, but I still want to make her happy."

"What about Jade?"

"I like her."

He got to his feet. "Avery would probably kill me if she knew I said this, but you should go out with Jade. That way you'll know."

I furrowed my brow. "Know what?"

"How you really feel about Kendall when you have options."

"I always had options. I didn't fall for Kendall because she was the only girl in town. That's insulting to her."

"Chill. I didn't mean—"

A knock at the door had us both looking at each other guiltily. Our workout sessions were our secret.

Another knock. "Fletcher?"

It was Avery.

"Just a minute," Fletch called out, then he arched a brow at me. "She's going to get suspicious if I don't let her in, and while I don't think she'd jump to the conclusion that I have a girl in here, don't take this wrong, but this little thing we're doing isn't worth upsetting her."

"Let her in," I said in resignation. It was going to be the first time I'd seen her since Kendall and I broke up Sunday. It was not going to be fun.

Fletch opened the door. Avery flung her arms around him, then quickly backed up. "Ew! You're all sweaty."

"Been working out. Come on in."

She stepped inside and her gaze fell on me. I shifted uncomfortably from one foot to the other. "Hey, Avery."

"You're working out, too." She said it as a fact not a question.

"Yeah."

She angled her chin. "For Jade?"

"No! For the gun show."

"I'm sorry," she said. "I was being snarky."

"I understand," I told her. "You're Kendall's best friend."

"But I'm also your friend." She came nearer. "How are you doing?"

I shrugged. "Mostly confused, feeling a little lost, but hanging in there. How's Kendall?"

"About the same as you." She leaned her hips against the back of the couch, crossed her arms over her chest. "I can't believe you guys broke up."

"Something happened. We weren't happy."

"Are you happy now?"

Not even the tiniest bit, but neither was I feeling pressure to meet someone else's expectations.

"Anyone want a root beer?" Fletch asked into the uncomfortable silence that was stretching between us.

"No, thanks. I need to go."

"I'm really sorry, Jeremy," Avery said quietly.

"Yeah, me too."

But at the same time, I knew Fletch was right. I hadn't fallen for Kendall because she was the only option. I'd fallen for her because of who she was, how she was. But that didn't mean that she was the only one I could ever love.

Chapter 29

KENDALL

Taking you someplace fun. Think steampunk.

I read once more the text I'd gotten from Chase an hour ago. After a few days of watching Jeremy and Jade taking their breaks together, I had agreed to go out with Chase.

But I wasn't sure what his text meant. I knew what steampunk was, had read a couple of books that Jeremy had recommended. I knew he loved the genre. But I still couldn't quite decipher why I was supposed to think about it. I'd tried calling Chase and gotten his voice mail.

Standing in my bedroom, I studied my reflection. I looked like someone about to have some fun. I was wearing a short red skirt, a lacy, white, layered top, and platform heels. Maybe we were going to a movie, although I didn't know of one out right now with a steampunk theme. Slipping my phone into my skirt pocket, I headed downstairs.

Mom was sitting on the couch watching TV, Bogart's head in her lap. I petted his head.

"This is weird," I told her. "Going out with someone who isn't Jeremy."

She gave me a lopsided smile, like she wanted to be happy for me but was sad as well. "I know it's hard, but it's good that you're not wallowing, that you have a chance to get out and have some fun. And Chase doesn't have to be the one forever. It's all right if he's just the one for now, for tonight."

"Is that what you think when you go on a date?" I asked. I was beginning to understand why my mom had waited so long to date after Dad died. It was like I was really saying good-bye to Jeremy, to what I'd had with him.

"I tell myself that it's okay to have fun. Took me a while to get to a point where I didn't feel guilty about wanting to live my life again. But my situation is a little different from yours. If there are no sparks on the date, that's fine. I try to find the enjoyment in just going out and doing things with someone else. He doesn't have to profess his undying love."

"I like Chase," I told her. "But I'm not totally crazy about him like I was with Jeremy."

"You can't compare them. But you might also be surprised. Sometimes the sparks start slow."

How did I not do that—compare them? I wished I knew. Especially since comparing Jeremy to other guys was what had started all our problems. If I hadn't become restless, bored with the summer, maybe I wouldn't have lost him.

"You don't compare these guys you're dating to Dad?" I asked.

She slowly shook her head. "There will never be another guy like your dad. I have to consider these guys in light of who *they are*. I know what I need to be happy."

I almost confessed about the ways I'd prodded Jeremy into changing. If I'd just left well enough alone . . .

"Think about all the different dogs you fall in love with at the shelter," Mom continued. "None of them are the same, and yet you find things about each of them to love. Some you might have a stronger connection to—like Bogart. But you can still love a dog that isn't like Bogart."

I shifted uncomfortably trying to understand all the implications of what she was saying. I could love a man who wasn't my dad. I could love another dog. I could love a guy who wasn't Jeremy.

The doorbell rang, and my heart gave a little thud. "That'll be Chase."

Mom followed me to the foyer, Bogart trotting along behind us. I opened the door and froze.

It was Chase. Although it wasn't. He was wearing a vest over a buttoned shirt, with some sort of cloth wrapped around his neck, and a dark brown coat that was more like a duster that cowboys wore. Goggles were perched around a top hat on his head.

With a wide grin, he gave me an appreciative once-over. "You look great."

I released a little self-conscious laugh. "I'm not in costume."

"I've got some stuff in the trunk you can borrow if you want, but it's totally not necessary." He crouched down and took Bogart's face between his hands. "Hey, fella."

I shouldn't have been surprised. I'd seen him with other dogs, knew how much he liked them. He looked up and past me. Then stood. "Mrs. Jones, I presume."

I felt myself flush. I didn't know why I was so nervous. Maybe because this was not only my first date since Jeremy and I broke up, but my first date with someone who my mom didn't already know, someone who hadn't hung around in my house before. "I'm sorry. Mom, this is Chase."

"It's nice to meet you," she said as though she meant it, although she was probably wondering what her daughter was getting into. "Are you off to a costume ball?"

"In a way. It's an annual get-together for those of us who appreciate steampunk. It's a lot of fun, pretty different."

My first thought was that I needed to call Jeremy and tell him about it. He would love this. He loved steampunk. Then I shoved that thought down because I could not think about him tonight. We were no longer together.

"Sounds interesting," Mom said. She leaned over and gave me a kiss on the cheek. "I want to hear all about it when you get home."

"Count on it."

Then she was ushering Chase and me out the door. When we reached Chase's car, I couldn't help but notice that it had a sizeable backseat, although I couldn't imagine myself back there taking advantage of it. He opened the trunk and produced a pair of goggles similar to his. "You can just drape these around your neck."

Feeling silly, I did. "I'm not really dressed for this."

"I didn't figure you had a Victorian dress lying around," he said, "but my mom is always attending fund-raising teas, so I borrowed one of her hats."

It looked a little like a short, red top hat. It had netting surrounding it that ended in a bow on one side. I settled it on my head.

"Fantastic," Chase said. "And really a lot of people won't be dressed up, so you'll be fine. Let's go."

He slammed the trunk shut and went around to his side of the car, slipped behind the wheel. I wandered to the passenger side as he started the car. He didn't open the door for me, but a lot of guys didn't do that anymore. *Don't compare. Don't compare.* I had a feeling that was going to be my mantra for the night.

Getting into the car, I bumped the hat on the roof and ended up taking it off and placing it on my lap.

With a screech of tires, Chase peeled out and I grabbed onto the edge of the seat. I was never going to complain about Jeremy's cautious driving again. I slammed my eyes closed. Of course I wasn't because I wasn't going to be driving with him again. Taking a deep breath, I opened my eyes.

"So where is this all happening?" I asked.

"Warehouse district." That was an old part of town where they had converted some of the warehouses into bars, shops, and entertainment venues.

I tried to think of something to talk about. "Okay, just so I don't come off as a fool, tell me how you know something is steampunk."

"It's just a world where everything is steam driven. There are even some stories with steam-driven computers. The costuming is usually Victorian, but it can be anything really."

"Well, in my steampunk world, it's obviously a short skirt and a lacy top."

He glanced over. "You look cute."

It took us a while to find a parking place. The warehouse district was hopping on Saturday night. When Chase parked, he got out of the car and waited on his side. Didn't come open my door. As I got out, I could see him fairly bouncing on the balls of his feet. This wasn't how I ever would have thought about spending my Saturday night, but he was excited about it. I was determined to be a good sport and not ruin his fun.

Besides I might have a blast.

We walked along the crowded street until we reached the designated warehouse. People dressed in assorted costumes, many of them with goggles, which seemed to be a staple for steampunk, were mingling around outside. Chase took my hand and a little shock of awareness went through me. It was only a hand, but it felt different, it was different. It wasn't Jeremy's. Chase led us through the crush of people to the door where he handed over some money for entrance. The backs of our hands were stamped and inside we went.

It was wildness!

As Chase took my hand again and we wended our way through the crowd, I felt a little out of place with my make-shift costume because obviously most of the people here took their costumes seriously. Some were really elaborate. One guy was dressed in something that looked like a metal skeletal frame. The room was dimly lit, smoke and fog swirling around. Music was blasting. Mechanical gadgets were displayed on various tables.

"Here we go," Chase said, and he led me farther into the alternative world.

I saw Darla, Tommy Simms, and a couple of other guys from the construction site sitting at the top of a U-shaped couch, a short table in front of them. Darla was wearing a flowing skirt, hiked up on one side, and a wide leather belt with some sort of metallic hooks joining it together. Tommy, Nathaniel, and Ethan only had goggles dangling around their necks. So not everyone was into dressing up elaborately.

Chase sat on the side perpendicular to them and tugged me down beside him, and I suddenly found myself facing Jeremy. I hadn't even recognized him. He was wearing what looked like a safari hat with goggles perched on it. He looked as uncomfortable as I felt. Nestled up against his side was Jade.

"I'm so glad you came," she said, but it was obvious she was talking to Chase instead of me. She wore tight leather shorts and a corseted top. It looked so snug that I didn't know how she could breathe. Her leather boots laced up past her knees. Goggles dangled from her neck. She wore a hat similar to mine but somehow it was more provocative, sexy, maybe because she was comfortable in it, or maybe because she had it at a rakish angle.

From her fingers, she dangled two yellow wristbands. "You have to be wearing one of these to buy alcohol. It means they carded you. I stole a couple from the bartender." More than a couple, because she was wearing one. So was Jeremy. It seemed so unlike him. We drank at private parties, but we'd never done anything in public. Of course just because we were wearing the wristbands didn't mean we had to buy or drink.

Without hesitation, Chase held out his arm. Reaching across the table, she wound one around his wrist and secured it. Then she arched a brow at me.

I didn't want to be seen as a spoilsport. So I stuck out my arm, and Jade attached a condemning wristband.

"Cute outfit," she said, although her tone was more mocking than complimentary.

Still, I said, "Thanks."

She settled back onto the sofa, so close to Jeremy that light couldn't have seeped between their bodies. I wanted to pretend that I was cool with this, seeing them together, even though it was killing me. "I had no idea this went on," I admitted.

"Yeah, it's an annual thing," Jade said. "Last summer was my first time to come. I love it. People who are into steampunk are so cool. Even if you aren't into it, it can still be fun, especially if we drink up." She stood and crooked a finger at Chase. "Come on. Your turn to buy."

"You okay with me going?" Chase asked.

Not really, no. She'd already stolen one guy from me. But again, I wanted to be cool. "Sure."

Getting up, he followed her into the dark world of

automatons. I felt really awkward, wished I wasn't here. I couldn't believe Chase had brought me. Had he wanted me to see Jeremy with Jade? Had he wanted to show Jeremy that I was on a date with him? Was he trying to make me face reality? In one way it seemed cruel and yet in another way, he'd given me the chance to prove to Jeremy that I was over him. Or at least pretend I was. The awkwardness thickened. I had to do something.

But before I could think of anything, Jeremy leaned forward. "How's Bogart?"

He couldn't have asked anything that would put me more at ease, that would make me stop thinking about the strangeness of sitting here with him when I was no longer *with* him. "Good. I still walk him every night." Alone. But that was okay. "Although I've had to shorten the distance. Sometimes it's a struggle for him to make it too far. I think it's because of the heat." Or at least that's what I told myself.

"Your mom still dating Mr. Morris?"

Even though tomorrow would mark a week since our split, he was asking questions like we hadn't seen each other in years. Was this what it would be like when we ran into each other in the dorm? We'd been so close and now we were practically strangers. "They had a date last night." Mr. Morris had picked my mom up at the house. I wanted to tell Jeremy how odd but how right it had seemed to see them together. But my feelings were too personal, a part of myself that I couldn't share with him anymore. At that moment, all that we'd lost hit me harder than it had before.

Over Jeremy's shoulder, I saw Chase returning. He was holding a tray of drinks. Jade followed along behind him, sipping a pink concoction. She slid onto the sofa and snuggled against Jeremy. Setting the tray on the table, Chase sat beside me and grabbed one of the drinks. It was in a cocktail glass and it looked like fog was rising from its surface. He handed it to me. I took a sip. It was very strawberry but I recognized the kick of something stronger.

"How do they make the fog?" I asked.

"Dry ice," Chase explained.

"Aren't you going to try one?"

"No, I'll stick with club soda since I'm driving."

Everyone else had helped themselves to a glass. Jeremy downed his as though it were water. I guessed he hadn't suffered too much after Scooter's party.

"Who's your designated driver?" I asked him.

He set the empty glass aside. "I'll be fine by the time we leave."

"You're fine right now," Jade said with a stupid wiggling of her shoulders. Standing, she took Jeremy's hand and pulled him to his feet. "Let's dance."

Then she led him to an area where people were doing a lot of bobbing up and down.

"That girl has way too much energy," Darla said.

The three guys from the construction site got up. "We're going to check out the babes," Tommy said by way of explanation as the other two wandered away. Then he went after them.

"There was a babe right here," Darla muttered, before finishing off her drink and reaching for another.

Chase slipped his arm around my shoulders and drew me in. "Sorry if it's uncomfortable," he said. "When Jade invited me and Darla, it didn't occur to me that she'd bring Jeremy. I'm a huge fan of steampunk and I just thought this would be something fun and different."

"It is, and I'm fine that he's here," I lied.

"We can leave if you want."

"Nah, it's okay. It's not like I can avoid him forever, especially with the gun show coming up."

"Let's walk around."

"Okay." I looked over at Darla. "Do you want to come with us?"

"Nope. Gonna defend our seating area and see that none of the drinks go to waste. But take one with you."

I did as she suggested. Liquid courage. Chase kept one arm around me so I was nestled up against him, making it easier to move through the crowds. Being this close to him was a little odd, though, because he was a little taller than

Jeremy, a little wider. As I drank more of the strawberry whatever, I became more relaxed.

We left my empty glass on the bar and danced for a while. I had to admit that it was fascinating to see all the various costumes and unusual decorations. Small hot-air balloons and zeppelins hung from the ceiling. Then we went back to our table. Ethan and Darla were talking. Jeremy and Jade had also returned and were doing that whole we-could-be-Siamese-twins-because-we-sit-so-close-together thing. I hated it. I should have told Chase I was ready to leave, but I didn't want to ruin the night for him since this only happened once a year.

Chase and I sat down on one of the couches.

"Any idea how long this party goes on?" Darla asked.

"All night, I think," Ethan said.

"They have to shut down the bar at two," Jade said. "Speaking of which: Jeremy, maybe you should go ahead and get us another round of drinks."

"Sure."

It was no longer my job to worry about him, but habits are hard to break. He looked so much older tonight with his unshaven jaw, his longer hair. I thought maybe he'd gained a couple of squint lines working in the sun, even with sunglasses. Still, I couldn't stop myself from saying low, "Are you sure? What if you get busted?"

His lawyer dad would kill him.

"I've got this," Jeremy said.

He got up and I watched until he disappeared in the crowd. But I couldn't shake off the feeling that this was a bad idea.

Chapter 30

JEREMY

Kendall's question about the designated driver had struck a nerve. Even now she was striving to control me, although I also recognized that she'd spoken out of concern for my welfare. I might buy the next drinks but I was switching to water.

I really wished I wasn't here. I especially wished that Kendall wasn't here with pumped-up Chase. I couldn't blame the guy for wanting to be with her. Even though she wasn't dressed up like Jade in something that looked like it could double as a torture device, she looked hot. And really uncomfortable around me.

I hated that.

When Jade asked me to come to this event with her, I'd thought it would be fun. I loved reading steampunk, but it hadn't occurred to me that Jade might have told several people at the shelter about it. I hadn't realized I'd have to suffer through watching Kendall with another guy.

I missed her. I would have loved bringing her to this party and walking through the room with her, pointing things out, sharing my passion for steampunk with her in a place where she could actually see so many of the things that appeared in the books I read.

Sharing all this with Jade . . . I didn't think she was really into steampunk. She just liked wearing the sexy clothes. And drinking alcohol like she was a fish. And breaking all the rules.

I looked at the wristband on my arm. It wasn't some protective shield. If the bartender asked to see my ID, if the cops raided the place—

What was I doing thinking of buying drinks when I was underage? This wasn't me. I needed some time to figure out what I wanted tonight, what I was willing to risk.

I decided to take a detour by the restroom. It was at the end of a long hallway. When I came out, I saw someone walking toward me with sure, long strides.

Jade.

I couldn't believe how provocative her outfit was. Her shoulders and arms were bare. I didn't know if she was heading to the restroom or just wanted to help me get the drinks.

"Hi," I started to say, barely getting the word out before

she placed both her hands on my shoulders and pushed me back against the wall.

Then her mouth was on mine like she owned it.

It was the first time we'd kissed. While I struggled to enjoy what should have been enjoyable, I was struck by how aggressive she was, like she was trying to conquer something. There wasn't a lot of giving and taking. It was almost combative. She didn't sigh softly like Kendall, and back here in the restroom hallway wasn't the most romantic of places. If I was honest, I'd wanted to be the one to instigate a kiss, maybe when I took her home. Not that I wasn't flattered by her interest, but the kiss didn't generate any sparks. For all her enthusiasm, it was without passion. It didn't make me feel warm, glad, or happy.

Hearing a small gasp, I pulled back. Over Jade's shoulder, I saw Kendall. My gut knotted up. Because of the dim lighting, I couldn't be sure, but she appeared to be a little green, like maybe she was about to be sick. Why had Chase brought her here tonight? Why had Jade picked this moment to plant a kiss on me? Why had I let her?

Kendall spun on her heel and ran off.

"Kendall!" I tried to set Jade aside, but she clung to me.

"You don't need her," she said.

Only I did.

"I knew things would be great between us," she continued. She ran her hands over my shoulders with a little

233

purr that almost turned my stomach. "I get you like she never will."

Only that wasn't true. No one got me like Kendall did. She got the real me. She'd fallen in love with me when I was just a geek. Jade had never looked at me twice all through senior year. Kendall hadn't asked me to change the core of who I was. That had happened because I'd let Jade's flirtation go to my head.

I was an idiot.

Chapter 31

KENDALL

Your fault, your fault, your fault.

My heart was breaking and some stupid little voice in my head was trying to convince me that it was my fault. I'd wanted girls to notice Jeremy. I just hadn't wanted them to kiss him. Or for him to kiss them back.

With tears blurring my vision, I fought my way through the crowd back to our table. I don't know what my face looked like, but Chase stood up and asked, "What's wrong?"

"Can we go?" I did not want to sit here and watch Jade making out with Jeremy. She was bold enough that she would do it right there on that couch, in front of us all.

Chase looked around as though he was trying to find the reason for my abrupt need to leave. Then he settled his gaze on me. "Sure."

I gave a quick little wave to the others as he took my hand and led me out of this crazy place. We didn't talk as we trudged to the car. He didn't open the door for me, and I was really glad. I didn't want him to do anything that reminded me of Jeremy.

I looked out the window at the passing night as we drove into my neighborhood. He pulled into my driveway, slid the gear into PARK, and left the engine idling. Putting his arm along the back of the seat, he turned slightly and studied me.

"I'm sorry for ruining your night," I said.

"I'm not a genius," he began, "but I assume you saw Jade and Jeremy up to something when you went to the ladies' room."

"She was kissing him. Up against the wall. I turned into the hallway and . . . surprise. I know we're not together anymore, but I just wasn't prepared for that. I wanted to be cool about seeing them together, but I couldn't be."

"This is on me. I should have gotten you out of there as soon as I saw him with Jade."

"It's not your fault. I just need to accept that things are different now."

Ironic since all summer I'd been searching for something different. But this wasn't what I'd wanted.

"Maybe tomorrow night we could do something a little more traditional," he said. "Go to a movie."

My stomach dropped. "I like you, but I don't think I'm ready to date. Tonight was—"

"A mistake," he interrupted. "A bad idea. Stupidity on my part. I thought being around other people would take some of the pressure off. But I'd really like to see you again."

"Oh, that's so sweet but I totally ruined tonight."

"Jade did that. I like you. I've wanted to go out with you since I met you. Let's give it another try tomorrow night. I'll even sit through a sappy movie."

Why was I hesitating? Things were obviously so over with Jeremy. He had Jade. "Okay, yeah. I'd like that."

"Great." He got out of the car, and I realized the conversation was over. I also realized he wasn't going to open my door. So I did it and stepped out. We were walking to the front door, when he took my hand, pulled me in, and kissed me.

It was so strange to be kissing someone who wasn't Jeremy. Had he felt the same when he kissed someone who wasn't me? Inwardly I groaned. How could I be thinking of him during a moment like this? I should be focusing on Chase, but I couldn't seem to let Jeremy go.

When Chase pulled back, he gave me an inquisitive look. "You were thinking about him."

"I'm sorry."

"Nah, it's okay. I know it's difficult at first after a

breakup. I'll just have to work harder to make sure you don't think about him tomorrow."

I didn't know if I'd ever not think about him. Chase said good night and walked back to his car. Jeremy never left without making sure I was safely inside.

I growled. I had to stop comparing. That was what got me here in the first place, what ruined my relationship with Jeremy. Comparing and controlling.

Chase took off, the tires screeching.

Inside, the house was dark except for a lamp on the table by the stairs. So Mom had gone to bed. I trudged up the stairs and into my room. Bogart was on his bed. I picked him up, put him in bed with me, wrapped my arms around him, and cried.

The tears had been building until they were an ache in my chest and a knot in my throat. It hurt to release them, but it hurt more to hold on to them. In a way, that was how I felt about Jeremy. It hurt to let him go, but it would have hurt more to hold on to him.

I had to accept that things between us were truly over.

Chapter 32

JEREMY

I woke up Sunday morning missing Kendall with an actual physical ache in my chest. With a sigh, I stared at the ceiling. My mom had gone to some yoga retreat in San Antonio to regain her Zen. My dad was in one of the Carolinas golfing with some buddies. While I wouldn't have done anything with them if they had been here, for some reason, I was really noticing their absence.

Without thinking, I reached for my phone to text Kendall—and stopped.

After seeing me kissing Jade last night, Kendall had probably blocked my number. She and Chase had been gone by the time Jade and I returned with drinks. I'd seen Chase get into his car at the shelter. I pictured him comforting Kendall in that huge backseat—

I was spared completing the image when my phone

signaled a text received. My heart kicked against my ribs with the thought that maybe it was Kendall. But it was Jade.

Pool at your house?

I didn't know why I hesitated to answer. After she'd initiated things last night, she'd kissed me several other times. On the couch, when we were dancing, while she was drinking. But the entire time I'd felt guilty about it, because Kendall had seen us. Then I felt guilty for thinking about Kendall while kissing Jade.

I finally replied with:

Yes.

Can I come play?

Along with the words was a picture of Jade's bare stomach, her belly button ring, and the bottom portion of her two-piece bathing suit.

I had two choices: be miserable all day or be distracted. Jade certainly knew how to distract. And she knew how to have a good time. I texted her my address.

When she arrived half an hour later, she had Melody with her. They stepped inside and stared at the huge foyer, the sweeping staircases on either side of it.

"Are you, like, rich?" Jade asked.

"No," I assured her. Shrugged. "My parents are."

"Wow." She glanced around and asked in a low voice, "Are they here?"

"No, they're out of town. Won't be back until late tonight."

She leaped at me. With a laugh, I caught her in my arms as her legs circled my waist. "We are going to have so much fun!" she announced.

I smiled brightly at her enthusiasm. "Yeah, I think we will."

Because she was latched on to me like a monkey, I carried her through the house to the pool, while Melody followed along. Once I set Jade on the tiled area around the pool, she gave me a big grin and tugged on my T-shirt. "This needs to come off."

"Maybe later."

"Now or we're going to push you into the pool."

Based upon where we were standing, that was going to take a lot of pushing. Still, I drew the shirt over my head and tossed it onto a nearby lounger.

With her finger, Jade outlined my ribs, the ridges along my stomach. "Nice. You are so totally going to win."

"Totally," Melody said.

I appreciated their confidence in me. "You want something to drink?"

"A couple of beers would be nice," Jade said as she stretched out on a lounger. Melody took one on the other side of her.

"Sorry, but I can't offer you a beer."

"Margarita?"

"Nope."

"Your parents don't drink?"

"They do, but they'd know if something was missing. I'd get into a boatload of trouble."

She pouted. "Are you afraid?"

"No, but this is their house. I need to respect their boundaries. Besides it's not even noon."

She rolled her eyes. "Okay, then, water, tea, something boring."

I went to the kitchen and grabbed a couple of soft drinks out of the fridge. When I returned, I handed them each a can and stretched out on the lounger beside Jade. She set her soda aside, got up, came over to my lounger, and straddled my hips. Then she leaned in and kissed me like we'd never have another opportunity because the world was going to end.

Gently I placed my hands on her shoulders and eased her back. "What are you doing?"

"Uh, duh! Making out."

I shifted my eyes to the side. Melody was wearing huge sunglasses. I couldn't tell if she was asleep or looking at the pool. It didn't matter. "Melody's here."

"Yeah, so?"

Before Avery got together with Fletch, Kendall and I often included her when we went places or did things. But we never made out in front of her. Maybe we'd sneak in a quick kiss if Avery wasn't looking or we were separated for a little while, but nothing like what Jade was suggesting.

"It's rude," I said.

With something that sounded like an impatient growl, she looked up at the sky, then glanced over at Melody. "Mel, do you have a problem if we make out?"

"Nah, go ahead."

Jade grinned. "See?" She moved in again, and I stopped her.

I didn't want to think about how I had suggested Kendall and I make out at Scooter's party, but then I'd had too much to drink, everyone was doing it, and it was dark. "She might not mind, but I do."

She gave her eyes an exaggerated roll. "I thought you were cool."

"I am, which is why we're not going to do this."

She sighed. "Then why am I even here?"

"To hang out."

"Boring. Let's go to the beach then."

Only I didn't want to go to the beach. I wasn't sure that I even wanted to be with her. Did we have anything in common, other than steampunk?

"Are you going to college?" I asked.

"Community."

"What are you going to study?"

"I don't know," she said impatiently. "What does it matter?"

"We only talk about parties and other people." She had lots of funny stories about other people, but I realized she didn't reveal a lot about herself. "I don't know very much about you."

She gave me a sexy smile. "You'll know a lot if we make out."

"But I want more than that. Don't you?"

"No, not really." She climbed off me. "Mel, let's go to the beach."

"Okay."

They started gathering up their things. I stood, a little relieved, a little disappointed and sad that Jade only wanted a surface relationship. "You don't have to go," I told them.

"Yeah, we do," Jade said. She walked over to me and tiptoed her fingers over my chest. "But don't worry. You're still on my make-out list."

Funny how that didn't make me feel any better. I saw them out, then returned to the lounger and stared at the sparkling water of the pool. I wondered what Kendall was doing, if she was as miserable as I was.

Chapter 33

KENDALL

As Chase drove us to the movie theater, I was determined not to compare him to Jeremy—not even once. I wasn't even going to think about Jeremy. Chase was totally different, his own person. He had his own way of doing things.

When he parked, I immediately opened the car door and got out. I caught up with him, smiled when he took my hand. He bought the tickets, then we stood in line for refreshments. He ordered two small, buttered popcorns and two drinks. I told myself that he was being polite, that we didn't know each other well enough to share, but maybe someday we would. I went to the butter stand that allowed for more butter to be added to popcorn and pressed the spigot five times.

I turned to him. "Do you want some more butter?"

"Nah, this is fine."

After we made our way to theater three, he guided us to seats in the middle of the first row.

"Hope this is okay," he said. "But you come to a theater for the big screen. If you don't sit in the front, then you lose the advantage of a big screen and it's just like watching a TV."

Okay, I didn't really get that but since he bought the tickets, I didn't feel like I could suggest that we at least sit where we wouldn't have to crane our heads back to see the entire screen. "This is fine," I said.

"Previews are my favorite part," he said.

I smiled. "Mine too."

"That and the popcorn."

He'd kept his promise and we were going to see a romantic drama. A romantic comedy or an animated movie might have been better for my mood, but I appreciated his attempt to do whatever I wanted. This morning when I woke up, I'd almost texted Jeremy with a simple, "Be happy."

If Jade made him happy, then I hoped things worked out with them. And here I was thinking about him when I'd promised myself I wouldn't.

The previews started up. Chase made comments on each one—"No way." "Definitely going to see that." "Dumb." "Maybe." "What were they thinking?"

When the movie began, he went silent and I breathed a

sigh of relief. I liked to get totally engrossed in the movie, escape into the fantasy.

After a few minutes, Chase leaned over. "Who is that guy? I've seen him in something."

He was one of those actors who always had bit parts, but had played a gazillion roles. I didn't know his name and couldn't think of anything specific I'd seen him in. I just shook my head.

Chase pulled out his phone. Was he searching IMDb? He was.

"Oh, yeah," he whispered. "I've seen him in a lot of stuff."

He turned off his phone. I decided if he asked about anyone else, I was just going to make up something.

"Want to grab something to eat after this?" he asked.

"Sure," I whispered.

"Pizza or burger?"

I shook my head. Really? We were discussing this now? "Pizza."

He settled back into his seat, and I was glad there were very few people around us. He shifted in his seat a couple of times, looked at his watch. I wished we'd gone to something he wanted to see.

"I don't understand what she saw in the guy," he said as we were leaving the theater.

I almost said, *He didn't talk when he took her to the*

movies. But in all fairness, they'd only shown about three minutes of the couple at a movie. For all I knew, they had talked.

"He accepted that she wasn't perfect," I said.

"I guess I can see that."

"I really appreciate that you took me to a movie that obviously didn't really interest you."

"I didn't mind making the sacrifice."

But if he didn't mind, should he have even mentioned that it was a sacrifice? His comment made me feel a little guilty even though he'd selected the movie.

At the pizza place, we ordered two individual pizzas because we couldn't find anything we liked in common.

Do not compare, I thought when our food was delivered.

"So next Saturday is the big day," he said.

I couldn't help but grin. "It is, and we have so much left to do. It's like it snowballed."

"I've seen you walking around with a big notebook."

"It has all the information and lists that relate to the event."

"You should get an electronic tablet."

"I have one, but I like actually holding on to something that is a visible, physical embodiment of everything that needs to be done. When I write something down, it becomes clearer in my mind and I remember it a lot easier.

I love being able to check off tasks."

"You can have a task list on a tablet."

"But it's not as rewarding as pressing a pen to paper and hearing that tiny scratch when you mark something as done."

"Whatever works for you, I guess."

I didn't think he was judging me, but still I felt compelled to say, "This works for me."

"It's going to be a great event. Although the gun show is going to rule."

"It's definitely the most intriguing part of the event."

We talked a little bit more about everything that was going to happen at the Bark in the Park event. I grew much more comfortable and less self-conscious. Our love of dogs, our wanting to help the shelter raise money was something we had in common. I remembered why I liked him, why I'd been willing to go out with him. He had a few quirks, but then so did I.

When we got to my house, he walked me to the door. I stood on the porch, shifting from one foot to the other, wondering if I should invite him in. He leaned in and kissed me, then put his arms around me and drew me nearer.

It didn't make my bones melt or my toes curl. I was comparing it to Jeremy's, so I shoved the thoughts away. I tried to pretend that I'd never been kissed before, that I had nothing with which to compare it. It was pleasant, nice. Maybe a little tentative as though he knew I might be tempted to compare it.

He drew back and smiled at me. "Better than last night."

So he was comparing, too.

"I had fun. Thanks for taking me out."

"Anytime. And I mean that. Literally. I'm just a text away."

"That means a lot to me, Chase."

"I'll see you around."

He walked off. I went inside, grimaced at the screech of his tires. It was comforting to have someone who was interested in me. We might not be perfect together, but maybe perfection was overrated. Or maybe it would come with time.

And when I was with him, I missed Jeremy just a little bit less. But I wasn't sure if I would ever not miss Jeremy at all.

Chapter 34

JEREMY

Saturday was the big day. Bark in the Park. The gun show. It was hard to believe that it was almost time for me to strut my stuff. Even harder to believe that I actually wanted to do it, for Kendall, and for the shelter.

Tuesday night I sat in a meeting room in city hall, where the shelter had gathered together all the volunteers, the gunslingers, and the vendors for the event to explain everything. Fletch was in a chair beside me, Avery on the other side of him. I knew she was trying to remain impartial, but she wasn't as warm toward me as she'd once been.

Terri stood behind a podium, projecting layouts of the event, explaining all the various areas and how they would be utilized.

"Friday night the city manager will allow us to begin setting up our event in the park," she explained. She pointed a red laser light at an area on the screen. "Here is where we'll have the gun show. Simms Construction will be building a small stage with a canopy the evening beforehand. We don't want our gunslingers to get sunburned. Jade Johnson"— Jade stood, waved like a beauty pageant queen, and smiled brightly at everyone before winking at me—"is in charge of the gun show. Saturday morning you need to report to her by nine thirty. You'll go onstage at ten. You'll have three two-hour shifts, with thirty-minute breaks between shifts. Please remember this is a G-rated event."

"*G* stands for guns!" Chase called out, and a few whoops sounded in the room.

Kendall, sitting in the front row, turned around and smiled. I wondered why they weren't sitting together, figured it had something to do with their roles in this event. The front seats had been reserved for those who were overseeing key elements of the day.

Terri went on to explain where all the other activities would take place, but I didn't pay a lot of attention. Although when they mentioned the poop patrol, I was glad that I hadn't gotten roped into that.

"Are there any questions?" Terri finally asked.

She answered the few that were tossed out. Then she adjourned the meeting.

"This gun show doesn't sound too bad," I said as we stood.

"Might even be fun," Fletch said.

"I'm going to check with Kendall on something," Avery said. "I'll catch up with you outside."

I thought about trailing after Avery but I didn't know if Kendall would appreciate it. We hadn't talked since the steampunk ball. Since then I'd written her numerous texts but deleted them all without sending them.

"—come with us."

Fletch's voice brought me back to the present. "I'm sorry. What?"

"We're grabbing a burger at B. S. Do you want to come with us?"

"That'd be great. I didn't get a chance to eat before the meeting."

"We'll meet you over there." He nodded as Avery left Kendall and began heading back to us. He met her halfway and walked out with his arm slung around her shoulders.

Kendall started talking to Tommy Simms. He was another one of the gunslingers. I thought about edging my way over, but a couple of other guys had suddenly queued up to talk with her. I didn't know why. Our instructions for Saturday were pretty straightforward.

"Let's go grab a pizza," Jade said, suddenly appearing at my side, rubbing my stomach like I was a genie in a bottle and could grant her a wish. She seemed to have no social cues about appropriate public behavior.

I wrapped my hand around her wrist to still her actions. I didn't want to hurt her feelings but I'd discovered she was just a little too brash for me. Since Sunday, we'd spoken a couple of times at the shelter but we hadn't gone out. "Thanks, but I have plans."

"Change them," Jade said.

"What?"

"Change your plans. Come be with me."

"That would be rude," I told her. Even though Fletch and Avery would probably understand. It was just a burger. "People are expecting me."

Okay, it was only two, but still.

Jade shrugged, then gave me a sly smile. "Just so you know, I'm going to give you a primo spot on the stage Saturday," she said.

"I appreciate that." Although I'd seen the plans for the stage and every spot was going to be pretty much equal.

"See you later," she said, and wandered off.

I looked back toward the front of the room. Kendall was gone and so was my chance to talk with her. It was probably for the best. Or at least that's what I told myself.

Chapter 35

KENDALL

I texted Avery to let her know I was running late. I'd finally managed to answer all the questions that some of the volunteers had and slipped out without catching Jeremy's eye. Not that he would have noticed me. He was pretty focused on Jade.

Chase was waiting for me, leaning against my car, feet crossed at the ankles, arms folded over his chest. "Hey," he said.

I arrived a little breathless. "Hi."

"Want to hit a pancake house?"

"Thanks, but I'm meeting Avery. We need to work out some details regarding Bark in the Park."

"This fund-raiser is really keeping you hopping."

We'd only seen each other when we worked the same shift at the shelter. We hadn't had any dates since

Sunday. "Yeah, but I love it."

"How about we catch dinner Saturday after the event?"

I welcomed the chance to have a distraction. I didn't want to sit around at home and have flashbacks of all the flirting I was certain Jade and Jeremy would do during the gun show. I smiled. "I'd love to."

"Okay, then. It's a date."

He walked off. I opened my car door, climbed behind the wheel, set the thick notebook with everything that needed to be done for the weekend on the seat beside me, and sighed. I'd been a little worried that Jeremy might try to corner me tonight, might talk to me, and I wasn't sure I could be totally cool about it. He'd looked so wonderful sitting there with Fletcher, so confident. It occurred to me that he might really have a chance of beating Chase and Fletcher. As far as I was concerned, of the six gunslingers, they were the top contenders.

My phone buzzed.

Avery:

Where are you?

I quickly texted back that I was on my way. Then I started the car and headed out. I'd almost said no when she invited me to grab a burger with her, except that I was hungry and didn't want to eat alone. She was always trying to include me in things she and Fletcher did but it was awkward being the third wheel. I couldn't believe she'd done it for months before she started falling for Fletcher. It was hard being the odd-numbered one in a group. Briefly I thought about inviting Chase, but I wanted to relax and totally be myself. For some reason, I couldn't do that with him. At least not yet. I told myself it was because we were still in that uncomfortable just-starting-to-date stage. Even though I'd never experienced that stage with Jeremy. I'd been comfortable with him from the moment I met him.

I pulled into the B. S. parking lot, got out of the car, and walked into the restaurant. I staggered to a stop when I saw Avery and Fletcher sitting in a booth with Jeremy. His back was to me. I glanced quickly around for Jade but didn't see her. Maybe she was in the restroom. She seemed to like hallways with restrooms.

I thought about retracing my steps and getting out of here, but Avery smiled and waved at me. Jeremy turned around and surprise washed over his face. He quickly masked it. I walked forward as though I were going to my execution. How could Avery do this to me? I was going to kill her.

Fletcher got out of the booth and slid onto the bench next to Jeremy. Avery glided over and stood up. She gave me a welcoming hug. "I'll sit across from Fletcher."

I wanted to ask her if this had been a setup, if she was trying to play matchmaker and get us back together, but my voice box seemed to be locked. Besides I knew if I said anything at all that it would come out snarky.

"Saturday is going to be so much fun," Avery said as we settled into the booth. Fletcher reached for the salt-shaker, set it in the middle of the table, and gave it a spin.

"Yeah," I said. "I thought you wanted to talk about that."

"I do, but why don't we grab some food first? I'm starving."

"Got it covered," Fletcher said as he climbed out of the booth. I reached for the shaker he'd abandoned, then pulled my hands back and sat on them, as I remembered Jeremy pointing out some of my control issues. I was working not to have them, but salt and pepper were supposed to stay together, not be separated.

Of course, I'd thought Jeremy and I would stay together forever, too. Look how that turned out. Maybe nothing stayed together.

"The usual?" Jeremy asked.

"Yeah, but I'll get it." I gave Avery a little nudge.

"I've got it," Jeremy said.

"At least let me give you some money." I started to open the small wallet that also housed my phone.

"I've got it," Jeremy repeated.

"I wouldn't feel right."

With a shake of his head, he slid out of the booth and followed Fletcher before I could give him anything. I turned to Avery. "Was this setup on purpose?"

"No, I didn't know Fletcher had invited him until he got here."

"You could have texted and warned me off."

"He's still my friend. Besides you can't avoid him forever. He's one of your gunslingers."

"He's not mine." Not anymore, anyway.

"You're going to run into him at college. Probably a lot since you're living in the same dorm. You might as well start practicing how you'll act when you run into each other."

Easy for her to say. She hadn't seen her boyfriend in a lip-lock with Jade.

When the guys returned, they distributed the food. A burger to me and a basket of fries to share with Jeremy. Only I wasn't going to share with him. I'd just have the burger. I checked it out. Layered just the way I liked it. Then my gaze shifted to that lone saltshaker, my fingers itched—

Jeremy picked it up and set it back into its place. My heart did this stupid, dumb flutter because that was so Jeremy—to know what was bugging me and to try to make it right. Then his gaze settled on mine, and he nudged the basket toward me. "Help yourself."

Just one. Maybe two.

"So I wanted to run this by you. Dot would like to feed

the crew readying the park on Friday," Avery finally said.

"What do you mean?" I asked. "Have them go to the restaurant on the beach afterward?"

"No, she'll bring the food to the park."

"That's awfully generous."

"You know she's an animal lover. So she wanted to do something to help out this weekend."

"I don't think it will be a problem, but we'll need to talk to Terri."

"That's what I thought but I wanted to get your opinion on it."

Right. Like we were going to turn down free food. I knew a lame excuse for getting me here when I heard it. If she hadn't told me that she needed to talk to me about something regarding Bark in the Park, I might have walked out when I saw Jeremy sitting here. Yeah, this had definitely been a setup.

Although I wasn't sure what she thought she would accomplish. Maybe letting us both put the breakup behind us. As she'd said, he was still her friend. While her first loyalty was to me, our breaking up had to make things difficult for her. I hadn't even considered that.

Nor had I considered how nice it would be to just be with Jeremy. He'd been my friend before he'd ever been my boyfriend. As we started talking about how we'd begin packing for college right after Bark in the Park, I feasted on French fries and finished off my burger. In a way I wished Jeremy and I had chosen different schools. It might have made things easier. On the other hand, I knew that if I ever needed him for anything, he'd be there. And I'd be there for him.

It was nearly eleven o'clock when Fletcher said he needed to go because he had to get to work in the morning. So did Jeremy.

"I enjoyed tonight," he said as we walked out to the parking lot.

"Me too. I thought it would be awkward when I saw you sitting there."

"I think they set us up."

With a smile, I leaned against the hood of my car. "You didn't know I was meeting them here?"

He shook his head. "No."

"Would you have come if you'd known?"

"I don't know." He shifted his stance, studied the ground for a few seconds before looking up. "It's strange not having you around. I keep writing texts to you and then deleting them."

"I wrote you some emails, but I didn't send them."

"What did they say?"

"Little things, silly things. Nothing really important. I'm glad we had tonight."

"Me too."

I shoved myself away from the car. "I should go."

He opened the door for me, and my chest tightened at the gesture. So Jeremy. I wondered if Jade appreciated all the small things he did.

I slid behind the wheel. He closed the door, and I rolled down the window. "Good luck Saturday."

"I'll see you before then."

"But we might not talk before then."

He gave a quick nod. "Right."

When he stepped back, I started the car, backed up, and headed for the street. Just before I reached it, I glanced into my rearview mirror to see Jeremy still standing there, hands shoved into his jeans pockets, watching me.

Chapter 36

JEREMY

I barely saw Kendall for the remainder of the week. Two reasons. Number one: she wasn't taking dogs out into the play area. I figured she was busy getting all the last-minute things done for Bark in the Park. Number two: most of the work I was doing was now taking place inside because the structure of the new wing was finished.

Jade was also scarce. All the emphasis this week was on the event that would raise money for the shelter.

So I was glad when Friday arrived and the crew headed to the park to begin setting up various stands and platforms, including the short stage on which the gun show would take place. I had to smile when I saw Kendall marching around, clipboard in hand, checking things off her list. She might have control issues but sometimes that was what was needed to get the job done. I couldn't have been more proud of everything she was getting accomplished.

"Hey," Jade said as she walked over and watched us putting the last planks in place on the stage. "Kendall says that we'll wait until morning to put up the canopies. Apparently there is some concern that they will get stolen."

"Unfortunately, I think she's right," Tommy said. He unfolded his body from its crouched position so he could better hammer nails into the platform and wandered over to Jade. "So is Darla around?"

"Yeah. She's helping to set up the food." I watched as Jade ran her hands along Tommy's chest, and wondered why I wasn't jealous or fuming or upset. I'd never seen her give him any attention before. Was it because he was suddenly expressing an interest in Darla? "I'm thinking you might win tomorrow."

He laughed. "And I'm thinking you're a tease."

Heading back over to the platform, he went to work. "Might want to keep your girlfriend on a leash," Tommy said to me when I joined him.

"She's not my girlfriend," I said.

"Thought you liked her."

"I do." I did. "But I don't love her. Sounds like you might have an interest in Darla."

"Like her, don't love her." He stopped swinging the

hammer and grinned. "But I'd really like to kiss her."

"Go for it."

"Maybe I will."

When we finished with the platform, we helped build some booths. Dusk was settling in when Kendall blew a whistle, announced we were done for the night, and it was time to grab some food.

A long line of picnic tables had assorted seafood and vegetables laid out on them. I started to reach for a plate when I noticed Kendall inspecting the platform. I headed over.

"It's solid," I said.

She spun around, looked guilty. "I know. I just wanted to look it over before I checked it off my list."

"How much more do you have to check?"

"This is it."

"Come get some food."

"I will in a little while."

"Why don't you save us a spot here and I'll pile some food onto a plate that we can share?"

"That's sweet but—"

"You ready to eat?" Chase asked as he came to stand beside her.

What had I been thinking? She wasn't mine anymore.

"Yeah, I am," she said. "Jeremy, do you want to join us?"

I shook my head. "Nah. I'm good."

Chase winked at me as he started to walk off with the girl I had once loved. "Tomorrow, dude. May the best man win."

I had a feeling he wasn't just talking about the gun show. Before then I needed to decide if I wanted to win Kendall back or let her go completely.

Chapter 37

KENDALL

I couldn't get out of working at Bark in the Park. Not that I really wanted to. I believed in the fund-raiser, understood the importance of the money we'd raise. The new wing was coming along nicely, most of the work being done on the inside now. Or so it seemed. I spent a lot of my shifts at the shelter avoiding looking over at the construction site, trying very hard not to search for Jeremy.

He'd be here today with the other gunslingers. They each had a designated director's chair with their name taped to the back, a jar for donations. This wasn't a body-building competition. We didn't expect them to stand around flexing their muscles. They were welcome to play with any dogs that came up to them.

But I imagined Jeremy flirting with the girls who brought their dogs over. Single-purpose Jeremy, who had always given me all his attention. I missed him so much. And that was crazy. Things were over between us. I was never going to get back what I'd had. We'd both changed.

I spent two hours assisting with the last-minute setup. Just before the event began, I took my place at the area where we had dogs for adoption crated. I would work two hours here, trying to entice people to adopt one of the dozen dogs we'd brought. I was pretty sure the puppies would go, but as always the challenge was finding a forever home for the older dogs.

I could see the canopy of the gun show tent from where I was, but just barely. I wouldn't be able to see the guys strutting their stuff. I wouldn't be able to see Jeremy.

"Ready for the big day?" Chase asked as he sauntered over.

"You bet." I squeezed his arm playfully. "Good luck raising the most."

He bent his arm, flexed those biceps, and grinned. "Not even a competition." Crouching, he ruffled the bichon that I had on a leash. "We still on for a date afterward?"

"Absolutely."

He straightened. "Great. It'll help me get through the long day."

"I only have two more hours and then I'm free to go."

"You're not going to leave all this, are you? Get your

face painted or get a balloon animal from the clown." His specialty was creating poodles.

"When my shift is done I'm going home to get Bogart. Then I'll be back."

"That works." He tapped his finger to my lips. "Kiss for luck?"

Why didn't I jump on that, jump on him, plaster my mouth to his? Why did a small part of me niggle and nag that I should be supporting Jeremy, that I should want *him* to win?

Waiting patiently, Chase angled his head at me like a thoughtful dog. What was wrong with me? When this whole thing had started, I'd wanted Jeremy to win. Now I was seeing Chase. Of course I wanted him to win.

Throwing my arms around him, I gave him a quick, hard kiss. Embarrassed by my enthusiasm, I stepped away, felt the heat warm my face. "Good luck."

He grinned. "I'll take another one of those when I win. See you later."

He sauntered off, toward the canopy. I could see the shadows of a couple of guys. I couldn't see them clearly, but I could have sworn that I recognized how one of them moved. I was pretty sure it was Jeremy.

I wondered if he'd be doing something with Jade later. I could see her sashaying around with a bullhorn and issuing orders to the guys.

"If the early arrivals are any indication, we're going to have quite the turnout," Terri said. She'd set up a little pen for the puppies. Now she was holding one of the goldens, letting it lick her face.

"Looks like," I admitted.

"I can't decide if the gun show really belongs," she said. "Seemed like a good idea when Chase suggested it, but now I don't know."

"If it brings in money . . ."

She shrugged. "You're right, although part of me thinks Chase just wanted to show off. He is so proud of those muscles."

"They are pretty impressive."

"So are you two dating?" she asked.

I felt the heat warm my face. "We have plans for afterward."

"He's a nice guy," she said. "Makes it easier after a breakup if there's someone to catch you. But then you have to worry about rebound feelings."

"We're just friends, really. I leave for school in two weeks."

"I'm going to miss you," she said.

"I'll miss you, too. And the dogs."

I glanced toward the canopied area. Jade rushed over to Chase as he approached, grabbed his arm, and began to propel him toward the stage. For all her flirtatious faults, she did seem to have a handle on how the gun show should be run.

I saw Jeremy, felt his gaze on me, wondered if he'd seen me kiss Chase. What did it matter? We both needed to move on.

Turning away, I got busy opening crates for people so they could get to know the dogs better. Today was about finding homes for these animals and raising money so we could help more of them. It wasn't about my crazy, confused heart.

Or wishing that I'd given Jeremy a kiss for luck instead.

Chapter 38

JEREMY

Seeing Kendall kiss Chase—even from here it was obvious that she initiated the move—had been like taking a punch to the solar plexus. Under any other circumstance, I might have liked the guy, but today I totally wanted to kick his butt.

I was even mad that he was teasing Jade about her seriousness in overseeing this event, not so much because he was giving her a hard time, but because he couldn't flirt with her if he was serious about Kendall. And if he wasn't serious about Kendall, then he was an idiot. It didn't help that I knew I was being a hypocrite because I'd flirted with Jade while I was with Kendall. I'd thought it was all harmless flirtation. But I was beginning to think there was no such thing.

"You know with that Wolverine-about-to-go-for-blood

look on your face," Fletcher began, "you're going to terrify the kiddies. Probably the dogs, too."

I glared at him just because I was in the mood to glare. "I want one of us to beat that guy."

"Go for it."

I wished that encouragement had come from Kendall. That she had walked over to wish me luck. Hell, I was here for her. She should have at least stopped by to acknowledge my presence. My rambling diatribe slammed to a halt.

She didn't owe me anything. We'd broken up. The fact that I was here for her—it didn't matter if she knew it. She still mattered. Her opinion mattered.

"All right, guys," Jade said through the bullhorn. "Sixty seconds before we begin, so take your places."

Each of us sat in a tall director's chair. I sat between Fletch and Tommy. Chase and Fletch had the bookend spots on the row. Nathaniel and Ethan were also in the lineup.

"Remember," Jade continued, "the winner is the one who collects the most money." She held up a ten and slid her gaze over to me. "So who gets mine? Impress me!"

I sat there while everyone else stood up and began flexing their biceps, showing off their guns. What was I doing here? This wasn't me.

I almost walked off the stage, but then I thought of Kendall and how important all this was to her. So I stood up. I was wearing the red muscle shirt that we'd bought when we were at the beach. The one she'd searched through mounds of unfolded shirts to find.

That seemed so long ago. A different time when we were different people. Or maybe we had just seemed different, because I still wanted now what I'd wanted then: for her to be happy. I wouldn't be with her forever. But I could still give her today.

Jade walked up the line, smiling at displayed muscles, grunts, and grins. Then she was standing in front of me. She arched a brow. "Let's see what you got."

I lifted my shirt until the hem tickled my lower ribs.

She gave me a really wicked smile. "Well, hello, abs. Maybe I'll see you later."

I let the cotton drop back into place.

She shifted her attention to Fletch. "You?"

"Won't even try to compete with that."

"You have to show me something."

"Only the guns." He flexed the muscles in his arms.

"I'm an abs kinda girl," she said, and with a seductive grin, she stuffed the ten into my jar. "You were holding out on me. We'll talk about that later."

Her interest in me had been waning, but I had it again. The thing was, I didn't want it beyond the contest. I didn't want to impress Jade. I wanted to impress Kendall. Everything I was doing today was for Kendall.

It always had been.

Chapter 39

KENDALL

Half an hour into the gun show, I was regretting that I hadn't set it up nearer to the adoption area. A nice crowd had gathered. Cheers and applause echoed toward the small grassy knoll where we were set up.

"We should have brought binoculars," Terri said. "People seem to be having way too much fun over there."

"Is there such a thing as too much fun?"

She grinned. "You're right. There isn't. All that enthusiasm has to bode well for donations."

"I hope so."

"Did you want to sneak over there and take a look?"

"When I'm finished here."

By the time my shift had ended, many of the animals had been placed with someone who we thought—hoped—would love them forever.

Another volunteer showed up to replace me. I went home to get Bogart. Mom had gone out of town to a spa retreat with some of her girlfriends. She wouldn't be back until late tomorrow night. I could have taken advantage of that if Jeremy and I were still together. I'd thought about inviting Avery over for a girls' night. Movies, doing each other's hair, talking guys. Like we used to do, but I wasn't really in the mood for a trek down memory lane. Besides, I figured she'd rather spend the time with Fletcher.

Bogart was lying on the cool tile in the kitchen when I got home. He looked up at me with sad, droopy eyes. But his tail was wagging.

"Hey, buddy," I said, kneeling down and petting him. "Want to go to the park?"

His tail wagged faster. When I reached for the leash hanging on a peg, he shoved himself to his feet.

"Yeah, you know, don't you?" I cooed as I snapped on his leash.

He trotted along behind me to the car. Lifting him up, I settled him in the front seat. It was so comforting to have him with me.

"I think I'm going to ask Chase to come over and we'll have steak tonight," I said as I slid behind the wheel and buckled up. "You'd like that, wouldn't you?"

He gave a little kerfuffle sound that could have been a bark of approval. The parking lot was packed when we got there. I'd thought about bringing him with me this morning, but I hadn't wanted him outside in the heat for most of the day, especially when I'd be preoccupied showing off the other dogs. So the great spot I'd had that morning was gone, and I ended up parking down the street.

It was a long, slow walk to the entrance of the event. I stopped by the adoption station. The volunteer who had replaced me was gone. Terri was still there, smiling brightly. We had only three dogs left.

"That's great!" I told her.

"I know. I think this has been our most successful event ever. Chase had a good idea with the gun show."

"Maybe I'll check it out."

"You do that. And enjoy the event. You've earned it."

I didn't know about that. I'd helped set it up, but she'd done most of the work. As I wandered over, Bogart traipsed along behind me. When I neared the canopied area, I saw Avery leaning against a tree, munching on a blue snow cone. I joined her.

"That looks good," I said.

"It is. Want some?"

"Sure." I took a bite, welcomed the coconut-flavored ice melting in my mouth. Bogart stopped at a water bowl. We'd set up watering stations throughout the area and one of the volunteers kept them full.

I nodded at the paw painted on Avery's cheek. "Cute."

"Darla is pretty good at painting faces. Some of these kids look like they're wearing dog masks; I couldn't go that far. But a paw? Sure. And the money is for a good cause. Speaking of money, it looks like your gunslingers are bringing in quite a bit."

"They seem to be having a good time." When someone walked by, they'd each strike up a crazy pose until money was dropped into a jar. Then they'd each slap hands, bump knuckles.

"I think they are. Fletcher is, anyway."

"It doesn't bother you?" I asked.

She shook her head. "I know he's mine."

I'd thought Jeremy was mine.

"Think I'm going to wander over and get a closer look," Avery said.

"I'll go with you. Come on, Bogart," I said, and tugged gently on his leash. He padded along behind me. My heart sped up as I neared Jeremy and his gaze landed on me. It was silly for me to react, but I figured I always would. The one that got away.

No, the one I'd pushed away, the one I'd wanted to change.

Avery and I stopped at the edge of the crowd, near the front so we had a better view. The guys were bunching and relaxing their muscles, making quarter turns. They dipped, crouched, got creative trying to outdo each other. I couldn't help but smile at their antics.

"Abs!" Avery suddenly shouted. "Show us some abs!"

Fletcher grinned at her. Lifted his shirt slightly until a hint of firm muscle showed.

"Wow. Impressive," I whispered to her.

"I know. You should see the entire package. He and Jeremy have been working out."

"What?"

She grimaced. "I wasn't supposed to say anything. Jeremy wanted to surprise you."

I looked at him a little more closely. He was wearing the shirt I'd bought him, so I could see his arms more clearly. They were definitely firmer, but I'd assumed that was because of all the construction work.

"Shirts off!" Jade suddenly yelled through the megaphone. "Shirts off!"

The crowd picked up the chant. Chase whipped off his tank without even hesitating and tossed it into the crowd. Some girl caught it and pretended to swoon. At least I thought she was pretending. With a broad grin, he leaned forward slightly, cupped his hands together, and made his muscles stand out. He had a really nice physique.

The chanting got louder until Tommy and Nathaniel drew their shirts over their heads. Ethan quickly followed suit, which just left Fletcher and Jeremy. They looked at each other.

"Do it!" Avery shouted, then laughed.

Both guys made little guns with their hands, pretended to shoot them, then reached down and grabbed the hems of their tanks. Slowly, so slowly, they lifted them up. Abs, chest, shoulders. Then the shirts were at their feet and they were flexing their muscles. The crowd erupted into shouts and applause. Girls rushed forward to drop money in their jars. I was impressed that they could move at all because I was totally frozen. Jeremy had never been a slouch in the physique department, but now the muscles along his stomach were more defined. I couldn't imagine the hours required to get that result in such a short time.

"Pretty impressive, huh?" Avery asked.

"Oh, yeah." I'd told him that I'd wanted him to beat Chase, and it seemed he'd taken my wishes to heart.

The crowd slowly dispersed until only Avery and I were standing there. A few more people began wandering over and I knew it wouldn't be long before we were once again surrounded. Avery approached Fletcher, while I eased up to Jeremy.

"Hey," I said quietly, while giving a little wave to Fletcher who just nodded and took a few steps away as though he thought we needed some privacy. Or maybe he wanted the private moment with Avery. "You look . . . great."

"Helps that we put on a little oil," Jeremy said, humble as ever, before crouching down and petting Bogart. "How are you doing, Bogie? Keeping out of trouble?" He looked up at me. "Looks like it's a successful event."

"Seems to be. Terri is pretty happy about it. We have only a couple of dogs left to be adopted."

He straightened. "That's awesome."

"It is," I said. My eyes drifted down to his stomach, back up along his chest until I finally met his gaze. "Jeremy, I really appreciate that you did this, especially after everything—"

"I knew it was important to you," he interrupted.

But not more important than you, I thought. *Than us.*

His hair was so much longer. I wanted to run my fingers through it. It had been my idea to grow it out. It seemed like I should at least be able to comb my fingers through it. I wanted to tell him I missed him, wanted to tell him I was sorry, wanted to tell him a hundred things.

He'd been the best boyfriend ever, and I hadn't realized it until it was too late.

Reaching into my shorts pocket, I pulled out a folded hundred-dollar bill. When I started pet-sitting for my neighbor, I'd put the first hundred I made aside, intending to do something special with it. I stuffed it into Jeremy's jar where an abundance of ones, fives, and tens fought for space. "Bye, Jeremy."

The hardest thing I'd ever done was walk off. I knew I needed to stop and say something to Chase, to thank him as well, to thank all the guys, but I couldn't. Tears were threatening. I kept going until I was way past the crowd gathering for another exhibition. Bending down, I picked up Bogart and snuggled against him. I needed comfort and he provided the best.

I became aware of something warm on my arm. I thought maybe it was my tears, but when I looked down, I saw the blood. "Bogart?"

I lowered him and myself to the ground. I started to examine him. Had he stepped on something sharp? It took me a moment to realize that he had a nosebleed. A very bad nosebleed.

Picking him back up, I started running for the car. Something was wrong, terribly wrong. I had to get him to the vet.

Before it was too late.

I sat on a bench at the vet's and stared at the drops of blood on my right sneaker. How had they gotten there?

As soon as I'd arrived, the staff had immediately taken Bogart back for some X-rays. I wasn't hopeful. He was old and there was too much blood. I wanted to cry but all the tears were caught in my throat, trapped in my chest. I ached. If I thought about it too much, I felt as though I was suffocating.

I didn't look up when I heard the door open. Didn't lift my gaze at the sound of footsteps. Didn't even move when someone sat beside me.

A large, slender hand wrapped around mine, interlaced our fingers, squeezed.

The dam of tears nearly burst at the kindness.

I shifted my gaze over slightly until I could see the familiar blond hair, the brown eyes. An unfamiliar dark-blue plaid shirt over his black T-shirt. Sleeves rolled up to reveal strong arms, arms he was supposed to be showing off.

"Jeremy, you're supposed to be raising money for the shelter," I said.

"I'll have my dad make a huge donation."

"I don't want you to have to ask him for something."

"Don't worry about it."

"If you're not there, they won't put money in your jar. You won't win."

With his free hand, he cradled my cheek. "I don't care about any of that. I saw you running off with Bogart. I knew something was wrong, figured you'd be here. Is he—"

"They're taking X-rays, looking him over. I want to be with him but they said not yet."

"What happened?"

"He got a nosebleed, a bad one."

"You should have come to get me, so I could have helped you."

How could I? How could I ask him for help when we weren't together anymore? Everything was so messed up.

"He's my dog, too," he said quietly.

I'd forgotten that Jeremy's name was on the paperwork. It seemed a lifetime ago.

Squeezing my hand, he said, "He's going to be okay."

I shook my head. "No, Jeremy, he's not."

"You don't know that."

But I did.

The door that led to the examination rooms opened. The vet's assistant smiled sadly at me. "Kendall, you can come back now."

Without a word, Jeremy got up and came with me. She led us to a room. Bogart was lying on the table, breathing heavily. He didn't even raise his head, but his tail gave two little wags.

I went over to him, buried my fingers in his fur, placed my face close to his. "Hey, sweetie."

"Dr. Syn will be with you in just a minute," the assistant said before quietly closing the door.

Jeremy came to stand behind me, his hand resting on the small of my back. For a minute, it was almost like old times, with him always there, always knowing exactly what to do to comfort me.

The door opened and Dr. Syn walked in. He greeted us, shook our hands, then set his laptop on the desk, opened it, and brought up an image. "Not good news, I'm afraid," he said somberly. "See this area here?" He circled a shadowy white spot in what was obviously Bogart's head. "It's a tumor."

He displayed another image—this one showing Bogart's chest area. "It's metastasized. You can see additional tumors here." He looked at me, his eyes as soulful as Bogart's. "You need to make a decision. Do you want to call your mom?"

I shook my head. "She's out of town. There's no reason to bother her." I looked at the X-rays, looked at Bogart. His eyes met mine, and I knew he knew. Somehow he knew. I stroked his fur, bent down, and kissed the top of his head. "You're going to see your pal soon."

Then I gave my attention back to Dr. Syn. "I don't want him to suffer anymore."

"Do you want to wait in the hall?" he asked.

I shook my head. "No, I'll stay with him."

Dr. Syn patted my shoulder, then left to get everything he needed.

I wrapped my arms around Bogart and said good-bye.

Chapter 40

JEREMY

I'd never had to put a dog to sleep. I didn't realize everything that needed to be done. Papers signed, arrangements for cremation made. I took care of everything while Kendall stood in the hallway and cried.

Broke my heart to see how badly she was hurting.

I'd seen her running from the park and had started out after her, but Jade had intercepted me, told me I couldn't leave. She'd made a big production out of it, when I knew that it didn't matter. They had plenty of gunslingers. No one was going to notice that I was gone. So I hadn't been able to catch up with Kendall at the park. But based on how fast she'd been running, I'd decided to try here first. I felt badly that I hadn't gotten to her sooner.

When I finished signing everything, I went over to her. "You ready to go?"

She gave a barely perceptible nod. I put my arms around her and drew her close. "I'm going to take you home."

"I can drive." Her voice sounded rough and raspy.

"I don't think that's a good idea."

"You don't have to be so nice."

"Yeah, I kinda do." Because she mattered to me. In spite of the fact that we'd somehow lost each other, she still mattered. She'd always matter.

Chapter 41

KENDALL

As Jeremy drove, I remembered that my mom had once told me that how much you loved someone had nothing at all to do with how long he or she was in your life. She'd been talking about my dad, about how they hadn't had a gazillion years together but she would never love another man as much as she'd loved him. Even though if she met someone now, he might be in her life longer than my dad had been.

Bogart hadn't been in my life long. But I couldn't have loved him more if I'd raised him from a pup.

When we got to my house, Jeremy hopped out of the car and dashed around to my side. I had the door partway open, but he opened it fully like he used to. I'd forgotten how nice it was to have that courtesy. I was exhausted. But I knew I wouldn't be able to sleep.

"Thanks," I said.

"I'll stay for a while," he said.

"You don't have to."

"I want to."

Once I got inside, I didn't want to be here, either. The house felt so empty. How could a dog take up so much room that when he was gone his absence was so keenly felt?

"Let's sit on the deck," Jeremy said.

"Yeah, that sounds like a good idea."

"You go on. I'll get us something to drink."

I didn't argue. I simply unlocked the sliding glass door, opened it, and stepped out onto the deck. I dropped onto a cushioned lounge chair and stared at the sky, thinking about the rainbow bridge where dogs were supposed to wait for their owners. I wondered if owners waited for their dogs. I so wanted Bogart to be back with his original owner.

I'd pick up his ashes in a few days. I knew exactly what I was going to do with them.

I barely noticed Jeremy coming outside. He sat on the lounge chair next to mine and extended a glass of lemonade toward me. I didn't remember us having lemonade. Lemons, yeah. So that meant he'd made it.

As I took a sip of the iced concoction, I realized that he made it very well. "Thanks."

"There was nothing else that you could have done," he

said. "Anything else . . . he was suffering—"

"I know," I said, cutting him off before he could list all the reasons behind my decision. I knew them all. "I don't feel guilty. I'm sad and maybe a little angry. I couldn't control what happened to him."

"But you did control it. You made sure his last minutes were peaceful."

They had been. Dr. Syn had given Bogart an injection. While I petted him, he hadn't even reacted to the needle. He'd simply drifted away. It was the first time that I'd been with an animal when he was put to sleep. I'd always avoided it at the shelter when we got an animal that was too ill for us to help.

"I think he knew where he was going," I said. "That he was going to be with Mr. Forrest now."

"Probably. Dogs can sense things."

Sitting up, I turned until my knees were almost touching Jeremy's. "I like to control things," I told him.

"I know."

"I think because I had no control whatsoever when my dad died. It was such a freak thing, you know? He was just driving along, approaching an overpass where some repair work was being done. . . . He was going to pass under it—and just as he gets there, it collapses. Hits him. Kills him. Instantly they say, but how do they know? And sometimes I think if I hadn't been dragging my feet that morning when he took me to school, if I hadn't forgotten where I put my backpack, if I'd been ready to leave when he first called for me—he wouldn't have been there at that precise moment."

Jeremy took the glass from me, set it on a nearby table, then held my hands. "Kendall, if you'd been ready, something else might have delayed him. The line of cars at school where he was dropping you off might have been longer. Maybe he stopped for gas, maybe there was a traffic light. He didn't die because you were searching for your backpack. Just like Bogart didn't die because you brought him to the park today."

Tears stung my eyes as I nodded. "In my head I know that. But I never misplaced my backpack again. I never misplaced anything again. Until you. I misplaced you."

"No, you didn't. I'm right here."

I shook my head. "I tried to control you, make you into what I thought I wanted. You changed and I lost you. You were the one thing that was perfect in my life, the one thing that I shouldn't have tried to control. I miss you so much."

Chapter 42

JEREMY

When we first became friends, I quickly figured out that Kendall had control issues. I'd always found them amusing. I'd had a hint as to what was behind them, but I hadn't realized how deeply they were ingrained. I should have.

"I'm right here," I repeated.

She slowly shook her head. "Not the Jeremy I fell in love with."

That hurt. Maybe it shouldn't have, but it did, because it meant she wasn't really seeing me. Or maybe I wasn't seeing me.

"What's different?" I asked.

"Your hair." She touched it, brushed the strands off my brow.

"Your jaw." She skimmed her fingers lightly over the brown bristles. I didn't know why my beard was darker than my hair. She tugged on my shirt. "Your clothes."

"That's all outside stuff," I said. "I can change it back."

"I don't want you to if you like it."

I did like the longer hair, the not shaving every day, the not worrying if my clothes got wrinkled. But that was just for now, maybe through college.

"When I graduate from college, get a job, it'll all change again," I told her. "But my appearance isn't really the issue, is it?"

She shook her head. "You stopped texting me throughout the day."

"And I started messing with other girls." That was hard to say. Even harder when the words echoed between us, when tears welled in her eyes.

"I never was one of the popular guys," I told her. "Girls never noticed me. Until you. Then all of a sudden this summer I had their attention. I thought it was cool. But things between us changed before that, Kendall. When you started hinting that I could make improvements about myself. I kept thinking about my parents and wondering if that was how their unhappiness with each other started. They pick at each other. Dad's wearing the wrong tie. Mom colors her hair and it's the wrong shade. Who the hell cares about ties and hair? But suddenly you seemed to care, and it bothered me. I tried not to let it, but it did. Even when you didn't say something point-blank, I began to feel like you didn't like the way I was."

"I know."

I shook my head. "No, you don't. Not really. You were the only one who ever accepted me the way I was."

"Jeremy—"

I touched my finger to her lips. Lips I'd kissed so many times that I'd lost count, lips I wanted to kiss again. But I had to tell her everything first, had to be honest with her, had to say things I'd never said out loud.

"Anytime my mom gets upset with me, she calls me a 'mistake.' My dad isn't so blunt, but he's not shy about letting me know when he's disappointed in me. I've tried my entire life to please them. To behave, to get good grades, to dress sharply, to act properly, to be what they want me to be. Then you started asking me to change things. Little things. I told myself they didn't matter."

I studied the lines on her palm, traced them, as though all the answers were there. "My parents got married right out of high school because my mom was pregnant. They both worked while they were in college, they shared babysitting duties. My dad's a successful lawyer but they fight all the time. I just wish they'd get a divorce, but that wouldn't be good for my dad's image."

"I didn't know," she said. "I mean, I knew they were hard on you, but—"

I lifted my gaze to her, and she went silent. "At first,

I didn't mind you suggesting that I change things. I know you like to be in control, but the more you wanted changed, the more I felt like I wasn't what you wanted. That I was about to travel my parents' path of being with someone but wanting someone different. Then we went to that stupid party. Jade and Melody were flirting with me. I thought, 'They like me the way I am.' And I wanted to be liked the way I am."

She closed her hands around mine. "Jeremy, I'm so, so sorry."

I stroked my thumbs over her knuckles. "Here's the thing, Kendall. They don't like me the way I am, because I'm not me when I'm with them. I'm still trying to be what I think they want instead of what I am. The only time I've ever been me is when I'm with you. I miss you, too, babe."

She released a sob, moved across to sit on my lap, and wound her arms around me. Crying, she held me. I rocked her. It was so good to have her back in my arms.

Now I just had to figure out how to keep her in my life.

Chapter 43

KENDALL

As I stood in the shower with the warm water cascading over me, I knew things between Jeremy and me weren't completely patched up. He'd kept his arms around me until I'd stopped crying. I'd been crying for what we'd lost, for hurting him, for thinking so much about what I wanted that I hadn't thought about what he needed.

There was so much more for us to discuss, to work out, but it had been a long day. He'd gone home to clean up. We considered going out to eat, but I was still an emotional wreck, so we decided to eat in. He promised to pick up some Chinese food on the way back over.

I didn't know where we were going to go from here, but at least he was coming back.

I picked up the shampoo, squirted some in my hair, went to set it back into the hanger on the showerhead.

Considered. Put it on the edge of the tub. Started to work up a lather. Stopped. Put the shampoo bottle back where it belonged. Took a deep sigh. Was it really such a bad thing that I liked for everything to have a designated place and to stay there?

I lathered up, rinsed, and turned my thoughts back to Jeremy. I'd told him that he'd changed, had thought he had. But the guy who had shown up at the vet's office, who had been there for me, was the guy I'd fallen in love with. His hair, his clothes didn't define him. The way he cared did. The way he knew when I needed him, the way he knew how I needed him, what I needed him to do.

Today I'd just needed his quiet strength as I said good-bye to Bogart. He hadn't interfered. He hadn't tried to take over. Jeremy didn't need to be in control. It took a lot of strength not to be in control. I wasn't sure I'd ever realized that before.

When I was finished with my shower, I slipped into a pair of soft shorts and a green, lacy T-shirt. Not bothering with shoes, I headed back downstairs, trying not to notice how quiet the house was. Stopping halfway down, I took out my phone, noted the time, and cursed. Bark in the Park would be over. Chase would be heading over here.

I texted:

Sorry. Not in the mood to go out. Had to have Bogart put to sleep.

Chase:

NP. Another time.

NP? No problem? Seriously?

I lowered myself to the steps and stared at his message. I'd lost my dog, and that was his response? He claimed to love animals, to care—

My cell phone dinged.

Chase:

Fletcher won the gun show. Dude had a sponsor. Not fair. We need rules next time.

I couldn't believe it. The guy who claimed to want to date me, to be only a text away, couldn't be bothered to come over and help me grieve, while the guy I'd broken up with was doing everything possible to ease my heart.

I heard a car drive up, looked out the window to see Jeremy arrive. For the first time since I'd lifted Bogart into my arms this afternoon, my heart soared. It felt so good to see him. Not because he was strikingly handsome in his shorts and maroon T-shirt. But just because he was here. I opened the door and smiled in welcome. "Hey."

"Hey." Grinning, he held up the bag. "Dinner awaits."

I wanted to believe everything was back to normal, but I knew it wasn't. Still, it felt like we'd made some progress. So I stepped forward and wrapped my arms around him. "I'm so glad you're here. Like, you cannot believe how glad."

"Me too, but I wish the circumstances were different."

I did, too, but I also wondered at the timing of everything. It was almost like fate. I might have never had Jeremy in my life again if I hadn't had to say good-bye to Bogart.

As we walked into the house, Jeremy put his hand on the small of my back.

"Chase texted me that Fletcher won the gun show," I told him.

"Yeah, I got a text from Fletch, too. He said Chase was pretty ticked off. Especially since I came in second, even though I left early."

I stopped walking and faced him. "That's great! If you'd stayed, you might have won."

"Nah. Fletch had it in the bag. Six three, remember?"

I pressed the flat of my palm to his stomach. "Six-pack."

He laughed. "Fletch has one of those, too."

"Avery told me today that you'd been working out."

"Just crunches, sit-ups, that sort of thing. Nothing much."

Modest, unassuming. That was the old Jeremy. The one I loved. He'd been lost for a while, but I was so happy to know that he was back.

I started walking forward again. "Should probably go get my car when we finish eating," I told him.

"If you feel up to it," he said.

"I think I will."

We set things up at the counter in the kitchen. Even though I hadn't told him what to order, my favorites were there: sweet-and-sour chicken, egg roll, and fortune cookies. I poured us two glasses of Coke, set them down on the counter, and slipped onto a stool. Picking up my chopsticks—Jeremy and I had taught ourselves how to eat with them—I moved my chicken around.

"Thanks for today," I said. "Everything, including the gun show."

"Any idea how much money was raised?" he asked.

"No. Terri did call after you left. She saw me leave in a rush, wanted to know if everything was okay. I told her what happened. That sort of stopped any talk about the events at the park. I'll get the news the next time I go in."

"You changed your shifts at the shelter," he said.

I had. I'd started working in the evenings after I walked Bogart, and on Sunday afternoon when I knew the construction crew wouldn't be around. "You noticed."

"Yeah." He stirred his General Tso's chicken. "My favorite part of the day was seeing you."

"My least favorite was seeing you with Jade."

"You should know that nothing happened between us." He held my gaze. "A couple of kisses, but nothing more than that."

"Same thing with me and Chase," I told him.

"How much do you like him?" he asked. "On a scale of one to ten, with ten being totally in love."

"Five before today. But then . . ." I showed him the texts.

"That's cold."

"Yeah. So I might have to drop him to a three. What about Jade?"

"Four." He furrowed his brow. "Maybe a three. She's a constant flirt, even when she's with someone. I never would have shown interest in her if she hadn't come on to me. I think I was just flattered. Which I'm not particularly proud of."

I'd only eaten about half my dinner, was actually surprised that I'd eaten that much. I shoved it aside. "I liked that she and Melody thought you were hot. I'm not particularly proud of that." I pointed to the fortune cookies. "Which one do you want?"

"You always get to choose first."

"I know, but I'm trying to let some of my control issues go."

"Don't change, Kendall. I love you just the way you are."

Tears stung my eyes. "Do you, Jeremy? Do you still love me?"

"I'll always love you. Even if we don't stay together forever."

"Oh, Jeremy." I buried my face in my hands, let the tears come.

"Hey," he cooed as he got up, came around, and held me. "I didn't mean to make you cry."

"I'm just an emotional mess today," I said as I sat straighter and swiped at the tears.

"Here." He nudged a fortune cookie toward me. "Check out your fortune."

I'd been eyeing the other one, but I was not going to be a control freak about cookies. I opened the packaging, broke the cookie in half, and unrolled the small slip of paper.

HAPPINESS COMES WHEN YOU LEAST EXPECT IT.

"That's so true," I said, handing him the fortune. "I wasn't expecting you to kiss me that night we went to the movies without Avery. But when you did, I was so happy."

"I couldn't believe you were surprised. I'd been thinking about kissing you for weeks."

"Are you thinking about kissing me now?" I asked.

He nodded. "But I don't know if you want me to, so I need a distraction." He opened his cookie, smiled, and handed it to me.

NOTHING IS GAINED IF YOU NEVER TAKE A CHANCE.

I looked up at him. Waited. He put his hand on the back of my neck, leaned in.

I held my breath. Closed my eyes. Felt his lips brush

302

mine like the flutter of butterfly wings before his mouth settled in more firmly. Familiar, yet not. Bolder, but the same. I couldn't explain it. It was as though we'd never kissed before, as though we'd kissed a thousand times.

He drew back. "I want to be with you, Kendall. You and no one else."

"Jeremy, like I said, I'm an emotional mess. So much has happened today. To be honest, it really hurt to see you with Jade."

"It hurt to see you with Chase."

"I'm not going to see him anymore."

"I'm not going to see Jade anymore. I'm not going to flirt with other girls. You have to know, Kendall, that the one thing that didn't change was how much I love you. I want to be with you."

"I want to be with you, too. Will you stay with me tonight?" I didn't want to be alone. I knew if I called my mom she would come home, but I didn't want that, either. I wanted to be mature, strong, and independent. But it would be easier if Jeremy were here.

"I wasn't planning on going anywhere."

We cleaned the kitchen, put our leftovers away in case we got hungry later. Then we went to get my car. We were quiet as we drove over to the vet's. My chest tightened as we pulled into the lot.

"Why don't you drive my car back?" Jeremy said.

"Yeah, okay." I handed him my keys, grateful that he understood I wasn't quite ready to be in my car yet. It had been Bogart's final ride.

Jeremy followed me. We were partway home when he flashed his brights. I looked in my rearview mirror and saw him pull into a car wash. I made a U-turn at the next intersection and returned to the car wash. I waited while he cleaned the inside of the car, then the outside.

It was so Jeremy to take care of something that he knew would be difficult for me. When we got home, he came over to me, handed me my keys, didn't say anything about what he'd done.

It had been a long day. It was late. When we got inside, I set the alarm, took Jeremy's hand, and led him upstairs to my room. Lying on my bed, I pulled him down beside me. His arms came around me, and I snuggled against his chest.

"The house is so quiet," I said, my voice low.

"I could sing."

"Don't take this wrong, but I've heard you sing."

He chuckled low. "Yeah, it's pretty bad."

"But I do appreciate the offer."

We were quiet for several minutes before I said, "Now that you've been at it for a while, how do you like construction?"

"Looking forward to being a lawyer. Construction is hot and hard."

"That should make your dad happy."

"Happy is not in his wheelhouse, but he'll be relieved. Until he realizes I'm not going to work for his law firm."

"Isn't it a little soon to decide that?"

"Nope. The one thing I have realized is that I like not having to deal with him all day. Not facing the pressure of having to please him has made working so much better." He skimmed his fingers over my arm. "Still going to be a vet?"

"Absolutely." I pressed my hand to his chest. "Why does it seem like we've been apart forever?"

"I don't know. But I feel the same way."

"Doesn't it make you worry that we're wrong for each other?"

"We're only wrong for each other if we let ourselves be," he said.

I rose up on my elbow so I could see him more clearly. I sifted my fingers through his hair. Then I lowered my mouth to his.

Mom wasn't coming home. We weren't in a cramped car. We were together. I knew that we weren't going to go any further than this. I was feeling vulnerable, raw. I think he was, too. We'd made some mistakes, but I believed we were willing to work through them.

Still, it was scary to think about, to consider.

Things had gotten out of whack so quickly before.

But it was reassuring to have Jeremy with me now, tonight, when I needed him the most.

Breaking off from the kiss, I snuggled against him, inhaling his familiar scent. We talked about things we wanted to do before we left for college. Summer had passed so quickly, more quickly than I'd expected.

I drifted off to sleep with him holding me.

Chapter 44

JEREMY

I woke up with a numb arm that was trapped beneath Kendall. Not that I cared. I could still feel the weight of her, and I had one arm that wasn't tingling. With my good hand, I brushed strands of her hair back.

Sunlight was streaming in through her windows. I liked how she looked when she was asleep. I could count her faint freckles, could see the way her nose twitched. I watched as she opened her eyes and a slow smile eased across her face.

"I'm glad you stayed," she said.

"Me too."

She sat up, stretched her arms over her head while blood rushed into my arm with a vengeance, but I fought to ignore it.

She rolled out of bed. "I'll make you breakfast."

She padded out of the room, while I stayed there for a minute wondering exactly where we went from here.

By the time I got downstairs, the kitchen was filled with the tantalizing aroma of bacon. Using the Keurig, I made some hazelnut coffee before sitting at the counter to watch her fry up some eggs. "What are you going to do today?" I asked.

"I don't know. Maybe go to a movie. I don't want to mope around but if I stay here, I think I will. What about you?"

"Have some plans."

"Oh?" She looked at me, and I saw the doubts in her eyes. She just nodded, went back to the eggs.

"Not what you think. Not with Jade or anyone else."

"You don't have to tell me what you're doing."

I got up, walked over to her, and put my arms around her waist, set my chin on her shoulder. "There's no one else. Not after yesterday. I can't tell you what I'm planning until I know for sure that it's going to happen. If it doesn't happen, I'll go to the movies with you. I should know in a couple of hours."

"That's kinda Jason Bourne-ish," she said.

I laughed. "Yeah, I'm a skilled assassin. If it works out, I think you'll like it."

While she finished with the eggs, I got the toast out

308

of the toaster, buttered it, and took it to the counter. She brought over the eggs and bacon.

"This is so domestic," she said as she hopped onto a stool.

"Maybe we'll get a house together our sophomore year so you can cook every morning."

She stilled, stared at me. It was something I could have said a couple of weeks ago and it would have caused no tenseness between us, but now we weren't completely comfortable with each other. The teasing was gone; the absolute trust had vanished.

I knew it would take some time to get that back.

"Want to tell me what you were doing all night?"

I'd barely walked through the front door when my dad started the inquisition.

"Not really," I said. I didn't think my dad would believe me, anyway, if I told him that all I did was hold Kendall. If he knew we were in bed together, he would assume we'd had sex. Not that I hadn't wanted to, but I'd understood that wasn't what she'd needed last night.

"You need to break things off with this girl if you want me to help you with your college expenses. I'm not going to stand by and see your life ruined."

It was ironic. If he'd made the demand a few days

ago, I could have told him that we'd broken up. Right now, though, I wasn't exactly sure where we were.

Following breakfast, I'd helped Kendall clean up the kitchen. Then I'd headed home. At that precise moment, I was wishing I'd stayed at her house.

"Dad, who I date, who I spend time with, who I love, who I ruin my life with—is my business. I know you didn't want to get married when you were eighteen. I know you think it was the biggest mistake of your life, that I'm the biggest mistake—"

"Son, I never—"

"Even if you never said it, I felt it. If Mom hadn't gotten pregnant, if you hadn't gotten married, where do you think you'd be right now? How much better do you think your life would be? Kendall, the girl I love, her name is Kendall, needs to control things, but we can't control everything. No matter how hard we try. Things happen that we're not expecting and we make the best of them. If you don't want to help me with my college expenses, don't. I'll get a job, I'll get a loan. You made your choices and if you're not happy with them, they're on you. Do something about it."

I turned to go to my room and nearly slammed into my mother. She was pale, her face horror-stricken. What could she say? She had told me I was a mistake.

"If you're not happy, you don't have to stay here because of me," I said quietly.

Then I headed to my room, determined that I would never look back and think that whatever happened between Kendall and me was a mistake. Whether we got back together or stayed apart, it wasn't going to be because I didn't know what I wanted, because I made a mistake.

Chapter 45

KENDALL

Movie it is. What time works 4 U?

The text came from Jeremy while I was sitting on the deck with Avery. I'd called to tell her about Bogart and she'd immediately come over. A true friend.

I wondered what Jeremy had planned that wasn't going to happen, but I was also glad that we were going to a movie. I replied:

This evening. Want 2B here when Mom gets home.

Be over in a bit.

"I haven't seen that smile in a while," Avery said.

I clutched the phone to my chest. I'd already told her about everything Jeremy had done for me the day before. "It was Jeremy. We're going to a movie tonight. Do you and Fletcher want to come with us?"

Smiling, she shook her head. "I don't think so.

Especially if you're getting back together. You could use some alone time."

"I don't know what we're doing, but it feels right to be with him."

She clinked her lemonade glass against mine. "I'm for anything that feels right."

The door that led into the kitchen opened, and Mom stepped out. "There you are." She glanced around. "Where's Bogart? He didn't greet me at the door."

Unfolding my body, I stood and touched her arm. "We had to say good-bye to him."

Her face fell, her eyes watered. "When?"

"Yesterday."

"You should have called me. I would have come back. You didn't need to be alone."

"There wasn't time. And I wasn't alone. Jeremy was with me."

"That's good," she said, hiking up her chin, but I could see a little quiver in her mouth.

"It's okay to cry, Mom."

"He was just a dog." Tears welled in her eyes, spilled over. "He was just a dog."

"But he was our dog." I stepped forward and put my arms around her. She hugged me tightly.

"He made me love him, dad-gum it," she said. "That's not fair."

"You probably made him love you, too, Mrs. J," Avery said.

"Still not fair," Mom said, pulling back and swiping at her tears. "But then that's just part of life." She patted my shoulder, furrowed her brow. "You said Jeremy was with you?"

"Yeah. We're going to a movie tonight."

"Are you back together?"

"I think we're testing the waters."

"Well, I hope you find them to be warm and lovely."

I wasn't actually sure what she meant. My mom often spoke in a New Age kind of way.

"I'm going to go unpack," she continued.

I figured she wanted some time alone to grieve the loss of Bogart. After she went inside, I sat back down on the lounge chair. "My mom was never a dog person."

"I think she is now," Avery said.

"I think you're right."

Avery swung her legs around. "I should probably leave so you can get ready for your date."

"Am I being naïve to think Jeremy and I might have a chance of making this work again?"

"I think sometimes you just have to trust your heart."

I knew if I asked my mom, she'd say the same thing. Sometimes it was hard to trust your heart when it was still bruised. But it had gotten hurt because I had tried to control things. Jeremy had changed. I could, too.

I'd never before experienced nervousness when I'd been with Jeremy. I didn't know why I was tonight as I waited for him to arrive. I was wearing white capris and a dark-purple top that draped over my chest. And I was pacing the foyer.

What if he'd changed his mind? What if he'd decided not to take a chance on us?

"You're going to wear a hole in the floor," Mom said.

I came to an abrupt halt. "Sorry. I don't know what to expect."

"Expect that life will have peaks and valleys. Relish the peaks and trudge through the valleys. Always appreciate if you have someone to trudge beside you."

"How do I know if it's the right someone?" I asked.

"Because he'll always be there when you need him the most. You won't have to ask. He'll just be there."

"How do I know if I'm the right one for him?"

"You won't. But he'll know."

"I'm scared, Mom. I think about going off to college and leaving you. I think about all the decisions I'm going to have to make. . . . What if I make the wrong ones?"

"Then you'll learn a lesson and next time you'll make

the right one. Life is never perfect, Kendall. It's not always neat, with salt and pepper shakers placed exactly where they belong."

I cringed. "I'm that obvious, huh?"

"I know you feel a need to control things, but we can't control life. Just live it to the fullest."

"I'll try."

"That's all any of us can do."

I heard a car drive up. I gave Mom a quick kiss on the cheek. "See you later."

I opened the door. Jeremy was wearing jeans and a light-gray button-up shirt. He'd shaved, styled his hair. He looked great.

He waved. "Hey, Mrs. J."

I realized Mom was standing in the open doorway. "Hello, Jeremy. Y'all have fun."

"We will." He took my hand and led me to the passenger side of the car. He opened the door for me and I slid into the seat. Taking a deep breath, I inhaled his wonderful scent.

He got behind the wheel and we took off. I didn't know why I'd been nervous. It felt so right to be here.

"So what's this other thing you wanted to do?" I asked.

"We'll do it another time."

"You can't give me a hint?"

"Nope. I want it to be a surprise."

"So you think we'll still be seeing each other after today?"

He slid his gaze over to me. "I'm hoping so."

I was, too. But I didn't want to jinx it by saying so.

As we stood in line to get tickets, I noticed someone in line in front of us. "Is that Darla and Tommy?" I asked.

Jeremy leaned around me and grinned. "Looks like."

"I'm glad. She's really nice."

"Tommy is, too. I think they'll work."

"I hope so."

Jeremy bought tickets to a romantic comedy. At the concession stand, he bought a large popcorn and medium drink. I took the bucket of popcorn to the butter machine. I usually hit the button five times. I did it four. Stopped. Backed away.

"You miscounted," Jeremy said. "You like five squirts of butter."

"I'm trying not to be obsessive with the actual number. Four is fine."

"Why not six? If you're only worried about the number of times you hit the spigot, why not shoot for more butter instead of less?"

I laughed. "You're right." I pressed it three more times.

As we walked down the hallway to the theater, he said,

"You don't have to change your habits for me."

"I try to control too much. I need to be more spontaneous."

"Kendall, all you need to be is you."

Oh, God, this was why I loved him. Because he accepted me, quirks and all.

Sitting in the back row, we watched the previews, giving each other a thumbs-up for the ones we were interested in, thumbs-down for the ones we weren't. From the moment the previews began, we never talked. We'd never discussed movie etiquette. Not talking during a movie was just something we shared.

Like the popcorn and the drink.

When we were finished with them, Jeremy held my hand. The movie started. I focused on it but I was also very much aware of Jeremy beside me. Being here with him was a peak in my life. It felt right, it felt good, it felt like we were where we were supposed to be.

On the screen, the main female character said something to her friends and I laughed. Jeremy went still beside me. I looked at him. He was studying me. Even in the darkened theater, I was very much aware of the intensity of his look.

Then he leaned in and claimed my mouth as though it always had and always would belong to him.

Chapter 46

JEREMY

After all that had happened between us, after the loss of Bogart and her grieving, I hadn't expected that Kendall would laugh tonight. But when she did, the lyrical sound swirled around me, seeped into me, and reminded me of all the things I loved about her.

How passionate she was about animals. How kind and thoughtful she could be. How obsessive, and even how controlling. But it was her controlling nature that had helped to make Bark in the Park a success.

And just like the first time that we'd come to a movie without Avery, I'd been unable not to kiss her. That she kissed me back gave me hope that we would still be together next weekend.

She slid her mouth along my cheek until she reached my ear and whispered, "I don't care about the movie."

"Me either."

Standing, I took her hand, pulled her to her feet, and led her out of the theater. Once we were out in the parking lot, she laughed again. I put my arm around her waist, drew her in, and kissed her.

A car horn honked, and we jumped apart. I realized we were actually on a path and holding up traffic. I grabbed Kendall's hand and we ran to the car. She laughed the entire way.

Once we were inside the car, we just sat there for a few minutes looking at each other.

"Want to go to the lake?" I finally asked.

She nodded. "But . . ."

"But?"

She looked over her shoulder into the backseat.

"Yeah," I said. "We might have changed a little but that didn't."

"What if we borrow Avery's car? It's as old as the earth but it has a huge backseat."

I thought of all my father's warnings, my parents' unhappiness. I thought about what I had with Kendall, what I wanted. "Okay."

She gave me a wonderful heart-stopping smile. Then she pulled out her phone.

Forty-five minutes later, we were at the lake, kissing in a backseat that gave us some room to maneuver. Not as much as I'd expected but still more than we had in my car.

"I can't believe your abs," Kendall said as she ran her hands over them.

"Now that I have them, I'll probably work to keep them."

"I feel badly that I nudged you into working out, that I made you think I was dissatisfied. Maybe I was the one who needed to change."

"The thing is, Kendall, we're both going to change. No one remains the same. I shouldn't have been bothered by the surface changes because I think you're okay with who I am."

"I love who you are."

Then she was kissing me again, I was kissing her. I thought maybe, just maybe, we were going to be all right.

Chapter 47

KENDALL

It was my last day, actually my last few minutes, to serve as a volunteer at the shelter. A few more days and I'd be heading off to college. I was saying good-bye to all the dogs, even the ones who had just been taken in, ones I didn't really know yet.

I heard the door that led into the lobby open, looked over my shoulder, and stared in surprise. "Mom?"

She looked really uncomfortable standing there, so I rushed over. "Is everything okay?"

She shifted from one foot to another. "A house needs paw prints to be a home. But I don't know how to do this, how to select the right dog."

I squeezed her hand in reassurance. "It's pretty easy. You just look at them until one touches your heart. You might not even find one today, and that's okay. You can't force it. Come on. Let's see what we have."

She stopped at each kennel, crouched down, and held out her hand for dog kisses. I didn't know why she'd never considered herself a dog person. She was a natural.

Near the end we found a cute, little miniature long-haired dachshund named Jake. He seemed to smile at her.

"Oh, I like this one," she said.

"Let's take him into the visiting room so you can see how he behaves."

She'd barely sat down before he jumped into her lap, licked her face. Mom laughed so deeply, so joyously that I knew she'd found her dog.

Two days later, I called Jeremy and asked if he would go someplace with me after work. He didn't hesitate to say yes. He didn't ask where. He just said yes.

When he pulled into my driveway, he was behind the wheel of a large sedan. He got out and grinned. "What do you think?" he asked.

"Where did you get it?"

"I convinced my parents that I needed a bigger car to get all my stuff to school."

"That's great."

"More than great. They actually agreed on something.

And they've started seeing a marriage counselor."

I squeezed his arm. "I'm so glad."

"Me too. It's been a long time coming." Then he gave me a sympathetic look. "Are you ready to go?"

"Yeah."

As he drove, I sat there holding a small wooden box. The people who had surrendered Bogart to the shelter had left their contact information, so I called them and they told me what I needed to know.

Jeremy turned off the main road and drove through a gate watched over by a stone angel.

"The section we're looking for should be near the end of this road," I said. "Near that big tree."

Jeremy came to a stop. He got out of the car, came around, and opened the door for me. I climbed out. He reached in and grabbed a garden trowel that I'd brought. We walked along the rows of headstones until we came across the name I was looking for.

I knelt down at the foot of the grave. Jeremy crouched beside me. With the trowel, he dug out some of the dirt, enough so that there was room for the box. I tucked it into place and we patted the dirt around it to keep it secure. A small plaque on top read:

BELOVED BOGART

ETERNAL FRIEND

I stood up. Jeremy put his arm around me.

"He's where he belongs," I said quietly. "Resting at his owner's feet."

Jeremy and I walked solemnly back to the car. When we reached it, I glanced back.

"I didn't know it rained today," I said.

"I don't think it did."

"But there's a rainbow."

"Maybe it rained wherever that rainbow really is," he said.

I shook my head. "No, I think it's the rainbow bridge and it was waiting for Bogart."

"I like that idea," he said.

He opened the car door for me, and I slipped inside, watched as he jogged around and climbed behind the wheel.

As he drove away, I realized that there are a lot of things in life that can't be controlled, a lot of things that shouldn't be controlled. A dog's love was one of those things.

Actually all love was one of those things.

"I love you, Jeremy," I said.

He grinned at me. "I love you, too, Kendall."

Settling back against the seat, I asked, "What should we do tonight to celebrate you getting a new car?"

"Let's go to the lake and check out this larger backseat."

With a laugh, I took his hand. "It's a date."

Three days to go before Jeremy and I headed to A&M. I was in my bedroom, considering what else I needed to pack for the university, when I heard a motorcycle roar into the drive. Looking out the window, I recognized the bike. What was Fletcher doing here?

Then he removed his helmet, looked up at my window, and I stared at Jeremy. I guessed that he saw me in the window because he waved for me to come down. Leaving my list, I hurried outside. "What are you doing?"

He grinned. "Fletch taught me how to ride a motorcycle." He pulled his wallet from his back pocket and showed me his license. "I even took the test for a Class M license so I'm all legal."

"Why?" I asked.

"Because from your interest a few weeks ago, I figured you wanted to ride one."

"You didn't have to do this for me."

"I did it for us. I was going to surprise you on your birthday, but I didn't want to wait any longer."

"Was this what we were going to do instead of a movie that afternoon when we got back together?"

"Yeah, but Fletcher had already taken off, so I decided to wait for another perfect moment. Then today I realized any moment would be perfect. Do you want to go for a ride?"

326

His words touched me. I knew not all our moments together would be perfect, but I figured most of them would be. I nodded. "Yeah, but I'm a little scared, too."

"So was I at first, but now I kind of dig it." He handed me a red helmet that I knew was Avery's. "Are you up for it?"

He was straddling the bike. He looked so sexy but I realized it didn't have anything to do with the bike or his hair or his clothes. It was him. The way he made me feel.

I took the helmet and pulled it down over my head. Then I got on behind him and wound my arms around his waist. He revved the engine a couple of times before peeling out of the driveway. I released a little screech as we headed up the street.

I held on to him tighter. Heard him laugh.

I didn't know where we were going. It didn't really matter. It only mattered that we were going there together.

Read a sneak peek of
Avery and Fletcher's story in

TROUBLE FROM THE START

"You can't just stand here, Avery. You have to get out there and flaunt it."

I wasn't quite sure what Kendall Jones, my best friend since forever, thought I had to flaunt.

"It seems a little late for all that," I told her. "We only have a week left until we graduate."

"Which is exactly why we're here," she said, removing the clip from her red hair, retwisting the curling strands, and securing them back into place. "Jeremy and I had our pick of three parties tonight. I knew this one would have the most people."

Because it was totally without chaperones. Scooter Gibson's parents were out of town and he had the key to his family's lake house so here we were, standing out by a magnificent pool, catching glimpses through towering trees of the moonlight dancing across the calm lake waters. Laughter, screeches, the din of conversation, and raucous cheers as girls stripped before diving into the pool competed with music blasting from speakers on the patio.

"I feel like a party crasher," I told her. "It's not like I was invited."

"You're with us. It's cool."

"I shouldn't have come."

"You're never going to get a boyfriend if you just stay at home."

I had been staying at home more since Kendall and Jeremy Swanson hooked up over spring break. They invited me to go almost everywhere with them, but I often simply felt out of place.

Kendall wrapped her hand around my upper arm. "Look, Avery, I want you to have what I have. But if that doesn't happen, you still need to go on a date. You can't start college never having been alone with a guy. You'll feel awkward."

As though I could feel any more awkward than I did now, standing around, experiencing a rush of hope that I might find a boyfriend of my own every time a cute guy glanced my way, only to be disappointed when he turned back to his friends. I longed for some guy to think I was special enough to kiss.

At seventeen I wasn't kissless but my one kiss had

happened at band camp sophomore year. I still shuddered when I remembered the tuba player pressing his puckered, chapped lips to mine. We'd gotten trapped with a spin the bottle game. I'd thought I would be perceived as cool if I acted like I was up for anything. Instead I discovered that some things just aren't worth it.

"You just need to get out there," Kendall continued. "Let guys know you're interested."

How was I supposed to do that? Wish a flashing neon sign? Not that I thought it would make any difference. I knew these guys, and they knew me. If we hadn't clicked after twelve years of being in school together, what made Kendall think it would happen tonight?

Jeremy was the newest kid in town, and it had taken six months for him and Kendall to start dating, although I noticed the sparks between them way before that.

"Yeah, okay," I said with far more enthusiasm than I felt. "I can put myself out there."

She gave me a quick hug. "You deserve to be as happy as I am."

"Here we go," Jeremy announced, rejoining us and handing us each a plastic cup.

Jeremy's family had moved here in the fall when his dad got a job transfer. He'd been bummed about not graduating with his friends. He'd started hanging around with us, and the three of us grew close. One night when we were all planning to go to a movie together, I'd faked being sick because I suspected he liked Kendall as more than a friend, and I was in the way. That night he'd kissed her, and the rest was history.

"Mmm," Kendall sighed, snuggling against him. "This tastes like an orange dreamsicle."

It did, but it also had a little kick to it. I had a feeling that it wasn't a melted ice cream bar. The two he'd brought each of us earlier had been strawberry something or other.

Jeremy slid his arm around her. He was tall enough that her head fit perfectly into the nook of his shoulder, like fate had made them to go together.

"Let's dance," he said in a low voice near her ear.

She looked at me, one brow arched. "He could be out there."

"Who?" Jeremy asked, clearly baffled.

"The right guy for Avery," Kendall said.

"Oh, yeah, he could totally be out there." Jeremy shifted his gaze to me. "Just avoid the house. It's make-out central in there. Don't want someone to get the wrong idea about what you're looking for."

"I'm not even sure what I'm looking for," I admitted.

"Someone nice like Jeremy," Kendall said. "And you'll have a better chance of meeting him if we're not here. Have fun!"

She handed me her drink and they wandered off.

Self-consciously I glanced around. Everyone else was already separated into groups, based on common interests—which usually involved gossiping about someone *not* in the circle. I didn't really feel like barging in. But I also didn't want to stand here alone like a total loser.

I ambled over to the nearest group of girls. They were giggling hysterically. While I'd missed the joke, I laughed, too, and tried to look like I was part of their gab-fest. Melody Long stopped laughing, which caused the others to stop as well, because she was the alpha in the group. Flicking her long blond hair, she turned ever so slightly and looked at me as though she was considering tossing me in the pool.

"Hi, Melody," I said, plowing ahead, even knowing that I was about to ram into a brick wall. "Isn't this a fun party?"

She narrowed her eyes. "Are you wired?"

"You mean feverishly excited about being here?" I smiled brightly, refusing to let on how much her barb had hurt. It wasn't the first time someone had hinted that I might be a narc. "You bet."

Blinking, she stared at me blankly. It was the same look she wore when we had a pop quiz in history.

"One of the definitions for wired is feverishly excited," I explained, realizing too late that I was making the situation worse, doing my Merriam-Webster's impersonation.

After drinking two fruity somethings-or-other I was finding that my mouth could work without any social filter.

Jade Johnson stepped in front of her. "She means wired like recording stuff for the cops."

"Why would I do that?" I asked, knowing exactly why they thought that and hating that they distrusted the police, that they distrusted me.

As Jade moved in, reminding me a little of a pit bull, she brought with her the fragrance of recently smoked weed, which explained why they were so paranoid. "Because your dad's a cop," Jade said, as though I didn't know what he did for a living. "I think you need to strip down so we know you're cool."

"Yeah," Melody said, brightening as though she'd finally figured out an answer on the pop quiz. "You need to show us you're not wearing a wire."

I thought about pointing out that my clothes—white shorts and a snug red top—weren't designed to hide much of anything. Instead, I just said, "Not going to happen."

Spinning on my heel, I walked away, their laughter following me, and this time I was pretty sure I was the joke.

I passed a group of three couples, but I wanted to avoid twosomes since I would stand out as someone no guy was interested in being with. I spotted two girls and a guy talking. They seemed harmless, but as I neared they began wandering off toward the house. Following after them would have made me appear desperate to be included.

Then I spied Brian Saunders leaning against a wooden beam that supported one corner of a cedar-slatted canopy. He was alone. I created a zigzag path to get to him because I didn't want it to seem obvious I was beelining for him in case he walked away before I got there. When I was three steps away, he was still there, drinking a beer. I noticed a few empty bottles at his feet and it occurred to me that he was still standing there because he was too unsteady to move away. But I was here now.

"Hey," I said brightly, moving in front of him so he blocked the view of the kissing couple stretched out on the lounge chair beneath the canopy.

For a moment he furrowed his brow, blinked, and I was afraid he didn't recognize me.

He blinked again, scowled. "I'll get to the problems tomorrow."

What was he talking about? Then I remembered that I'd given him an extra assignment to work on the last time I tutored him. "Oh, I don't care about that."

He brightened. "So I don't have to do them?"

"They're always optional, but if you work them out then you're more likely to learn the material—God, could I sound any more geekish? I'm sorry. I didn't come over here to talk algebra." Please don't ask me why I came over. *Eager to look like I belonged* wasn't a much better reason.

But he seemed to have forgotten I was even there as he took another sip and shifted his attention away from me. "Do you think Ladasha likes Kirk?" he asked.

I turned in the direction he was looking. I was hardly the one to tutor him in love, although his question seemed to be a no-brainer. Ladasha—who actually spelled her name La-A—always got the leads in the school plays and was moving to New York after graduation to pursue acting. At that particular moment, though, she was in the pool with her legs wrapped around Kirk's waist like he was her life preserver. "Uh, probably," I finally answered.

"She is so amazingly beautiful," he said.

"Yes, she is." She was probably the most beautiful girl in our graduating class.

"I'm going to tell her," he said, and staggered away, leaving me feeling even more self-conscious, as though everyone would figure out that I couldn't hold a guy's attention for two minutes.

Sighing, I returned to the spot where Jeremy and Kendall had left me so that at least they could find me easily. No way I was going looking for them. I wasn't sure all they were doing was dancing. Their relationship had seemed to have gotten intense fast. I was happy for Kendall. She deserved a great guy like Jeremy. He was the one who got invited to the party, and he'd included his girlfriend's best friend. A lot of guys wouldn't be that thoughtful. I'd come because senior year was supposed to be memorable, although at that precise moment I felt stupid and uncomfortable standing all alone while holding two plastic cups filled almost to the top. I chugged down Kendall's. Maybe with a little more alcohol, I wouldn't be bothered by the fact that since I'd spent way too much time studying and not enough partying, I didn't know any of these people well enough that they were going to include me in their little circles.

It had been that way for most of high school. I had so wanted to fall in love, or at least in like, before I graduated. Now I needed to admit that wasn't going to happen, but that was okay. The sea at college would contain a lot more fish, and no one there would know my dad was a cop. He wouldn't be coming to the university to hold assemblies with the theme "Dare to Say No." I loved my dad, loved that he was one of the good guys, but my dating life sucked.

That would all change at college, I was sure. I'd meet someone fantastic and fall in love. That had always been my plan, what I'd dreamed of when no one invited me to dances. I was going to be a late bloomer but I was going to bloom spectacularly.

Glancing around, I spotted a trash can a couple of feet away. I crushed the cup and lobbed it—

Missed. For some reason it irritated me. I should be able to hit a trash can. I wandered over, bent down to pick up the cup. The world spun and I staggered back a couple of steps.

"Whoa, brainiac. Careful." A strong hand gripped my upper arm, steadied me, and managed to send a shiver of awareness through me.

I jerked my head up to find myself staring up at Fletcher Thomas. Staring *up* at him because, at six foot three, he was one of the few guys taller than I was. The lights from the Japanese lanterns circling the pool barely reached him. It was almost as though he hadn't quite escaped the darkness from which he'd emerged. His black-as-midnight hair was shaggy, long. His dark brown eyes were almost invisible in the night. Stubble shadowed his jaw, making him seem unreasonably dangerous, although his reputation managed to do that for him.

I was pretty sure that he would eventually end up in prison. When he bothered to make an appearance at school, he was usually sporting bruises or scrapes, grinning broadly as he said, "You should see the other guy." He seemed to live for getting into trouble.

"Thanks, but I'm fine. I don't need help." Irritated, I worked my arm free of his grasp. How dare he mock my intelligence, which I doubted he had much of? As a member of the honor society, I was obligated to tutor at the school a couple of nights a week. I'd spent many a night waiting for Fletcher Thomas to show up for a math tutorial.

He couldn't be bothered, so if he didn't graduate, he got what he deserved. "And there is nothing wrong with being smart. You should try it sometime."

"Hey now, retract the claws. I was just trying to save you the embarrassment of a face-plant."

"While insulting me at the same time. Or trying to. I'm actually quite proud of my academic record." Could I sound any more like a snob? There went my mouth again, social cues disengaged.

He didn't seem the least bit offended. His eyes were twinkling like he found me humorous, and that irritated me even more. I took a long swallow of my drink, hoping he'd take the hint and go away.

"You know that drink is about three-fourths whipped cream vodka, right?" he asked.

I licked my lips, savoring the taste. "So?"

"So the reason it tastes like candy is to get girls drunk."

"I'm not drunk." I took another long swallow to prove my point, even though I realized I was way more relaxed than I should have been standing in the presence of a guy who had a reputation for showing girls a good time in the backseat of a car. Although I'd never figured out the car part, since he rode a motorcycle. Maybe he took them to the junkyard and found some beat-up vehicle there.

"Isn't this party a little wild for you?" he asked. "Figured read-a-thons were more your style."

"Guess you don't know everything," I said.

"Oh, I know plenty, genius," he said.

"I'm a few IQ points shy of being a genius. Your trying to goad me by referring to my intelligence is a little juvenile."

One side of his mouth curled up into a grin and his gaze swept over me as though he was measuring me up for something that was definitely not childish. My stomach did this little tumble like I was back in gymnastics class—which I'd left behind during seventh grade when I'd shot up to a ridiculous height of five foot ten, well on my way to the six feet I'd finally top out at. Gymnasts are usually small, but then so are most guys in seventh grade. And eighth. And ninth. It wasn't until tenth that some started catching up to me. I hated towering over them.

"You're graduating first in the class, aren't you?" he asked, surprising me with what seemed like genuine admiration in his tone. That and his smile made it hard to hold on to my annoyance with him.

"Third." The announcement had come a few weeks earlier. "Lin Chou and Rajesh Nahar are one and two."

"You got robbed."

Was he sticking up for me? It was kind of sweet, but I also knew that I hadn't gotten "robbed."

"Not really. They're way smarter than I am." Which he would know if he was in any of our advanced classes.

And I didn't mind coming in third. It meant that I didn't have to give a speech during the graduation ceremony, but my grades were still high enough that I could get into any state-funded college I wanted—and the one I wanted was in Austin. I'd been accepted a month ago. I couldn't wait until mid-August when I could head down there and be surrounded by people who cared about academics and grades as much as I did. I took another long swallow of the dreamsicle.

He narrowed his eyes. "You should go easy on that."

"I'm not a novice to alcohol."

"So that's not why you staggered earlier?"

"Just lost my balance."

He brought a brown bottle up to his lips and gulped down beer. I hadn't even noticed he had one until that moment. When I realized I was transfixed by the way his throat worked as he swallowed, I lowered my gaze and noticed how his black T-shirt clung to a sculpted chest, washboard abs, and hard-as-rock biceps. Suddenly I felt warm. Why was I noticing these things? I couldn't deny that he *looked* hot, and while I'd come here hoping to catch a guy's attention, I just didn't want it to be some guy with whom I had absolutely nothing in common. I knew he'd been held back at least one year, so studying wasn't a priority for him like it was for me. Fletcher tossed his empty bottle back into a bush.

"Don't you care about the environment?" I scolded him.

"You're not one of *those*, are you?" he asked.

Ignoring his question, I walked over to the bushes, crouched, and tried to see into the darkness, but I suddenly felt light-headed and dropped to my butt.

Fletcher hunkered beside me, balancing on the balls of his feet, his forearms resting on his jean-clad thighs. How did he manage that? I'd bet money he'd already swigged down way more than I had. "You okay?"

"Yes, just—" I realized that I'd finished off my drink. Everything suddenly looked far away, like I was viewing it through a tunnel. The cup slipped from my fingers and onto the grass.

"You need some fresh air," he said.

"We're outside," I pointed out. "It doesn't get any fresher than that."

His fingers folded around my elbow and I was struck by how large his hand was, how strong, how warm against my skin. With no effort at all, he helped me to my feet. "It's better by the lake."

He curled his arm around my shoulders, pulled me in just a little, and I had this insane thought that we fit together like pieces of a puzzle. I liked his height compared to mine. He made me feel normal, when I often felt like a giant. He guided me over the uneven expanse of land that led down to the lake. When we reached the bank, he didn't release his hold, and while I wouldn't admit it to him, I was grateful because suddenly nothing seemed solid beneath my feet.

I knew I'd had too much alcohol too fast on a too-empty stomach. Snacks weren't nearly as abundant around here as the drinks.

"Take a deep breath," Fletcher ordered.

I did, and I could smell the brine of the lake, the sweetness of the wildflowers, the dankness of the dirt, and Fletcher. His was an earthy fragrance, nothing artificial, all male. With his arm around me, he was overpowering my senses, until he was almost the only thing I was aware of.

"Better?" he asked.

"Yeah." There did seem to be more air here. I could hear the breeze stirring the leaves in the trees around us, feel it wafting over my skin. I turned slightly in his embrace until we were nearly facing each other. His nearness was making me dizzy. His hand came up to cradle the back of my head, and he settled my face into the crook of his shoulder. I had that same crazy faraway thought that we fit. I could hear his heart pounding—felt it thumping through his chest, sending tiny little shivers over my face.

"Don't drink if you can't handle your liquor," he said, his voice low enough that it didn't disturb the chirping crickets. "There is always some guy willing to take advantage."

"Like you?" I asked.

"Exactly like me."

Don't miss the companion novel to

THE BOYFRIEND PROJECT

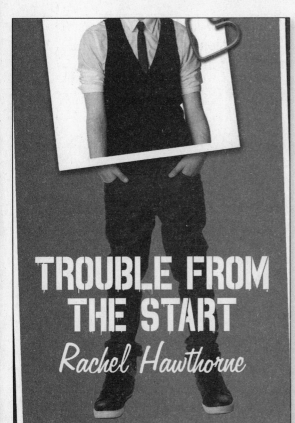

Avery is the clean
living, super-smart
daughter of a cop.
Fletcher can't seem to
outrun his bad–boy
reputation.

But when Avery's dad
takes Fletcher in as a
foster child over the
summer, Avery starts
to see the sweetness
beneath Fletcher's
damaged exterior.
What happens when
the good girl falls for
the bad boy?

YOUR *PERFECT SUMMER* STARTS HERE

ONE PERFECT SUMMER

Rachel Hawthorne

LABOR OF LOVE *and* THRILL RIDE

Read two sweet stories by
RACHEL HAWTHORNE in one paperback bind-up!